The Vibrations of Words

The Vibrations of Words

Second Edition

Ettore Grillo

Strategic Book Publishing and Rights Co.

Strategic Book Publishing and Rights Co., LLC
USA | Singapore
www.sbpra.net

For information about special discounts for bulk purchases, please contact Strategic Book Publishing and Rights Co., LLC. Special Sales, at bookorder@sbpra.net.

ISBN: 978-1-949483-24-6

TO MY UNCLE
SALVATORE GRILLO

ACKNOWLEDGMENTS

I thank my love Kim Hyunok, a Korean poet. She spurred me to write the second edition of this book and helped me proofread it precisely.

I thank my Uncle Salvatore Grillo, who gave me inspiration, and the great souls that told me about vibrations and resonance of words.

I thank the staff of the publishing house SBPRA and, above all, the vice-president Bruce Martin, who has always been friendly to me.

Contents

PREFACE

Any person of average intelligence, if he knows a particular field well, can write a thematic book easily, for instance, on gardening or on cooking. But things get complicated when he aims at expressing what he harbors in his heart. In this case, he has to find the proper words to convey his feelings and emotions. Words are supposed to mirror the mind, but sometimes they misrepresent concepts and feelings. Some states of the soul are even inexpressible. It may also happen that written words are unclear and inevitably give rise to misunderstanding.

In the past, whenever I attended important meetings, I worried about finding the right words to express my ideas. The same happened to me at school. When I was a student, sometimes I couldn't express in words what I had in my mind. My difficulties were so great that a teacher of mine spurred me to answer his questions in the Sicilian dialect, because what mattered for him was the concept, not the form.

How does one start to write a book? I feel a fire inside myself, a volcano filled with magma ready to erupt. How can I turn my ideas and feelings into written words?

Once there was a great Italian poet who withdrew from the world. His name was Giacomo Leopardi. He was a nobleman. Secluded in the tower of his gorgeous manor house, he wrote wonderful poems.

Maybe I should do as he did to create good writing. I should isolate myself to write my book, I thought.

I talked with a friend of mine, who was a critic, about literary work that springs from the solitude of the author.

She said, "If you seclude yourself, your writing will not be good. It will be dead writing. Conversely, if you live in the world, you will write something good and interesting to readers."

She went on, "Words are like seeds. If you sow good seeds, they will sprout and flower. If you sow bad seeds, they will produce poisonous weeds. Passing from mouth to mouth, from ear to ear, or from eye to eye, good words will spread their beneficial energy to the whole universe, while bad words will pollute the air. Words are like boomerangs. Good or evil, the fruits of your words will come back to you. So you have to be careful about what you write."

I pondered on what my friend said. I recalled an episode that caused quite a stir in my hometown when I was a high school student. A girl had committed suicide in her car. I still remember her blue car and even the number plate. She had fired a gun against her head. A book was found close to her. She had read that book before committing suicide. Was it possible that the book she had read gave rise to her self-destruction?

Suicide has many causes. In this case, one of the causes could have been the reading of that book, whose words were not favorable to life.

I want mine to be a living and wholesome book that generates good energy and improves the lives of those who will read it.

A friend of mine, who was a lawyer in Palermo, used to go to a bookstall and purchase a randomly chosen book. He said that a book bought by chance opened him to new horizons. Someday, if someone picks up my book randomly from a bookstall, he will come in contact with the vibrations of words.

MEMOIR

PART I

When I was a university student, I used to spend my spare time with my girlfriend, Giulietta. I also used to stroll on Via Roma with my friends, chatting with them about this and that. We had been four inseparable friends since childhood. Maybe our height, which was above average, made us form a group. When we walked in the street, our height, fair complexion, and light brown hair made us look like Nordics living in Sicily.

One evening I received a call from my Uncle Salvatore. He asked me to come to his old house, which he still used, though he lived in a gorgeous new apartment.

He had received many proposals from people interested in purchasing his old house. They wanted to demolish it to construct a new apartment block, but he always refused to sell the house, which he had inherited from his father. According to him, one should never sell an ancestor's house.

He enjoyed withdrawing to the rooms where he had been born and grew up. There he used to write, pray, listen to music, and meditate. Now, at the age of ninety-two, his sight was weak, and he got tired in front of a computer. It was not easy for him to write and proofread. He trusted and loved me like a son.

Usually the front door of his house was kept open until night. My uncle locked it when he went back to his apartment. The building was quite large. From the main door, a white marble staircase led to the upper floors. At the top of the first flight was a landing with two doors. The door on the right side was always open, but nobody walked through it. However, it was possible to glimpse two rooms full of old stuff in the darkness. In these rooms, my grandfather's brother used to live. He was called Uncle Vanni (a diminutive of Giovanni). He stayed there until he immigrated to the United States. Since then, nobody had inhabited those rooms for at least fifty years. The furniture, the bed, the couches, and the console table with its fine-framed mirror were covered and carefully protected with wide white sheets when he left. Uncle Vanni's personal belongings were still there, intact and untouched. They looked like silent witnesses of a presence long gone. They were still waiting for the improbable return of their owner. The balcony that overlooked Via S. Agata remained shut.

My grandfather loved his brother and kept hoping that he would come back from America someday. They corresponded with each other by mail until the end of my grandfather's life. As for me, I had shivers of fear whenever I passed by those two rooms. I felt as if the souls of my ancestors haunted that gloomy place.

On the left side of the landing, a door led outside to an area full of rubble due to a bombing during the Second World War. Another left revealed a staircase to go down to a space first used as a stable and then as a garage for parking and maintaining trucks.

At the beginning of the second flight, on the left side was another room used as a cellar. At the end of the staircase were two locked doors. One led to the rooms that had once been used for the shipping company established by my grandfather, the other to a room where my youngest uncle, Michele, used to live. On the top floor was the kitchen that Uncle Salvatore also used as a living room. He had transformed one of the cupboards into a bookcase. Although it was an old house, he maintained it quite well. The walls had been painted white, and many light bulbs had been installed. In the kitchen was a glass door to the terrace and two small windows about two meters from the floor. The roof was covered with old Sicilian style tiles. My uncle loved light, and for that reason he never hung curtains.

Uncle Salvatore was a thickset man. His hair was still thick in spite of his age. He didn't use shampoo. When he soaped his face, he also soaped his scalp. Whenever he talked, his thin lips had a faint smile, so sometimes you felt as if he were teasing you.

As soon as he opened the door, I gave him the customary kiss on his cheek, and then we climbed the iron staircase to the kitchen. He sat down in his rocking chair, and I took a seat on a chair. There was a laptop on a small desk in front of me.

"What's up?" I asked.

"Yesterday, I had a meeting with my brothers. We had some arguments, and my youngest brother, Michele, claimed he had made our family's fortune. He has written a memoir, which he plans to hand out to his brothers, sisters, nephews, and nieces. In it he sets forth his truth about our company and how he made our family wealthy."

"Do you think things happened differently?"

My uncle got heated. His face turned red, like fire.

"Yes, I do! The truth is different, indeed. I made the wealth for our family, not him. Therefore, I want you to help me write my memoir, which I will hand down to my children, my siblings, and their children. I want you to type my memoir with this laptop. I'll dictate the actual facts to you."

"Okay, Uncle Salvatore, I'll do as you want. I am ready. How long do you think it will take to finish the entire memoir?"

"Two or three days will be enough."

"We can meet here at about eight in the evening. Usually, I study until six o'clock, I eat something, and then I go for a walk with my friends in Via Roma for an hour. So eight o'clock in the evening will be the right time."

My uncle nodded and opened a folder with some handwritten sheets of paper. Then, he turned to me.

"The title is *Salvatore Gagliano's Memoir: A Reply to the Memoir of Michele, His Younger Brother.* I dedicate it to Gagliano brothers and their family members. Benedetto, are you ready to write?"

"Yes, I am! Let's start our significant work, Uncle Salvatore. I am already excited."

"Okay, Benedetto. The memoir written by Michele, who considers me the main culprit of the missed merger of our companies, makes me set forth my version of facts.

"It is unfortunately true that in the past my brothers and I were not in the habit of recording our decisions and making them official. That was too bad! If so, now we would have much more evidence. Although Michele's memoir doesn't contain inaccuracies, he just tells the recent facts, not the story of our companies from the outset. I am the eldest brother and the founder of Gagliano Angelo Haulage Company."

I blindly typed on the laptop what my uncle dictated. I didn't have evidence to judge whether the truth was from his brother Michele or from him. Both of them were my uncles, my father's brothers, and I respected them. Perhaps both Uncle Salvatore and Uncle Michele were right. They just reported two different phases in the history of Gagliano Angelo Haulage Company in their respective memoirs.

Uncle Salvatore dictated in a calm and low voice. His words were seemingly detached, but they vibrated with inner energy and denoted the fiber of a great businessman. He spoke with no hesitation.

Then, he went on, "Our company came to light in the month of July of the year 1930, after I, the undersigned, was discharged from military service, precisely at the end of the month of June of the year 1930 . . ."

"Is it necessary, Uncle Salvatore, to write so many details? I think it is important to describe how things happened, passing over the minutiae. It doesn't matter whether the company was born at the end of the month of June or at the beginning of July."

"This is my style! Everybody has his own way of talking and writing. I want to be myself, the person who I really am. On the other hand, if people get bored while reading my memoir, they are free to give up reading it. Anyway, I want you to type what I dictate!"

I looked at my uncle, dumbstruck, and I winced. Nevertheless, I didn't retort. I had been brought up to show respect to my elder relatives. I looked at his lips, which were thin, like two knife blades. Quite soon, he noticed that he had hurt me with his dry tone and authoritarian manner, and then the expression on his face softened.

"Let's take a break. I'll make a pot of tea. An acquaintance of mine brought me special herbal tea from India."

He got up from his rocking chair and headed for the stove. The kitchen was made of bricks and tiles decorated with blue floral patterns. After a while, tea was ready. My uncle poured it into two finely decorated ceramic cups on a silver tray, and I tasted it.

"This tea is excellent! How did you make it?"

"I sweetened it with honey from our land. It is one hundred percent natural. Moreover, I squeezed a lemon from our garden and added some mint."

"I didn't know you were so good at making tea."

"You didn't know? I am also a good cook!" he added with pride. "If you like, tomorrow evening I want you to try a special dish. I'll prepare macaroni with tomato sauce, eggplants, and salty ricotta. As for wine, I have some special old bottles, but we shouldn't drink alcohol now, because we must be sober to write well. Let's drink wine after we complete the memoir. In two or three days, we will be able to finish our work, and you will enjoy a unique bottle of all-natural red wine aged in a Sicilian oak barrel. Now, let's go on writing."

I sat down on the chair and started to type again.

"When I got back home from military service, I was an expert mechanic. My father trusted me blindly and allowed me to transform his small business, which was based on transportation and delivery by animal-drawn vehicles. In installments, I purchased our first truck, branded SPA, which had the capacity of twenty-five quintals, and registered it in my father's name. So, the firm Gagliano Angelo Haulage Company came to light."

My uncle had a lump in his throat. Thinking back to that remote past, he was moved to tears. For a while, he couldn't keep dictating. I wanted to interrupt him again, due to the abundance of details in his report. Why does the amount of quintals matter? Why does the brand name matter? Those are insignificant details, I wanted to say to him. But I didn't do that, lest I hurt him again.

"Maybe we'd better stop our work now and go home," I said.

"Are you getting bored?"

"No, I am not. But I have something to finish. Let's continue tomorrow evening, and don't forget to cook macaroni, as you promised."

The truth was that I didn't want my uncle to get tired. After all, he was ninety-two years old.

"Okay, let's adjourn until eight o'clock tomorrow. During the day, I'll prepare tomato sauce and fry the eggplants in my apartment. I will boil macaroni here, but it will take just fifteen minutes."

"Let's go together. I'll walk you home."

My uncle's residence was across the street. It was an apartment on the top floor of a new building. His second wife, twelve years younger than him, was waiting for him. I said good night to my uncle, kissing him on both cheeks in Italian style.

At eight o'clock the next evening, I knocked on the door of the old house. My uncle came down soon. Apparently, he was waiting for me eagerly and was happy to see me at the exact time.

"I have already made a special sauce, but first we have to continue writing the memoir. We'll eat macaroni after we finish our work or at break time, according to the situation."

I sat down on the chair in front of the laptop, and my uncle started to dictate slowly, sitting in his rocking chair with sheets of notes in his hands.

"The activity of our haulage company went well from the outset, for our customers trusted us. Our firm was preferred over the others because our truck never had a breakdown, thanks to my good and continuous maintenance. At that time, all trucks needed maintenance, and not all drivers were able to do that. I apologize if I am self-important. But I have the duty to say such things because you nephews were not born at that time, and your fathers were too young to remember what I did for our company.

"After I bought our first truck, many haulers tried to compete with me. They thought it was easy to maintain trucks. But seventy years ago, believe me, the maintenance of a truck was very difficult.

"The other firms competed with me fiercely. The main competitors were Gioia, Campisi & Casalino, Bonasera Giuseppe, Barilà Rosario, and Nicosia Mario. None of them succeeded. Their trucks stalled on the road very often. They couldn't survive. Their firms closed down!"

"How was it possible, Uncle Salvatore, that their trucks stalled on the road, and yours was always in perfect working order? Did you have a special truck?"

"No, I didn't. But I had a good maintenance schedule. At that time, many vehicles had problems with their cooling systems. The fan belt broke down frequently, so the engine couldn't cool properly. I invented and made a special fan belt that never broke, so my truck was always running well while those of my competitors stalled."

"Yes, you were really smart, Uncle Salvatore! You were also a good engineer. All of us are indebted to you. Now let's take a break. I am hungry and looking forward to tasting your macaroni with tomato sauce."

"Okay, save the writing on the computer, and let's sit at the table."

My uncle took out a white linen tablecloth from one of the drawers and laid it on the table. Then he set the table with silverware, two plates and a fine white ceramic bowl at the center.

"Come here and smell it!" he said.

He had already brought tomato sauce and raw basil leaves in a glass jar from his apartment. When he twisted off the top, the smell was irresistible.

"Try it!"

He put a small amount of tomato sauce in a spoon and handed it to me.

"Wow, delicious! Do you have a special secret recipe?"

"Yes, I have my secret for making good Sicilian tomato sauce."

"Can you give me the recipe? If you don't mind."

"I chop the green onions into small pieces and fry them for a few minutes with olive oil. Then I add salt, peeled tomatoes, and a half teaspoon of sugar. This small amount of sugar is very important, because it removes the sourness of the tomato. Finally, I season the sauce with two teaspoons of raw olive oil and some basil. Our traditional Sicilian basil has small leaves. The fragrance of this basil is unique. But the real secret is these three things: first, to have good ingredients, second, to love cooking, and third, to love those who you are cooking for. In the end, love is the basis of everything, including cooking!"

We ate macaroni with gusto. A glass of good wine was needed, but my uncle said no.

"Now, let's keep writing the memoir. We need a clear head to do that."

I sat on my chair, and my uncle began to dictate again.

"In the meantime, our firm expanded. Your father, Francesco, fifteen years old at that time, helped in the business. My brother Luciano quit his apprenticeship as a cabinetmaker and joined the business. Michele, my youngest brother, was twelve years old and kept studying.

"When Michele finished middle school, he enrolled in the technical high school of Castelferrato, which was almost thirty kilometers from Isola. At that time, public transportation between the two cities was not good. Therefore, many times I took Michele to Castelferrato with my red Moto Guzzi motorcycle, which had a five hundred CCs engine."

Reliving those remote times, he kept silent for a while due to intense emotion. And then he reordered his notes and kept dictating.

"Therefore, the family workers at Gagliano Angelo Haulage Company—in fact, the firm was in my father's name—were we three brothers: Salvatore, Luciano, and Francesco, your father. We managed the firm in this way until the year 1935. Nevertheless, we all felt the need to enlarge our company to benefit our future families.

"In 1935, the war between Italy and Ethiopia broke out. Everyone hoped for good business opportunities in that faraway land where the New Italian Empire was supposed to be born."

"I think your story is going to a byroad. You should be more specific about what you did at that time."

I felt my uncle might get angry again because of my interruption, but this time he didn't. I heaved a sigh of relief.

"Dictate to me, Uncle Salvatore, the happenings of that time, one by one."

"Okay. We three brothers worked in our small company. Michele, the youngest, was still a student, but he was also helpful in the business. The firm was too small to feed four future families. Sooner or later, we all would get married and have children. We needed to enlarge our business. Is the story clearer now, Benedetto? Is it more specific?"

"Yes, it is. Keep dictating what happened. I feel it will be interesting."

"To grow our small firm, I decided to embark on an African adventure. I purchased, in installments, a Fiat truck with a capacity of fifty quintals at a bargain price. With this truck I boarded a ship bound for Africa in early February 1936.

"As soon as I arrived in Ethiopia, immediately I started working because I had to pay the installments which came due every month. We Italians worked well, despite all kinds of danger. I was lucky. God protected me, and I emerged unharmed from many difficult situations. Sometimes my actions put me at risk, but miraculously I avoided bad encounters with rebels.

"One night, I planned to leave Addis Ababa with my truck for one of the Italian army outposts. I was eager to work and get paid for deliveries. For me it was no problem to travel at night. I had a strong body and could drive for a long time without sleeping. Two other trucks were supposed to travel with me. I was about to leave when an acquaintance of mine from Isola came close to me and whispered in my ear, 'Don't leave tonight!' I still remember the family name of my fellow citizen, Di Prima. 'Why shouldn't I leave? My truck is ready to leave, fully loaded!' I said. 'I overheard that you have to drive through a gorge to get to the outpost.' 'Don't worry, our army protects us.' 'No! The army can't control all over the country. Somebody told me that rebels kidnap truck drivers and then, after cutting off their testicles, they kill them,' he said with his eyes wide open.

"Hearing my fellow citizen's words, I turned pale. I didn't set off that night, and it was my salvation. The other two trucks that left Addis Ababa that night were ambushed. The drivers were kidnapped. Their bodies were never found. I am sure that an angel disguised as my fellow citizen Di Prima saved my life!"

"I didn't know it was so dangerous to travel in Africa at night."

"It was wartime, and we Italians were occupying Ethiopia."

"How long did you stay in Africa?"

"Just for three years."

"Not so long."

"I didn't stay in Ethiopia for a long time. At the beginning, I worked very hard and earned a lot of money. The revenues were good until military operations were underway. In 1937, the war in Spain escalated. In Ethiopia haulage decreased more and more. A war in Italy was also feared. The government cut spending on Africa."

"So what did you do? I think it cost a lot of money embarking and disembarking your truck."

"Yes, you are right. It cost a lot, so I kept working in Africa. One day, I received a letter from my brother-in-law, Domenico Milano, who informed me that he had received an offer from Fiat to establish an authorized car dealership in Isola. My brother-in-law wanted me to return home to create a business called Gagliano & Milano Car Dealers. The offer was alluring, for we would be exclusive dealers in Isola. Moreover, I was a skilled engineer and could assist customers with the maintenance of their cars."

"I guess you were hesitant after you read your brother-in-law's letter."

"Yes, I was. I enjoyed staying in Africa. I loved African people, and many native Ethiopians were my friends. Nevertheless, I appreciated the letter from my brother-in-law very much. I considered his proposal to create a new company together as a sign of affection, not as a matter of business. In Africa I was still working well, but the horizon was turning dark."

"Did you come back to Isola at last?"

"Not right away. But, in February 1939—three years after arriving in Ethiopia—I decided to return to Italy.

"Upon my arrival in Isola, I agreed with my brothers and my brother-in-law to create the Fiat car dealership. We signed a contract with Fiat and immediately began our business activity."

"What about your truck, Uncle Salvatore? Did you close down your haulage business after signing the contract with Fiat?"

"No, I kept my truck. But during my stay in Africa, the firm, previously under my father's name, changed into Angelo Gagliano & Sons, formed by my father and my three brothers, Luciano, Francesco, and Michele."

"What did you do at that point?"

"I created an individual firm under the name Salvatore Gagliano Haulage Company. Therefore, in 1939, I was involved in two businesses: my individual haulage firm, and the Fiat car dealership in partnership with my brothers and my brother-in-law.

"We continued our activities with two separate haulage companies and the car dealership in partnership until 1940, when Italy entered the war."

"Did you go to the army? Your memoir is very thrilling. If it continues like this, we can publish it."

My uncle nodded and smiled silently.

"My life's story is like a novel. But now, let's go on, for I have to hand over my memoir to my brothers as soon as possible.

"When the war broke out, all the young men were recruited. My three brothers joined the army."

"How about their haulage company? You told me that when you set off to Africa, they created the firm Angelo Gagliano & Sons."

"Yes, they had formed a firm with my father. So, while they were in the army, only my father was in charge of the company."

"How could your father manage to drive the trucks and take care of the company? I think he was too old."

"Yes. He was old and also sick. Your grandfather's disease was very serious, and day by day he was getting worse. In 1941, because of the terrible cancer which was destroying him, my father couldn't manage the haulage company anymore. He needed frequent treatments. He also underwent surgery. In Isola, the hospital was not well organized for such complex surgical operations. It was necessary to take your grandfather to Palermo and Catania. I accompanied him to those hospitals even during the bombings."

"Didn't you go into the army? Why were your brothers called up, and did you remain in Isola?"

"I was the eldest brother. My age group was not called up, yet."

"With the bombings, could you manage Salvatore Gagliano Haulage Company?"

"Yes, it was still possible to work, even in wartime, but I neglected my business to stay close to your grandfather and take him to the hospitals. On the other hand, the firm Angelo Gagliano & Sons went adrift. My father asked me to merge the two firms: Salvatore Gagliano Haulage Company and Angelo Gagliano & Sons. He wished me to manage the newly merged company as best as I could. I was the only child who remained at home and the only one who could manage the business with care. Obviously, I was indispensable at that time. Without me everything would have been lost. I don't want to give the impression that I am a self-important person, but that is the truth. During the war, I was the one who shaped the destiny of our family's business."

"Did you hesitate before merging the two companies?"

"I accepted my father's request straightaway. I obeyed him. I couldn't say no to him. First of all, he was my father, and secondly, he was very seriously ill and unable to take care of his business."

"I think your father could find a good manager instead of you."

"No, in wartime, it is impossible to find a good and honest manager."

"What happened to your individual firm? Did you keep running it well?"

"As I told you, I obeyed my father. The consequence was that I entered in partnership with Angelo Gagliano & Sons and closed down my individual firm in April 1941."

"When you formed the new merged company, it was your father who gave you his shares?"

"No. When we merged the two companies, the valuation was fair. My individual company was worth one fifth of the new company. The name of the new company was Angelo Gagliano & Sons: Salvatore, Luciano, Francesco, and Michele. I started working with all my might to honor the commitments. At that time, I could count on a few able workers and truck drivers. Above all, I took good care of the commitments with the Italian army."

"What were your tasks with the army?"

"The most important thing was the transportation of ammunition and supplies for the garrison in Isola. Under my management, we increased our equipment. With the earnings, we bought several properties. In 1942, we bought the house called Piazza, the storehouse named Termini, and another house called Trimarchi."

"Did you have a special reason to buy the real estate for your business?"

"Yes, of course. I bought strategic assets. Trimarchi was the new building for the trading of Fiats.

"Unfortunately, in 1942, your grandfather died. So I was the only one in charge of the business at that time."

"Were your brothers still in the army?"

"Yes. It was wartime. The Anglo-Americans had not landed in Sicily, yet. My brothers were far from Isola. Your father, Francesco, served at the motor vehicle depot in Palermo. He couldn't come to Isola. Nowadays, a freeway links Isola to Palermo, and in an hour and a half you can cover the distance between the two places. But at that time, it took at least four hours."

"Did any of your brothers come home on leave?"

"It was wartime, Benedetto! It wasn't easy to get permission to come back home. I was alone, but I didn't lose heart. As a pine tree battered by strong winds that withstands the storm and gets vigor from the heavy rain that brings water and nutrients to its roots, I turned difficult situations into good opportunities for my brothers and myself."

At that moment, my uncle broke off his narration for a few minutes. He closed his eyes, opened them again, and then looked at me.

"Now, I recall my sister Angelina's words: 'In life, you can go in many directions, but keep in mind one thing, be sincere! Be honest in your life!'"

"Is your sister Angelina a good trader?"

"Yes, she is! She is a good person, too. She has a brave heart for new business and love for her husband and children."

"What is the secret to be a good trader?"

"My sister Angelina used to say, 'It is difficult to make the first million lire. After that, money will make money.'

"To become a good trader, you must love money. In our town, there is an old proverb: If a poor man finds a cent in the street, he will say, 'It is nothing.' If a rich man finds a cent in the street, he will say, 'It is better than nothing.'

"If you don't waste money, you can be a good businessman. To earn money, first you have to love money, not for itself but for what it represents. Money is God's gift. Do you know how to play chess?"

"Of course, Uncle Salvatore."

"Well, someday we'll play chess together, and I'll show you that a pawn is also important, for sometimes with the help of a pawn you can checkmate the opponent. One cent is like a pawn. It can be added to another cent, and more cents can make a euro. It's important to get into good habits. Being thrifty is a good habit, for sure.

"Difficulties can happen in business. It is usual for a businessman, but overcoming them leads to success. It is like being at the helm of a ship. There is no problem when you sail in calm seas. But, even though large waves overwhelm you, if you are alert and can control the helm well, you will be able to survive and overcome all difficulties at last.

"Predicaments in life are like storms in the ocean. You can't avoid them unless you opt for sailing near the coastline. If you want to sail the oceans, you have to be ready to cope with all sorts of obstacles! So be thrifty and strong, and then you will succeed. My sister, Angelina, even after she became a billionaire, didn't get out of the habit of peeling unprinted stamps off envelopes and reusing them."

"When I studied the classics at school, I learned about a poet who wrote that the secret of a good life lies in living the moment. His motto was carpe diem. I think he could be right. In fact, we don't know what is going to happen the following day. Who knows whether we will be alive or dead tomorrow! Therefore, it is better to enjoy life here and now. I can't understand those who sacrifice themselves for a goal. Why should we be thrifty when we can spend money and enjoy life?" I said.

My uncle was pleased with my question. He had the air of someone familiar with this issue.

"There are two ways to live life. One, you have just described: As human beings are not immortal, they can enjoy life fully. After we die, we can't live this kind of human life anymore. So why should we waste our life by making sacrifices and enduring hardships, even though our future is nebulous and uncertain? The other is the way of religions. Most of them maintain that the true life is the afterlife. In Christianity, sacrifices and sufferings are needed to live in heaven after death. In the Middle Ages, Christians tortured their bodies to receive blessings. Nowadays, there are still the cloistered nuns who live secluded from the world."

"What is your opinion about life? How should we live? For this life or for the life to come?" I asked.

"I follow the middle way, known as Buddha's way. He taught us to avoid extremes. It may seem to be an easy way, but it is very difficult to live in the middle way. It is a balanced, peaceful, and natural way of life. As for me, I live for both this life and the afterlife. It means that I enjoy this life and also I live religiously for the next life."

"Aren't you Christian, Uncle Salvatore?"

"I am open to all religions, and Buddhism is one of the religions I love. All religions have their value, but what matters is a person's moral code, which is engraved on the human heart. I abide by this code in my daily life. We've digressed much. Now let's go back to our main work, my memoir, for I want to finish it this week."

"Okay. I am ready to type."

"As I said before, after my father's death, I remained alone in the business. Despite the war, our firm kept working with our trucks, which never stalled due to my maintenance. The only running trucks at that time, besides military trucks, were ours. Our firm earned a lot of money, since I managed the company owned by all four brothers. I took the initiative to buy more real estate. I wanted to invest and get good profits. Those properties were the fruits of my hard work.

"In 1943, we bought the land of Berardi in partnership with my father-in-law, Romiti, and my brother-in-law, Domenico Milano, in equal parts. In 1942, we bought the building near Via S. Giovanni, where a cinema was built later. Afterward, I bought several properties: stores on Via Venezia in Isola and on Via Etnea in Catania. I bought these properties in Catania with the help of my brothers who, in the meantime, had come back home from military service in 1943."

"During the war, Uncle Salvatore, you managed the family business, and with the earnings you bought many real assets for the families. Have you ever had the temptation to buy something just for yourself?"

"No. The love for my brothers prevailed over any desire for myself. When you love somebody truly, you can't betray him. Furthermore, my father taught me to be honest, and I followed his teachings. I am an honest man, and I hope you will follow in my footsteps. Keep in mind that the money of a cheater is like the money earned by gambling, it doesn't last long."

"What happened after the war was over? Did you continue your partnership with your brothers and brother-in-law?"

"After wartime, we resumed our Fiat car dealership. We all thanked God for being alive, despite all the dangers of war. Our partnership went on in good harmony until 1949. Then misunderstandings arose among the brothers, and we had rows. So, we decided to split our business again. The firm Angelo Gagliano & Sons disappeared, and two smaller firms emerged, one under the name Gagliano Brothers, for Luciano, Francesco, and Michele, and the other as Salvatore Gagliano Haulage Company. Only as car dealers did we remain together. The shareholders were four brothers and our brother-in-law, Domenico Milano. The name of the company was Gagliano & Milano Car Dealers.

"Now, I want to tell the truth to everybody, especially to my children and nephews, who don't know why I left a prosperous company with many customers and established another smaller business in competition with the former. I was aware that my individual firm would face hardships in getting new customers, but I had confidence in the success of my business. Now, I will set forth the causes of our quarrels. I want to reveal the culprit of the demerger of the company."

(At this point in his memoir, Uncle Salvatore cut out his narration about the family businesses. The reasons will be exposed at the end. But I wanted him to continue to tell me the story of his life. The meetings in the kitchen of his old house became a daily routine.)

"I want us to keep meeting, Uncle Salvatore. Your life is dramatic and full of adventures. I am sure that we can make a good book with your memories. The title of the book may be *Conversations with Uncle Salvatore* or something like that."

"Leave aside the title for now. What matters in a book are the contents, not the title."

"We have plenty of contents from your life. What do you think about the plot of the book?"

"The story of my life is divided into two branches: an interior life and an exterior life. The former consists of monologues, the latter of relations with the external world. Nevertheless, I want to emphasize that the ultimate nature of phenomena is different from the way it is perceived by our sensory organs. In fact, our minds are involved in putting the world into existence. Everything depends upon the mind. Remember that! If you switch off your mind for an instant, the world disappears. With different minds, we have different worlds."

"From the outset, I sense this book will be stodgy."

"I don't care whether the readers will find this book boring or profound or not."

"Okay, let's do as you like. However, I think it is better to divide the book into chapters. Do you agree with me?"

"Yes, I do! Let's start with my inner life. Then, the plot of the book will unfold naturally."

MEMOIR
PART II

Uncle Salvatore and I kept meeting in the kitchen of his old house every night for almost twelve months. We planned to make a book with his memoirs. I was sure it would be fantastic.

As our meetings took place in the kitchen, sometimes he prepared a special dinner: risotto Milanese, spaghetti Bolognese, and so on. On a few occasions, he even baked a pie. But we seldom drank alcohol, although he had excellent wine in his cellar. According to him, we should be sober to write well.

A Chinese proverb says, *A single conversation with a wise person is better than ten years of study.* It suits me. My conversations with Uncle Salvatore broadened my mind. Listening to him was like reading hundreds of books. At last we made the book. His story looks like an unexplored ocean. By sailing it, new lands will rise from the mists, rich in mysteries and adventures.

CHAPTER I
RELIGION

"Besides managing your business, Uncle Salvatore, have you ever done something spiritual? I think business is important for human society. It is indispensable. Since the beginning of the world there have been traders. There is spirituality in economics, too. But I want to know whether you have ever searched for God and the metaphysical world or not. You are ninety-two years old by now, and your life will not last much longer. Have you ever asked yourself what is going to happen after you die? Will everything of you disappear into thin air? Will your soul and spirit be buried forever along with your body in the gorgeous family tomb you have built?"

My uncle nodded, slowly raised his arm, and pointed his finger at the cupboard.

"Those drawers contain my journal about religion, my travels, and my life. At the bottom of the lower drawer on the right side of the cupboard are my notebooks about the Gospels. I have tried to give the right interpretation to the Gospels. I wanted to discover the deepest teachings hidden in them. Please, go get the notebooks from those drawers."

I headed for the cupboard, opened the drawers my uncle had pointed out, and took out the handwritten notebooks, which were numbered one to twelve, and then I put them on my desk. Notebook number one was entitled *Gospels—My Way of Living*. I handed it to my uncle, who leafed through the pages, gathered his thoughts, and began to dictate.

"Starting from nothing, I have become very rich. Hence, I have asked myself, 'With all these riches, do I deserve the kingdom of heaven?' In fact, in the Gospel it is written: *It is easier for a camel to pass through the eye of a needle, than for a rich man to enter the kingdom of heaven* (Matthew 19:24). What does this passage mean to you? Do you think I have sinned by accumulating wealth on behalf of our families?"

"In my opinion, in that passage, Jesus wanted to say that you must create riches on behalf of others, not only for yourself. You have built the fortune of our families. This was a good action, because now we are rich, thanks to you."

"My interpretation is different. With money we can buy external things, not the inner world, and the kingdom of heaven is linked with the innermost heart. To be close to God, the heart should not be spoiled by the lust for wealth. At the beginning of my life as a rich man, I was sure that I could purchase everything with money. But over the years, I came to realize that I couldn't buy love, friendship, or the esteem of others. In other words, I couldn't buy feelings. I couldn't buy invisible valuable things for my soul."

"You are right, Uncle Salvatore. It is the right interpretation. In fact, you can buy a comfortable, expensive bed, but not an easy peaceful sleep. You can purchase a voluptuous woman with sensual lips, but you can't buy her love. With money you can't buy peace of mind or a warm heart. To get to paradise, you must know that money is useless. If you think you can buy salvation, you are in a worse situation than the camel trying to go through the eye of a needle."

"During Martin Luther's time, the Catholic Church allowed the rich to purchase indulgences to go to heaven. Martin Luther and the Gospel itself showed that the way to the kingdom of heaven is different. Faith is much more important than money. The widow's mite is more worthwhile than the offering from a rich man, according to the Gospel. The widow donated with heart everything she had, while the rich man donated a part of his wealth just to show his power. It is important to understand that money, riches, and power can't give you happiness. Sometimes, people who are in power or rich are the unhappiest. Furthermore, it is quite easy to lose power and riches."

"Can you explain to a hungry African boy that money is not worthwhile? Without money, he can't buy food to survive. Most youngsters of my age daydream about a nice car, riches, and beautiful women. They wouldn't understand your idea about the uselessness of riches."

"I don't mean that money is useless. However, when I stayed in Ethiopia, I noticed that the Africans had smiling faces and enjoyed life more than wealthy Westerners, though they didn't have enough money. Many suicides happen in rich Western countries. I don't think suicides happen among the poor Africans in such high numbers."

"I don't think so. We don't have sufficient statistics on that issue."

"We don't have exact data. You are right, but keep in mind that the rich have to defend and protect what they have. If a rich man slackens the reins, he will lose control of his assets and others will take advantage. One day I read somewhere in the Bible, 'The more goods you have, the more people will try to devour them.' But don't ask me to give you the exact reference for this passage. I forgot."

"Not all the rich struggle to protect their wealth. In Isola, a few rich men live without working. They own land and other properties, and their tenants pay rent to them every month. Therefore, they don't have to defend their riches, as you said."

"Things are not as simple as you think."

I shook my head in disagreement.

"Benedetto, I'll give you an example. In our city was a duke who owned a large estate between Isola and Capodarso. He lived in a gorgeous palace on one side of Piazza San Francesco. Whenever he walked in the street, all the people bowed when he passed by. In wintertime, he used to wear an overcoat with a black lamb fur collar. He looked like a lion and was revered by all his fellow citizens because of his noble birth and his palaces, lands, and money. A friend of mine, when he was a young apprentice carpenter, used to go with his boss into the duke's magnificent palace for carpentry work. If he met the duke in the palace with its many rooms, bathrooms, and halls, he didn't even dare to look at him and stood as if petrified. Fifty years later, things were reversed. My friend became a rich businessman and bought the duke's palace. In the meantime, the unlucky nobleman got poor and ended his life by shooting himself in the head.

"In my life, I used to be a good businessman. Business was my passion. This was my exterior world, but deep down, I have been searching for the metaphysical sphere of existence since I was a little boy."

"How did you search for God? Did you follow a precise plan? From where did you start? And now, after so many years, have you come to a conclusion?"

"Your question is really interesting!" he said, smiling in such a way that I couldn't make out whether he was kidding me or not. "If God exists, he is infinite. Humans, with their limited minds, can never see or understand God unless he wants to show himself to them. When I look at the sky on a starry night, I feel like a speck of dust in comparison with the universe. Is it possible to understand the infinite, boundless universe? Of course not. Remember! You can invest billions of euros in the search for God, but you will waste your money. Sometimes a poor person can overtake you in such a quest. Do you remember the widow's mite I just mentioned? Therefore, I didn't plan or invest money in my search for God. I thought God would benevolently show me the right way to follow to meet him. Perhaps he could appear to me in my daily life, through situations, nature, and people I met. Actually, everything comes from God."

"Quite often, Uncle Salvatore, things happen apart from God's will. We believe that fortunes, misfortunes, and happenings come from God, but they just happen. The ancient Romans used to say *homo faber fortunae suae*, man is the maker of his fortune. The thought that God is behind daily life is wrong. Our reasoning and fears bring God into existence. He doesn't exist outside us. Whenever we try to prove God's existence, we make a gap between the logical sphere and the ontological one. That is, through our mind and reasoning, we create an entity whom we give the name God."

"Everything is possible. You may be right. Who knows!" said my uncle.

I went on, "Once I read in *Awake*, the Jehovah's Witnesses' monthly magazine, that the creation of living beings is the result of God's project and cannot be ascribed to chance. But last year, my father took me to Portugal to visit the World Expo. There was an exhibition of minerals. On admiring that collection, I noticed that some minerals naturally had artistic shapes similar to animals and plants. They seemed to have been fashioned by a great sculptor. Therefore, Uncle Salvatore, is it not possible that chance and Earth's inner energy gave rise to living creatures, and God doesn't exist at all?"

"I don't exclude anything. We don't know the truth. We can just guess."

"If you agree with me, and you also believe that it is impossible to prove the existence of God, how did you follow your quest?"

"While searching for God, I turned off my thinking mind. I tried to access my being that feels life's music. I realized that my intellect was not enough to understand God. I had to put aside philosophy. By logic we can't reach God. To be with God means that we live the mystery and miracle, which are nonlogical. Music, art, and literature don't proceed logically. They just come from inspiration. I am convinced that something intangible and mysterious happens when one composes a piece of music, paints a picture, or writes a poem. Perhaps the inspired artists are close to God more than we may think. However, if you can't prove the existence of God or his presence behind the events of life, you can't prove the contrary either. You can't rule out that God manifests himself through those whom we come across in our daily life. Starting from this basis, I have been following the stream of life in my quest. Maybe life itself will make me meet God, I thought."

CHAPTER II
THEATER

"One day, on the corner of Piazza San Francesco, I came across an old friend of mine, Pietro. He was a Protestant pastor. I have known him since I was a child. When we were boys, we both frequented Catholic Action in the Church of Santa Rita. Often, we played ping-pong there. Have you ever met him?"

"No, I haven't, Uncle Salvatore. I didn't even know about the Church of Santa Rita. Where was it?"

"It was on Via Verona. Once, our city was constellated with churches and monasteries. How beautiful Isola was with all those places of worship!"

My uncle looked very moved by his memories. I stood up and brought him a glass of water. Then he went on.

"Over the years a few churches were demolished to broaden the streets, others naturally collapsed due to neglect. The Church of Santa Rita was razed, and that area was turned into a modern broad street. The church and our meeting place vanished. I couldn't meet Pietro often. I saw him occasionally. Our relationship loosened and we confined ourselves to saying hello. That day, God was probably showing himself through the fortuitous meeting with Pietro."

"Uncle Salvatore, it was not God! It was coincidence to make you meet that old friend."

"We don't know the truth, God or coincidence. Let me tell the story, and then feel free to think whatever you want."

"Okay. Do you mind if you describe your friend Pietro, so that I can write something about him?"

"No, I don't. As for his physical appearance, Pietro had an athletic body with black eyes and straight hair. His main trait was wittiness. He had the ability to tell jokes for hours and to recite poems in Sicilian dialect. All his friends enjoyed listening to him. He had been a sincere Catholic. Later, he abandoned Catholicism and became a Protestant pastor. A restless soul hid behind his playfulness.

"That day I was heading for the bank, thinking about my business, when he stopped me. 'How are you doing?' Pietro said with a big smile. 'I'm doing well,' I replied. 'Would you like to act in a play?'

"I opened my eyes wide. I couldn't quite believe my ears. 'Acting as an actor?' 'Yes, of course,' Pietro answered.

"At that moment, I recalled my brief career on the stage. The first time I acted was when I attended primary school. I had been selected for emceeing a school show. The performance was successful, though I was too shy for playing that role.

"A few years later, another teacher chose me to emcee a show again. I rehearsed many times, and the teacher was enthusiastic about me. But on the day of the show, I didn't go to the small school theater. The audience was waiting for me. A schoolmate of mine looked for me everywhere. When he found me, he begged me to go to the theater, but I was more stubborn than a mule. I didn't go. In the end, the headmaster called my father, who beat me and forced me to go there. But the show was already over when I arrived."

"How was it possible, Uncle Salvatore, that you left the audience waiting? I thought you were a serious person. Didn't you care about others?"

"Actually, I was odd at that time, but I was just a boy. Often we treat children as if they were adults. Indeed, the concepts of seriousness and punctuality are not so important in a child's mind as in an adult's. Anyway, even though I didn't act normally, I couldn't do anything to act well at that time. My shyness prevented me from facing the audience. Maybe I didn't deserve my father's thrashing."

"Was only your shyness to trigger that shameful action toward your teacher and the audience? Maybe there was something deeper that you don't want to tell me. We are writing your memoir. Tell me everything honestly, please."

My uncle sighed and then nodded.

"Yes, there was something more. You are extracting it from my unconscious mind, as a dentist does when he pulls a painful tooth from the patient's mouth."

"Tell me everything as if I were your psychoanalyst."

"My mother influenced my life much. She liked matter-of-factness. She didn't consider music, theater, art, and singing as practical aspects of life. In her opinion, these were evanescent. Only studying was important to her. By getting a degree I would get a good position in life. Actually, I owe much to my mother, who forced me to study. But in regard to those nonpractical activities, such as music and theater, she was not of much help to me. I was conditioned by her."

"So, do you think your father's beating was unfair?"

"I think so. But I don't want to judge anybody. Sometimes I also beat my children for some reasons. We are imperfect human creatures and can make mistakes."

"Go on, Uncle Salvatore. Consider me your confessor. Tell me about your mother. She was my grandmother, but I didn't know her because she died before I was born. I am curious to know something about her. Somebody says that character is hereditary, and the lineal descendants have some similarities."

"My mother was a good mother and wife. Thanks to her, I kept studying and acquired the habit to be independent. 'Go your own way!' she used to say to me. 'To become successful, you must rely on your education and inner energy, not on the connections you establish with others. You have to shine with your own light, not with reflected light.'"

"According to you, Uncle Salvatore, aren't social relationships vital to be successful?"

"They are important, but not essential. Success depends on one's inner strength, capacity of insight, and knowledge. Wisdom is also very important.

"Now, getting back to my mother, I can say she was a great woman, but very serious. I remember that whenever I laughed, she used to say *risus abundat in ore stultorum*, laughter abounds in the mouths of idiots. Because of her, I equated laughter with foolishness. Do you think I could be an actor or an emcee with such a point of view?"

"I can understand you. Tell me some other episodes about your upbringing."

"I remember, when I was a child, my mother took me to a piano lesson. It was the first and the last lesson to me. Then, she didn't take me there anymore. I asked, 'Mom, why don't we go to piano lesson?' She answered, 'The teacher said that you were not cut out for learning the piano.' In my opinion, she realized that learning the piano would take away time from my study, which she considered more important than learning music."

"Keep talking, please, Uncle Salvatore. Your telling is interesting."

"In my childhood I was beaten by everybody: teachers, parents, and schoolmates. When I fought with other boys, I always lost, even when they were younger than me. I lacked the aggressiveness to win. My face was like a punching bag for training boxers. Everybody trained on it. There was a teacher who, besides slapping my face, had a sharp preference for pulling up my ear. Sometimes he pulled so hard that I thought my ear would come off. He also liked to dig his thumb and forefinger into my cheek and then twist so hard and long that the pain seemed to have no end.

"When I attended high school, again I was asked to emcee a musical show in a church. The strange thing was that the more introverted and complex I was, the more I happened to be the center of attention. On this occasion, I didn't leave the audience waiting. I emceed the show with outward calm and naturalness, though anxiety burned inside me.

"Another time, I was asked by my school friends to play the role of the judge in a play about a trial against a first-year student. In the play, I repressed anxiety and strove to look witty and spontaneous. That was my last experience as an actor. Almost thirty years went by from that play, until my friend Pietro asked me to be an actor again."

"Did you accept his proposal? Your life has interesting hidden aspects."

"Although I was shy, I was excited by the idea of acting. In fact, inside me two opposite tendencies clashed with each other continuously. One pushed me to withdraw from the world, to stay alone, far away from all human beings, while the other spurred me to live fully, have friends, and enjoy life in the world. Fortunately, the latter tendency prevailed, so I accepted Pietro's invitation. He gave me the role of Commander Lieuvin in the play *It is Midnight, Dr. Schweitzer* by Gilbert Cesbron. We were six actors, including Pietro, who played the role of Dr. Schweitzer.

"First of all, we had to memorize our parts. Pietro gave each actor a script. We met once a week in one of the rooms of the Protestant church. Pietro was proud of that beautiful church. In Isola almost everyone was Catholic, so he met with many difficulties in building that large and elegant Protestant church. Its floors were white marble. In the main hall assigned to worship, there were almost three hundred blue chairs. Other rooms were used for meetings and leisure time. We sat around a table and read the script loudly. The other actors were much more professional than me. They read the script with ease. I felt like a schoolboy that read a schoolbook instead of an actor in a play. My reading was cold and dull. I couldn't identify with my character. I was about to give up. I said to Pietro that I was not the right person to play that role."

"I think, Uncle Salvatore, you are an indomitable man who never gives up."

"Yes, it is true, but at that time I felt I couldn't act. However, things turned better. 'Don't worry. Relax, Salvatore. I will help you to be an actor,' said Pietro with a broad smile.

"Encouraged by his words, I kept going to the Protestant church to attend the meetings with Pietro and the other actors. The most difficult thing was that I had to act the part of a commander. Military language is dry, harsh, and authoritative, while my way of speaking was quiet, slow, and humble. In fact, I was a meek person, against war and any kind of violence. Surely, I was not the right man to give orders. I didn't like when someone, including my parents, ordered me to do this or that, so I didn't want to give orders to others.

"One day I met a friend of mine who had studied in a theater school in Venice. 'What should I do to play the role of Commander Lieuvin?' I asked. He advised me to read the script at home looking at myself in front of a mirror. By doing so, I would be able to be more natural in my gestures. His advice was good for acting, but at that time the most important thing to me was to have a tone of voice fit for a commander.

"I talked about my situation with another friend of mine. He was an attorney enthusiastic about theater. He had directed some plays. When he was a student, he used to emcee musical shows and events in the theater of our town. 'You can't play that role,' he told me with a harsh tone. 'Why not?' I asked him, while my throat became dry. 'There is no difference between ordinary life and stage acting. A comedian can't act as a tragic actor, and vice versa. To be General Lieuvin on the stage, you must have the spirit of a commander. In other words, you must be an authoritative person in your daily life. If you are meek, you can't act as a strong, hard man. So forget the theater. It is not for you,' he said firmly."

"Did you give up, Uncle Salvatore? Did you follow the attorney's advice?"

"No, I didn't, even though within Pietro's theater group more than one actor was skeptical about my acting. Speaking generally but looking at me, one of them said that a person who was not conceited couldn't be an actor. 'To be an actor, conceitedness is basic. An actor should enjoy the pleasure of being admired by the audience. Whoever is not conceited had better stay at home instead of on stage,' he added sarcastically.

"His words chilled me. In fact, I was not a conceited person. Only Pietro continued to trust me. 'Don't worry. Be tranquil. I bet you will become a good actor,' he said.

"It also happened that I lost my voice sometimes. I don't know whether it was due to emotion or to my vocal cords. Even for this problem, Pietro reassured me. He said that the matter of losing my voice would be solved if I ate a salty sardine before acting. In the following days, I practiced the script at home in order to memorize it. The more I read it, the more I realized that my friend the attorney was right. I couldn't be both a lion on the stage and a rabbit in daily life. I needed to be an authoritative man. I didn't have a split personality to act a completely different person from me on the stage. A donkey can't run at the same speed as a horse, nor can a crow soar and dive like an eagle.

"Reading the script, I looked into myself. I noticed that my shyness was not innate. It was something I had acquired. My awkwardness and uneasiness were not parts of my mental structure. They were like a dark veil between others and me. That veil was an artificial superstructure, not a fixed component of my mind."

"Did you suffer from anxiety, Uncle Salvatore? Often anxiety takes us away from life and pushes us to give up and flee people and situations. I predict that you dropped your endeavors to be an actor."

"I suffered from anxiety at that time, but I didn't want to give up theater. Looking inside myself, I discovered that flight increases anxiety instead of diminishing it. At first, fleeing from a difficult or unpleasant situation can alleviate anxiety, but it is an illusion. The avoided situation gives rise to a sense of inadequacy and creates lack of self-esteem. In most cases, the lack of self-confidence generates new anxiety."

"I think, Uncle Salvatore, it was a sort of vicious circle. Your anxiety generated lack of self-esteem, and vice versa. What did you do to get out of that situation?"

"The answer is contained in one word, perseverance. I just persevered with my endeavors to be an actor. I didn't blame myself for my shortcomings. I kept practicing. With days and months passing by, the tone of my voice became louder and firmer, not only on the stage but also in my daily life. The amazing thing was that the improvements on the stage influenced my social relationships. The tone of my voice, which had been low and calm for more than thirty years, changed considerably. I realized that the submissive tone of my voice didn't come from my real nature. It was just a habit I had developed since the teenage years. At that time, I strove to emulate well-mannered gentlemen that talked in a low voice. But, by repressing my voice I repressed my emotions and feelings as well. Over time, I even became cold. Actually, tone of voice and expression of emotions are connected. A person with a closed and depressed mind speaks little and in a low voice, while a person with an open and cheerful mind talks a lot and aloud."

"Therefore, Uncle Salvatore, the way we speak influences our life! Is it true?"

"Yes, it is. Speaking naturally is fundamental! Spontaneous words express internal emotions and can cure anxiety and other personality disorders. These kinds of ailments appear when you are too cerebral and think too much before speaking. In this case, your speech is too reasoned. You hide yourself when you speak with an overload of reasoning. You flee from yourself, and it creates anxiety and mental illness. Tone of voice is connected to character, definitely."

"So, don't we have to think before speaking? If we speak rashly, we can make mistakes. Don't you think so?"

"I agree with you. But I wasn't spontaneous at all. I was too repressed and thought too much before speaking. Nothing is good if it is too much."

"I think it is possible for a general to speak in a low voice. Deep down, what matters is the contents of the orders he gives, not the tone of his voice."

"I don't think so, Benedetto. To command a platoon or a company, you need a strong, authoritative voice, otherwise the troops won't obey you. A general's order must be sharp, without hesitation. To play the role of Commander Lieuvin, my tone of voice should be commanding. Later Pietro asked me to use gestures to express the character's personality. Then, he corrected my movements. He recommended me not to step back while I was acting. 'Moving your feet back,' he said, 'is the worst thing you can do on stage.' What I learned from him I applied to my daily life as well."

"The strong man you are now is due to your theater experience?"

"In a sense, yes. There is no difference between daily life and theater. Both are life. The person on the stage is the same person at work. Actually, whenever I was involved in a difficult situation, I had the tendency to step back. Theater taught me to do the opposite. It gave me a new motto: *Never step back! Instead, cope with the obstacles, both in theater and in daily life.*"

"So far, you have told nothing to me about your relationship with the other actors. Who were they? Did you feel comfortable with them?"

"No. I felt quite awkward with one of them, but I used this situation as a base to find out the lowest common denominator for all human beings."

"What is it, Uncle Salvatore?"

"About thirty years ago, I travelled to Kathmandu. While I was crossing the bridge from Durbar Square to Ratna Park, I stumbled across a dusty young man lying down with his arms toward the sky and a bowl for alms next to him. People passed by and almost stepped on him. The bowl was dented and empty. Nobody cared about him, and his bowl continued to be empty. The young man was in the midst of the crowd, and you needed to be careful not to step on him. He didn't look like a human creature.

"What is the lowest common denominator for everybody? What is the common element between that poor man, who looked like an urban waste, and an educated person or a king or a politician? A great musician and that wretched being of Kathmandu are both men. Why so much difference between them? Who knows what feelings harbored in that guy, alone and abandoned by everybody? He was without money, with the street for a house and the moon for a night lamp. Certainly, he would not live long. Did that man have a soul and self-awareness? Or was he like a dog which lacks a soul, according to theology? And does the soul exist really?"

"You made too much digression, Uncle Salvatore. How can I write your book and give it a tidy form if you fly from the topic, theater, to your travel to Nepal?"

"The difference between a philosopher and an ordinary man is that the former wants to know the why of things and ponders on what happens to him and around him, while the latter doesn't care about the meaning of life. Personally, I want to understand the core of everything. As I told you before, there is no separation between theater and life, for theater is also life. Coming back to that young man of Kathmandu, at that time I asked myself: If the soul exists, why does it agree to be imprisoned inside a body?

"I think the soul exists and is different from the body. Similarly, material things and immaterial things are different. In other words, you can't touch the soul, the immaterial.

"Assuming that the soul is something different from the body, I wonder when it enters the body. At the moment of conception, or at the moment of birth? Everybody knows that nowadays it is possible to freeze embryos which maintain their vital strength. Does it mean that you can freeze the soul inside an embryo? It is illogical to think that the immaterial and subtle soul, which is eternal, would agree to be frozen along with the embryo and imprisoned in it for a long time."

"Yes, it is really illogical. However, I ask you to be concise, otherwise the layout of the book is not good. It is too messy. Fifteen minutes ago, we were talking about theater, and then you abruptly switched the topic into the soul."

My uncle looked at me with eyes full of surprise. He had the habit of thinking that everybody should be attuned to his opinions. Whenever someone dared to object to him, he masked his indignation. He was much disappointed if someone didn't agree to his ideas or actions. Then, he turned to me with an easy voice and a forced smile.

"You must know that life and nature are not based upon order. Sometimes a mess is harmonious and beautiful. For instance, first look at a modern garden with a well-maintained lawn and well-trimmed trees, and then go to the forest and see a mess of brambles, wildflowers, bushes, and different species of trees. What an amazing variety the forest has, compared with a modern garden! I want to do like this with my memoir. Let's jump from one topic to another. Don't worry. I will return to the theater pretty soon. In fact, the topic soul is connected to theater. You'll know it later! Let's go on now."

"I see. Do as you like. The book is yours, not mine."

"In accordance with the above reasoning about embryos, it is logical to presume that the soul enters the body at the moment of birth. But where does the soul live? Throughout the body, within the brain, or in the heart? Wherever the soul may be, surely it can't express itself without a body. To write my memoir, my soul needs my body's vocal cords to convey the words you are typing on the laptop. Without using his hands, a painter can't transfer the feelings and emotions of his soul to the canvas. The body is needed!

"As for the house of the soul, we can rule out that it is throughout the body. As we all know, parts of the body can be implanted into another body. Does it mean that you can also implant a part of the soul? Of course not! If the soul is inside the body, there should be a way to perceive its existence. Someone says that meditation is the only way to meet the soul. We will discuss that later. Now, let's go back to the topic from where we started."

"What topic, Uncle Salvatore? You are confusing me and my writing with your digression."

"The topic of theater, of course. As I told you before, I felt uneasy within the theater group."

"Why couldn't you feel at ease? You were all friends!"

"Except Pietro, we hadn't been friends for a long time. But an underlying reason made me feel anxious. 'Does everybody have a soul?' At that time, I asked myself."

"Of course, everybody has a soul! What are you talking about, Uncle Salvatore?"

"My question is not weird! Assuming that the soul exists, is it present in all human beings, or are there people without a soul? According to Jehovah's Witnesses, only one hundred and forty-four thousand people will go straight to paradise after they die. What about the remainder? They believe that all the others die and lie in the ground without any feeling or sensation. Nevertheless, the dead are in God's memory. He will wake them up. According to them, there are two different categories of humans: God's chosen people and ordinary people.

"If we examine billions of people's bodies, regardless of race, we can see that their organs are identical. Brains, hearts, lungs, sensory organs, hands, arms, fingers, and so on are the same. My deduction is quite clear. Since the bodies of human beings are identical, their souls are identical, too. That man in Kathmandu, that urban waste, filthy and dusty, lying on the bridge like a sick, scabby dog, also had a soul like the other human beings. What do you think about that?"

"I don't know. Your reasoning is too complicated for me. Nevertheless, I don't want you to lose your train of thought. Keep talking. We'll gather up the threads later."

"Okay, Benedetto. According to the Buddhists, the condition of a soul depends on its karma. Today's life is the result of actions performed in this or past lives. The early Christians believed in reincarnation, which is synonymous with metempsychosis. Some passages of the Gospel seem to asseverate that: 'As he passed by, he saw a man blind since birth. His disciples asked him, 'Rabbi, who sinned, this man or his parents, that he would be born blind?' (John IX: 1-3).

"I don't want to talk about complicated theological issues that may confound you more and more. Therefore, to make things easier, write like this: Everybody has a soul. The difference between souls that suffer inside their bodies like the case of the man of Kathmandu and souls that seem to enjoy a happy life doesn't affect the basic principle that a soul is present inside every human being.

"Now, assuming that everybody has a soul, I ask myself whether the quality of the soul is the same in all beings, or does the quality change from one individual to another? Is it true that there are noble souls and low souls, bad souls and good souls? What relationship can be possible among different types of souls? Let's take a serial killer as an example. Is the quality of his soul the same as that of ordinary people? It seems that the former has a low-quality soul.

"We don't know whether the capacity to discriminate good and evil depends on our willpower or on the quality of our soul. The Apostle Paul says that the inclination of human beings toward evil overcomes their free will. Let's see what he writes in his letter to the Romans: 'I want to do what is good, but I don't. I don't want to do what is wrong, but I do it anyway.' (Romans 7:19). 'So I find this law at work: Although I want to do good, evil is right there with me.' (Romans 7:21). The Old Testament shows the same features of the human soul: 'The Lord smelled the pleasing aroma and said in his heart: Never again will I curse the ground because of humans, even though every inclination of the human heart is evil from childhood. And never again will I destroy all living creatures, as I have done.' (Gen. 8:21)."

"Uncle Salvatore, that is your opinion. Mine is different."

"Okay, express yourself freely. Tell me whatever."

"I have read a book by an American philosopher, and I agree with him. He asserts that the quality of our soul depends on data stored in the files of our reactive mind. These data are the imprints piled on the basis of different reactions to external stimuli. He calls these imprints engrams and says that they are engraved on our reactive mind when we are unconscious. In other words, all living beings are born with the same type of soul that is prone to good, but engrams give rise to mental diseases, delusions, distortions of thought, and bad actions. Good and evil originate from our thoughts which are affected by engrams. According to him, if we discharge the bank of reactive engrams, all mental diseases, neurosis, manias, and vices will disappear. We will be what he calls *clear*."

"Yes, I know this theory. I also know about a Russian writer who talks about the 'chemistry of the soul.' He says that man is a machine, void of free will and drifted by circumstances. A famous French writer wrote about man who is born pure and good, but society turns him into a bad creature. According to a less famous friend of mine who showed me his unedited book, man is born with an inclination to evil, and, through the educational system, society makes him good."

"Who is right, Uncle Salvatore?"

"I don't know. Only God knows the ultimate truth. However, I ask myself how should I behave whenever I come across a person with a bad soul? Should I avoid any contact with him? What should be the fate of bad souls? Should they be driven out from good society? Let's see what the Gospel says about them. It seems that bad souls should be burned in the fire. Bring the Bible, please, Benedetto. I want you to read a passage from the Gospel."

I took the Bible out of the cupboard and handed it to him. He opened the Bible and gave it back to me.

"Read this passage aloud, please."

"I read, 'The kingdom of heaven is like a man who sowed good seed in his field. But while everyone was sleeping, his enemy came and sowed weeds among the wheat and went away. When the wheat sprouted and formed heads, then the weeds also appeared. The owner's servants came to him and said, 'Sir, didn't you sow good seed in your field? Where then did the weeds come from?' 'An enemy did this,' he replied. The servants asked him, 'Do you want us to go and pull them up?' 'No,' he answered, 'because while you are pulling the weeds, you may uproot the wheat with them. Let both grow together until the harvest. At that time I will tell the harvesters: First collect the weeds and tie them in bundles to be burned; then gather the wheat and bring it into my barn.'" (Matt. 13:24-30).

"What is the meaning of this parable?"

"The good seeds symbolize the good persons, while the weeds represent the wicked persons. On the Last Day, the evil ones will be sent to the eternal fire of hell. On hearing these words of Jesus, we remain perplexed. It seems that we are facing a very cruel God, as the torture reserved for bad souls is awful. They are thrown away into a furnace of fire, where they suffer and cry for eternity. Does a sentence to eternal fire come from a compassionate and merciful God? Is this the way God treats his children?

"Another cruel episode is reported in the Acts of the Apostles. The early Christians used to have all their goods and money in common. Two elder Christians, husband and wife, wanted to do the same as the other Christians. They sold their land and deposited the proceeds at the feet of the Apostles except for a small amount of money which they kept for themselves. They told the Apostles that the money was the entire sum derived from the sale of the land. Actually, they didn't tell the truth. The punishment of this lie was the death sentence on both husband and wife. In my opinion, the lie told by the two Christians, Ananias and Sapphir, didn't deserve capital punishment. Is it possible that God is so cruel and doesn't have any sense of proportion between the committed sin and the punishment?"

"I want to raise an objection to your reasoning, Uncle Salvatore. In my opinion, the fear of God is not always negative. Indeed, it prevents many people from committing bad actions. On the other hand, if God exists, he is like a father and we humans are like his children. Have you ever seen a father, any father, who never reproaches his children? If parents punish their children, it happens because they love them, not because they enjoy punishing them. When Jesus says that sinners will be tossed into the eternal fire, his words come from his love toward us. Sometimes deadly sins are prevented because of the fear of God."

"Inside that drawer are more notebooks. Please, stop typing for a while and bring me them."

"Of course, Uncle Salvatore, I'll get them. But, if you care to know my opinion, this work is a waste. Nobody will be interested in your talking about the Bible. Furthermore, it makes your memoir too boring. Surely, nobody will buy your book. Let's go back to talking about theater."

My uncle's tone was quite resolute. "They who want to read my book will read it, otherwise they will switch to something else lighter. There are millions of books. Now, let's continue our work!"

"Okay, Uncle Salvatore, I am ready."

"If we read the Gospels carefully, we'll find many passages that may give rise to discussions. One of these is given by Jesus's genealogy recorded by Matthew. The genealogy implies that Jesus was a man, not God. Why does Matthew report Jesus's genealogy? He starts with Abraham and ends with Jacob, who was the father of Joseph. Joseph's wife, Mary, gave birth to Jesus, who is called the Messiah. If Jesus was the Son of God, it is nonsense to report his human genealogy!"

"Are there other passages of the Gospel that make you doubtful?"

"Yes, there are. Another passage relates to Jesus's siblings. I am convinced that Jesus had both brothers and sisters."

"Uncle Salvatore, you are very lucky, indeed."

"Why?"

"If you had been born at the time of the Inquisition, you would have ended your days burning at the stake like a roasted chicken."

My uncle laughed loudly and could barely refrain from guffawing. Looking at him, I was proud of my wisecrack.

"Let's have a break! Shall we make an exception? I want us to try a glass of good wine from my special reserve."

He went downstairs and came back with a bottle of wine. The neck of the bottle was coated with red sealing wax. My uncle said that the sealing wax prevented the air from passing through the cork. Moreover, it was a guarantee of authenticity. He poured the pink wine into two fine crystal glasses.

"This wine is from our land in Vittorino. It is the best wine on earth. Cheers to the success of our book and our life!"

My uncle drank it all in one swallow, while I preferred to sip that delicious wine which tasted like Olympians' nectar.

"I know all the secrets for making good wine. Do you want to know my secret?"

"Of course, Uncle Salvatore!"

"Well, after I wash the oaken cask with very hot water, I disinfect it by burning a small thread of sulfur inside it. While the wood is still hot, I pour a bottle of good whiskey in the cask and roll it for a while. Then I throw away the whiskey. The cask keeps the flavor of the whiskey for a long time and transmits it to the wine. You need to bottle the wine from the cask at the right time, when the moon is propitious and the wind blows from the north. Now, can you understand my secret? It is simple, isn't it? Shall we go back to our work? We have much to write today!"

"Okay, keep talking, and I'll type."

"Once, if a Christian dared to question the official interpretation of the Holy Scriptures, he was considered a heretic and risked being burned at the stake. Those days are gone, and freedom of speech and thought can't be questioned anymore. I want to remain as a Catholic all my life, but it doesn't mean that I follow the mainstream doctrine blindly.

"The thought that some of Jesus's words might be wrong induced me to deepen my quest. The core of the evangelical message is love toward everybody, friends and enemies, good souls and wicked souls. So, why are there contradictory passages with regard to the wicked souls in the New Testament?

"A Lutheran theologian named Rudolf Karl Bultmann proved that the Gospels are not Jesus's biographies, but rather apologetic scripts of the primitive Christian church. The Gospels were written many years after Jesus's death, after having been passed along orally. When the Gospels were written, their contents were reinterpreted by those who wrote them."

"I don't think so, Uncle Salvatore."

"Trust me, for I have researched this topic deeply. Did the ones who wrote the Gospels maintain fidelity to Jesus's original message? Personally, I believe that Jesus was a very great master. The passages from the Gospels that tell of a severe God who punishes human beings by sentencing them to eternal fire can't have come from Jesus's mouth. They are a mistaken reinterpretation of his message.

"Should we avoid any contact with so-called wicked souls? Jesus taught us to love everybody, especially our enemies. What is Jesus's opinion about good and evil? Mark describes the most meaningful passage of the Gospels on this issue: When Jesus started on his way, a man ran up to him and, kneeling at his feet, asked him: 'Good Master, what shall I do to have eternal life?' Jesus said to him: 'Why do you call me good? Nobody is good except one: God' (Mark 10:17-18). How should we interpret this passage? The answer is that nobody on this earth can claim to be a good person, only God is good."

"Uncle Salvatore, what should we do when we come across someone who doesn't observe the commandments given by God? I think that if we cut relationships with wicked souls, sooner or later we will remain alone. Evil is a part of human nature, and few people can declare themselves pure beings."

"Yes, you are right, but now I want to get back to the topic of theater. There are no watertight compartments in life. Religion, economics, literature, theater, music, and so on are connected. They are different aspects of human life. It is like changing scenery on a stage. The scenes change, but the play is still the same."

I heaved a sigh of relief. I couldn't stand listening to such deep religious subjects anymore.

"Speaking frankly, I prefer the topic of theater. Most old people are interested in religion. Youngsters have other interests. Your book will be read only by the old!"

My uncle didn't say anything about my idea on religion, but his facial expression denoted that he disagreed.

"In the group of actors was a person who had committed a few heinous crimes in the past and had been jailed for a long time. He made me feel uncomfortable. What to do? And what would my fellow citizens think about me when they saw me acting on stage with such a man who was considered a wicked soul?"

"I, too, would have been embarrassed. My friends are students and don't like to stroll in the street with a porter or a hod carrier. So, what did you do?"

"After thinking and thinking, I finally came to the conclusion that the predisposition to good and evil was present in everybody. Nobody could claim to be a good person on earth. Therefore there was no reason why I should have felt uncomfortable when I acted on the stage with one that had a very bad reputation. Yes, it was true that he had committed those crimes. But who was I to judge him? Furthermore, I trusted Pietro. If he had admitted the ex-convict in the theater group, he must have had his reasons."

"I wouldn't have acted with that villain on a stage. Everybody in Isola knows the story of that notorious criminal."

"At that time I followed my heart. I kept practicing with the ex-convict, and with time we became friends. He repented what he had done in the past. As days went by, my awkwardness on the stage because of him vanished.

"After one year of practicing, finally the day of the performance came! The theater was small, and the audience was mostly friends and relatives of the actors. It was a hard trial, a real challenge to me. To win my battle, I should have avoided being conditioned by the audience. Therefore, I acted as if nobody were watching me. Whenever I needed to turn my body and eyes toward the members of the audience, I looked at them as a wholeness, not as individuals. I never looked at the expressions on their faces, otherwise I would have been influenced by their responses."

"How was the play? Successful? How was your acting? Were you satisfied?"

"The outcome was a success, a complete victory! The audience gave a standing ovation. We performed the same play two more times: once in a small parish hall, and the other time at Isola City Theater. I never imagined that I would be able to act at the municipal theater of my hometown!"

"Congratulations, Uncle Salvatore! What happened after that? Did you continue to act on the stage?"

"Yes, I did. We kept meeting once a week. After our first play *It is Midnight, Dr. Schweitzer*, we continued to practice in one of the rooms of the Protestant church. We planned to perform another play, *The Trial of Jesus*. This time, there was a new actor, a boy called Renzo, who was not endowed with a good intellect, though he was able to read and write. Previously, he had acted a small part in another play. We were discussing how to organize the play *The Trial of Jesus* when Renzo raised his finger and asked to talk. 'No!' shouted both Pietro and the director. 'Renzo, don't say anything! Shut up! If you want to stay here with us, you must be silent all the time. Do you understand?' said Pietro.

"Renzo's face turned red, and he remained silent. I was tempted to say something to Pietro and the director about their suppressive attitude toward the boy. But, I didn't, lest I upset the group's peace. It was my mistake. I should have said to them, 'Everybody must be allowed to express his ideas. Who do you think you are? Why did you talk to Renzo so harshly?' If I had said what I wanted to say, maybe they would have explained. On that occasion, I suppressed my anger. Repressed emotions don't bode well! My grudge against Pietro and the director was put away into my unconscious. It lay there silent and later burst out. I felt that our group was getting more and more professional, and the feelings of friendship were left behind. I had joined the group not to become a professional actor but to stay with some friends and enjoy togetherness. Now, things were becoming different. I perceived that there was less and less warm-heartedness. If one of us was not right for a role, the director didn't allow him to go on.

"I was supposed to play the role of Jesus's prosecutor. One day I was in a bad mood because of legal arguments with my brothers. The director found me too calm and quiet. To play my role well as a prosecutor I should have shown a stern face. 'You should watch television more,' he said. Obviously, he wanted me to follow the examples of the actors who acted on the small screen, but I thought he wanted me to change my lifestyle. 'I don't watch television,' I answered curtly. 'I prefer to read books, write, study, and listen to music. If you don't like me as an actor, feel free to choose another person that can play the role better than me!'

"The grudge I had put in my unconscious since young Renzo had been hushed came out abruptly. I was digging a rift between the other actors and me. 'You are too quiet,' said an actress sitting close to me.

"Another young actress opened her mouth to say something, but I immediately shut her up. 'Each one can give what he has,' I spoke out. 'I can't give what I don't have. This is my character!' I looked forward to the end of the meeting.

"My experience with theater was over, but it was precious. As for Pietro, I consider him a good teacher and a dear friend. Thanks to his theater I changed my lifestyle and became the strong man that is sitting in front of you now. I learned that nothing and nobody is worthless. Every person we come across is a guide from heaven. Both friends and enemies appear and disappear on the stage of life to teach us something new and necessary."

CHAPTER III
THE PROTESTANT CHURCH

"Pietro and his sister invited me to take part in the meetings at their Protestant church. The Protestants call their ceremony 'service' not Mass, as the Catholics do. Pietro used to name the function in the Protestant church 'worship'. I was happy to go to their church with them."

"I thought you were Catholic, Uncle Salvatore. How could you attend two different religious rites?"

"Usually on Sundays I go to Mass at the Catholic Church of San Paolo. I was baptized and raised in that parish. My grandmother was a sincere Catholic. I found her in church every evening. She used to sit on one of the pews in the front row. Whenever I entered the church, I looked for my grandmother, and once I spotted her, I sat close to her. She was the one who guided me to religion and godliness since my childhood. Now I can't live without religion or rather without my constant quest about the spiritual world, which is the basis of the universe and life."

"You haven't answered my question yet, Uncle Salvatore."

"I am about to answer you. Be patient! As I told you before, I am open to all religions. Although I was raised as a Catholic and I am still a Catholic, in the religious field I follow the example of Alexander the Great. He is renowned for having founded a great empire but is less known as a practitioner of many religions. Whenever he conquered a new territory and met new populations, he didn't confine himself to paying respect and homage to their divinities, he also worshipped their gods and made sacrifices on their altars.

"I didn't have a preference for this or that religion. According to my viewpoint, there is only one religion in the world; only the ways of worshipping the divine differ."

"Only one religion with different denominations? Do you mean there is one religion which belongs to the world? To humankind?"

"Yes, I do. In fact, worships differ from one population to another, but the ultimate goal of religions is the same."

"Do you practice your ecumenism in the Christian field, or include non-Christian religions as well?"

"In my search for God, I have attended Catholic and Protestant churches, Sikh and Hindu temples, Islamic mosques, Buddhist temples, and so on. When Pietro invited me to join him in his church, taking part in the worship was natural to me.

"The Protestant church was modern. Pietro had been in charge of the building. On the front of the church was a cross as high as the entire facade. But, unlike the Catholics, the Protestants didn't make the sign of the cross when they entered or left the church. I noticed that their prayers were reduced to just one, the Our Father. Inside the church there were no images except on the stained-glass windows.

"As soon as I entered the hall of the church, I was showered with a rain of religious songs. Almost three hundred people were singing in front of the blue seats arranged in the shape of an amphitheater, facing a platform on which there was a lectern. There was no altar in the church—another difference from the Catholic Church. The faithful sang with ardor as if they were possessed, for almost half an hour. They didn't confine themselves to singing but they also raised and waved their arms.

"I liked that kind of music and those songs. The text was projected onto one of the walls of the hall. Reading the words, I sang with them. I had already seen a similar worship when I attended the meetings of the Catholic Charismatic Movement. In the Protestant church, I sensed something intimate and familiar. Then the assembly fell silent. From time to time, a voice popped up. Someone, as if he were in ecstasy, gestured and praised the Lord."

"Uncle Salvatore, I guess that the Protestant ceremony is completely different from the Catholic one. While Mass is a fixed rite with standardized words and prayers, in the Protestant church, apparently, the worship is based upon music and songs."

"Yes. Music and songs preceded spontaneous prayer. Later, during the break, I asked Pietro why some persons were enraptured when they praised God. 'Some of us,' answered Pietro, 'have special gifts or charismata. They feel God inside themselves. They say and express what they feel. But I want to stress that it is not God that speaks through them. In fact, the person is the one who speaks through God's inspiration. Try and notice the subtlety. To help you to understand the concept, I'll tell you a story. Last year, one brother got up from his chair and said, 'I feel God inside me, as it happened to Noah when he crossed the Red Sea.' He kept talking for a while, and then he sat down. Soon after he got up again and said, 'Brethren, I feel God inside me, as it happened to Moses when he crossed the Red Sea.' It means that the mistake about the name of Moses, who actually crossed the Red Sea, was not made by God talking through that man but by him. Indeed, it was not God that talked, but our brother spoke through God's inspiration.'

"Then Pietro emphasized, 'When inspiration comes, God is not the one who speaks. The inspired person uses his own words. The Holy Scriptures were not written by God. Humans wrote them through God's inspiration.'

"That evening our conversation got more and more complicated, but I didn't want to get trapped in complex theological issues. In my opinion, those songs and music stimulated the emotional center so that the congregation felt an urge to get up and praise God and Jesus. Songs and music have vibrations. Whenever we listen to a piece of good music, don't we feel our heartstrings vibrate?"

"Do you know the phenomenon of resonance, Uncle Salvatore?"

"Yes, I do. But I want you to talk about that first."

"Okay, I'll tell you what I know. A friend of mine is taking guitar lessons. One day, she was experimenting with her teacher. They set two guitars at a certain distance from each other. Then, the teacher plucked the E string. To my friend's surprise, the E string on the other distant guitar also vibrated. It vibrated, though nobody touched it!"

"Did only the untouched E string vibrate, or did the other strings vibrate, too?"

"I am not good at playing the guitar, so I can't know about that. She told me that the E string of the other guitar vibrated. I don't know whether some other strings vibrated or not."

"Continue your talking. I am interested in it," said my uncle.

"Afterward, they repeated the experiment with the G string, and the same phenomenon occurred. The G string on the other distant guitar vibrated, too. The inference is that two strings must be attuned to resonate."

"It is very interesting! Music creates vibrations that can generate both positive and negative effects. Also words have vibrations."

"Do you think music can stimulate negativeness?"

"Yes, I do. Once I knew a lawyer from Palermo who had studied the occult for a long time. He asserted that youngsters' deaths, mostly due to car accidents, were caused by the kind of music they had enjoyed all night at the disco. According to him, those rhythmic sounds triggered negative vibrations, or rather resounded harmfully in the youngsters' bodies and souls. They had accidents because they were full of negativity which they had absorbed through the vibrations of bad music all night."

"I don't think so, Uncle Salvatore! I often go to the disco. I assure you that I have never perceived such negativeness there."

"Obviously, nobody has proved my friend lawyer's theory. I hold him in great esteem, and I respect your opinion, too."

"I think every piece of music makes our body and soul vibrate. Apparently, those people in the Protestant church were enraptured with their own singing."

"I agree with you. In fact, I noticed that a few worshippers spoke as if they were in ecstasy, but only after singing, never before."

"Something similar happened to me, Uncle Salvatore, when I was a member of the Catholic Catechumenal Movement. Songs and music were basic for Catechumens. After they sang and read passages from the Holy Scripture, they all sat down silently for the *resonance*. They let the songs and the scripture resonate inside themselves. During the *resonance* only professed members were admitted into the room or the chapel. The doors of the meeting place were shut. Then the worshippers expressed their innermost feelings under the effect of the songs and the reading of the scripture. Apparently songs, words, and music produce vibrations. They resound inside the body and the soul. Now tell me what you know about resonance and vibrations."

"I have studied this topic for a long time."

"I am hanging on your every word! Tell me everything, and don't skip anything."

"The first time I came across resonance and vibrations was after I bought my first SPA truck. I have talked about that truck in the first part of my memoir. Do you remember?"

"Yes, of course, Uncle Salvatore. But what does your truck have to do with resonance? Are you going off the subject again?"

"No. Let me tell what happened. Can you see those two small windows? Well, whenever I warmed up my truck's engine in the square in front of my house, leaving it on and in neutral, my mother leaned out of the terrace and shouted, 'Salvatore! Turn off the engine! The windowpanes are rattling because of your truck!'

"I looked up at my mother with surprise, doubting her words. Maybe my mother doesn't want me to drive this truck. Surely she is making an excuse, I thought. Actually, she didn't like new technology. Furthermore, she was always worried about me when I drove my truck.

"One day I left the truck idle with the engine in neutral, the brakes on, and four big wedges against the wheels, and then I went to the kitchen where my mother was cooking. All the windowpanes were rattling! My eyes grew round. My blood froze. How is it possible? There is something eerie behind the rattling, I thought. 'Go and sell that goddamn truck right away! It doesn't bring us good energy. I don't feel good with this rattling,' said my mother with an angry face."

"Uncle Salvatore, insofar as I know, windowpanes are thick and well-set in the window frames. It is impossible that they can rattle."

"Seventy years ago, windowpanes were thinner than nowadays. Furthermore, they lay a little bit loose in the grooves of the windows."

"I get chills of fear, Uncle Salvatore. What did you do to solve the mystery?"

"At that time, I had a friend who helped me with debt collection. He was a lawyer and also a member of an esoteric society. He had studied the occult for a long time. I had an appointment with him. I wanted to entrust him with two past-due bills so that he could recover my money. His house was Baroque style, opposite the Palace of Prefecture. After I entered at the iron gate, a path, flanked by flowering plants and deciduous trees, led me to the main door. The house served as his office as well, which was in a large room on the left after the entrance. His desk was very simple, compared with the magnificence of the house. The windows of the room were adorned with reddish colored drapes. Opposite the desk were a couch and an upright black piano. The lawyer, Bruno, was quite tall, had an olive complexion and black, bright eyes. When he was in court, he pleaded his cases with great enthusiasm and heart. He was a handsome man married to a blue-blooded woman.

"We talked about the bills for a while, and then I brought up my issue. 'Bruno, something strange happens to my house when my truck is in neutral with the engine on. The windowpanes in the kitchen rattle. The windows are a little far from my truck. How is it possible? You have been studying the occult for a long time. Tell me the reason. Do evil spirits haunt my house?'

"While I was talking, Bruno smiled and glanced at me mischievously as if I were one of his peasant clients with their heads full of superstitions. 'Don't be afraid! There are no ghosts in your house. Now, I'll show you something unusual.'

"He got up from his chair behind the desk, headed for the piano, sat on the piano stool, and tapped on one key. Then he turned his head back to me. His black eyes were bright like those of a little boy. 'Now, pay attention to what I am doing. Look at the thin crystal hanging from the chandelier. I will tap the F-sharp key, and then the thin crystal will vibrate.'

"I kept my eyes fixed on the chandelier, but I was quite skeptical. I doubted that the crystal would vibrate without touching it. Bruno hit a key, and then the thin crystal vibrated like a leaflet in the wind. 'Can you see?' 'Yes, of course!' I answered with open mouth. 'Now I'll play a piece of music. Keep your eyes fixed on the crystal while I am playing the piano. Tell me whether it vibrates or not.'

"This time the thin crystal remained still. Apparently, only when Bruno hit the F-sharp key would it vibrate. 'There is nothing diabolic,' said Bruno. 'It is a physical phenomenon. Including human voice, every sound creates vibrations which are propagated through sound waves that can even cross walls. A part of the vibrations comes back to you through reflection. Next time, instead of leaving the engine of your truck in neutral, rev it up a little. The windowpanes of the kitchen won't rattle. After that, come here again. I will tell you something more about the interaction between sound and matter, music and religion, sound and the creation of the universe. I predict that your mother won't shout anymore.'"

"It's very interesting, Uncle Salvatore. Did you try what the lawyer told you?"

"Of course I did. I asked my mother to check the windowpanes. Then I parked the truck in front of my house as usual. I revved the engine a little bit. My mother leaned out of the terrace, and her face was quite relaxed and smiling. The windowpanes didn't rattle!

"On Saturday evening, I met Bruno at his home again. As usual, he was very kind to me. We sat on the couch. A beautiful blond maid with a lacy white apron and white gloves brought us two cups of coffee on a silver tray. She waited until we finished our last sip. Then she put our empty cups on the tray and went out of the room with a slight bow. 'Bruno, I did as you said. This time the windowpanes didn't vibrate. Could you explain to me the reason?' 'Yes, of course. Wait a minute.'

"Bruno went to another room and came back with an old musical instrument that looked like a violin. 'This instrument is called *viola d'amore. Amore* means love, but it has nothing to do with love. This kind of violin has fourteen strings. Seven strings are located in the upper part and seven below. The player of the *viola d'amore* plays only the strings on the upper plane, while those below vibrate in sympathy with the upper strings. 'Is it possible for sounds to make any object vibrate?' 'Yes, of course. But the object must be sensitive to the sound's frequency. In the case of your truck, the windowpanes could vibrate only when the engine was in neutral. Changing the frequencies of the engine sound made the windowpanes indifferent to it. Something similar happens to the human ear. It can perceive sounds only if the vibrations are rapid enough but not too much,' Bruno explained fluently.

"I was fascinated by Bruno's words. Suddenly I recalled the Bible. Creation happened through God's words. I inferred that sound existed before the creation. 'Do only mechanical sounds vibrate? What about human voice?' I asked Bruno. 'Human voice also vibrates and has an effect on inorganic matter. Everything vibrates in the universe. Once, there was a baritone who was able to break a light bulb through the vibrations generated by his voice, and a soprano who could even spill wine from a glass with her high sound.' 'Are these effects generated just by singing or screaming? Or can those who speak in a low tone of voice influence an object, too?' 'Yes, every word creates vibrations, not only spoken sounds but also written words have an effect on objects. Words have vibrations which change their frequencies according to not only the tone of voice but also the quality of words. Good words produce sound and positive vibrations, while spiteful slanderous words have dangerous and negative vibrations.'

"Then he raised his forefinger as he did during his summations in the court of law and looked me in the eyes. 'Always keep in mind what I am going to tell you and never forget it. Words can create life! And they can destroy life! The Great Architect of the Universe created the world through his words.' 'Who is the Great Architect of the Universe?' 'Sorry, I thought you were a brother of mine. By the way, would you like to join our lodge? We practice brotherhood. I'd be happy to have you as one of our brethren. Moreover, as a member of the lodge, you will be able to learn more about this topic, vibrations.'

"I was intrigued by Bruno's proposal, but I couldn't accept it. At that time, one of the lodge members was a relative of mine with whom I had disagreements. I would have been embarrassed to meet him in the lodge. I was his enemy in reality, so I couldn't be a brother to him in the lodge. I made an excuse to avoid that situation. 'No, thank you, Bruno. I am honored by your proposal, but I can't accept. I am too much involved with my job.' 'Okay, do as you like. But keep in mind that the door of our lodge is always open to you if you change your mind. Now, I'll give you a special gift. This Indian booklet talks about sound and vibrations. It's for you.' 'Thank you very much, Bruno.'

"Bruno wrote a heartfelt dedication on the first blank page of the booklet and handed it to me. Then he walked me to the door. When I arrived home, I read that booklet right away. It was really interesting. According to the author, the creation happened through the vibrations generated by sound waves. Every sound needs percussion to be produced, but the primordial sound was not percussed. It was like the burning bush Moses saw on Mount Sinai. The fire was not from the bush, because it didn't need fuel to blaze. Actually, many myths put a sound or a word at the base of the creation. John's Gospel says that *Logos,* which can be translated as word, preexisted life and everything.

"Starting from the mere vibration of the windowpanes in the kitchen of my house, I came to deeper topics related to music, sound, and vibrations. I realized that there are two kinds of vibrations. One is a direct consequence of a percussion, the other is due to a sympathetic process as it happens in the musical instrument *viola d'amore*. Our souls also have strings that vibrate through sympathy."

"Uncle Salvatore, I learned at school that Sanskrit is the oldest language in the world. Its distinctiveness lies in the special vibrations that occur when words are pronounced in Sanskrit."

"Every language creates vibrations," replied my uncle.

"Yes, it is true. But in Sanskrit, the vibrations are greater. Mantras spoken in Sanskrit help purify Earth's atmosphere."

"There are mantras in all languages. One Sunday I went to Comiso, a town near Ragusa, with a few friends of mine. During the Cold War, there was a missile site near there designed to strike the Soviet Union. A Buddhist monk came from Japan to pray for world peace. After the Cold War was over, the monk remained in Comiso and built a pagoda. On that day, we went there to attend a Buddhist ceremony. I noticed that his prayers were based upon the repetition of the same mantra. Hundreds of times we repeated the same words and beat drums. Those words were like melodious music. I felt my heart open to peace and love. I think the chanting of mantras can create vibrations favorable to peace. Was it possible that the mantras of that Japanese Buddhist monk contributed to the peace between the two superpowers?"

"Yes, I think so. However, not only mantras but also the prayers we say in the Catholic Church have powerful vibrations. Long ago I used to join the Benedictine Sisters of Isola who in the early morning sang psalms. Singing psalms resonated in the air and vibrated in my heart. It was like a purifier."

Then my uncle looked at me with his unique, mischievous smile.

"What are you trying to hide? Do you want to talk about religion again?" I asked.

"No, I don't. I just want to talk a bit more about the Protestant church and then about gibberish, which is the next topic."

"Okay, let's start a new chapter."

CHAPTER IV
GIBBERISH

"When I attended worship in the Protestant church, I never felt the urge to stand up and praise God or Jesus. The strings of my soul were not attuned with those songs and music, so they couldn't vibrate. Evidently, the worshippers in the church felt some vibrations that I couldn't feel.

"One evening, after almost ten people had praised God, the pastor in charge of the church, whose melodious voice stood out, went to the lectern. He sang like a tenor, with a warm and powerful voice. He was quite short, black-haired, and had an Irish redheaded wife a bit taller than him. His four children, two boys and two girls, were in church. One of them played the keyboard. The others sang in the choir. All four resembled their mother. The pastor began the biblical study by talking about the interaction between music and religion. 'The book of Revelation, or Apocalypse,' he said, 'tells of an angel who plays the trumpet. There is closeness between religion and music. Famous is Saint Augustine's saying, *he who sings prays twice*. It means that if one praises God by music or songs, his prayer is more effective than prayers made of spoken words. Music is a universal language. Everybody can understand and feel it. Even with the extraterrestrials we can communicate through music. Music is a path toward God. I can't imagine paradise without music.' Maybe he is right. Music is a way to get close to God, I thought.

"As I searched for an answer to my basic question, is there life after death? I couldn't miss this important path to God, music. But what to do? At that time I was sixty-three years old. My hands and brain were too stiff to play a musical instrument. Nevertheless, I wanted to study music. So, I started learning the piano."

"Good job, Uncle Salvatore! I have never met an old man who started learning to play the piano. Young people's brains are nimbler than elders'. Fingers are not very flexible after a certain age and arthritis sets in."

"Yes, you are right. There are some parts of our brains we never use. Through my endeavors to learn the piano, I noticed the difference between brain and soul. Obviously, I can't prove it scientifically, but sometimes intuition leads to discoveries that can't be attained by science. When I strove to play the piano, my soul could feel the music, but my brain was not nimble enough to catch up with my soul's feelings. It was not able to make my fingers play the notes on the keyboard smoothly."

"Now your story becomes interesting to me. I want to listen to your endeavors to learn the piano. Tell me. I'm all ears."

"When I started to learn the piano, my first homework was to render my fingers independent from one another. Usually we don't do these kinds of movements. When one plays the piano, one's fingers must obey the orders given by the brain quickly. At first it was not easy for me to do that, but with patience and perseverance I succeeded in making my fingers more flexible."

"The musical notes are seven, Uncle Salvatore. The number seven is magic. I think the most amazing things in the universe are expressed by the number seven."

"Yes, seven is the number of the creation! The colors of the rainbow are seven! The number seven recurs in the Holy Scriptures and in life many times. In Eastern culture, the symbolic number seven is present as well. There are seven chakras or energy points in our body. In Korea seven is a symbol of good luck. I could continue to list sevens, but it is better to stop here.

"I learned the structure of the staff, but I couldn't read the notes quickly. When I practiced what I had learned from my piano teacher, my slowness was the main obstacle. I could spot and read the notes, but my playing was not smooth. I often paused when I passed from a measure to the next. Later, when my teacher added the metronome, the problem became more complicated. I couldn't follow the tempo, and every knock of the metronome was like a knock in my brain. I hated the metronome!"

"You have been a great traveler. Often you traveled abroad. When you were in foreign countries, how did you practice the piano?"

"It was a big problem. For at least one third of the year I was abroad. Later, in India, the idea of taking piano lessons occurred to me."

"You have iron willpower, Uncle Salvatore!"

"Yes, but my willpower was not enough at that time. I couldn't play the piano for more than ten minutes. It was a stumbling block. After playing the piano for a short while, my brain overheated. It was like a small car engine at maximum rpm. I was too old to start learning the piano, but I didn't want to give up. In my dictionary there is no giving up.

"In the Protestant church, the meetings took place on Thursday evenings and on Sundays. On Sundays I preferred to attend Mass at the Catholic church, and I continued to go to the Protestant church every Thursday evening.

"One evening, after nearly a half hour of singing, something extraordinary happened. The pastor who led the worship first started to stammer and then uttered a series of incomprehensible words or rather sounds. It was gibberish, which lasted for almost ten minutes. His words recalled an unknown dead language. I had never seen anything similar in the Christian world. Long ago, attending Catholic Charismatic Movement meetings, I heard about speaking in tongues. But I had never seen someone who spoke in tongues.

"The pastor seemed to be in a trance. He was perspiring and pale. His wife sat close to him, motionless as a statue, with her gaze turned forward.

"When the ceremony was over, I approached the pastor and asked him, 'What happened to you?' 'I had a fire inside my chest. It is possible to keep it under control, but it is better to let this inner fire out,' he answered. 'What kind of fire is it?' 'Our church was established in Wales at the beginning of the last century. From there it spread all over the world. It is related to the church of the early Christians. The gift of the Holy Spirit and speaking in unknown languages are described in the Acts of the Apostles.' 'What does speaking in tongues mean?' 'It means speaking in an unknown language. He who speaks in tongues experiences a special communion with God. To learn about this topic, I recommend you study the Holy Scriptures. At the beginning, there was only one language for all humankind. Then, due to the building of the Tower of Babel, God confused languages. Later, on Pentecost day, the Holy Spirit descended into the Apostles who spoke in an unknown language which everybody was able to understand,' the pastor said."

"Did you inquire into the pastor's gibberish?"

"Yes, I did."

"What conclusion did you come to?"

"The pastor's gibberish made me suspicious that it was due to the vibrations of the music and songs which resounded in his heart. He convulsively expressed the so-called communion with God."

"Do you rule out that the Holy Spirit talked through the pastor's voice?"

"No, I don't. But I am still a bit skeptical about it.

"A few years later, during one of my travels to India, I had a chance to know another kind of gibberish. This gibberish was a way of giving vent to the innermost thoughts and emotions buried in the depths of the mind. Actually, we hide repressed emotions inside ourselves.

"It is said that the etymology of the word *gibberish* comes from Gibraltar, a British overseas territory whose inhabitants spoke in a language mixed with English, Spanish, Hebrew, Arabic, and Hindi whenever they didn't want foreigners to understand their conversation. Another theory says that the word *gibberish* comes from the name of the Arabic alchemist Geber who used it as an incomprehensible jargon. At Osho Ashram, in India, gibberish consisted of speaking nonsense words in unknown languages. Its main function was to throw away the garbage inside our mind."

"Uncle Salvatore, everybody has some kind of madness inside! Is it possible that there are persons with a completely clean mind?"

"Maybe enlightened persons, saints or mystics. I don't know about that. I can only tell you about myself and the garbage in my mind. Many times in my life, I wanted to scream loudly and give vent to my emotions, but I couldn't do that. If so, people would have considered me mad. When I was a boy, sometimes I used to say nonsense words and unarticulated syllables long before I heard about gibberish. At that time, maybe I did gibberish unconsciously to let out my repressed emotions."

"I want to know something more about gibberish. Could you say something more?"

"Sure. We can't know ourselves well if we don't throw away all the garbage we have inside. To do that, we need to express our repressed emotions. When I did gibberish at the Osho Ashram, in India, I shouted nonsense words in an unknown language. After doing gibberish for one hour, I felt empty inside and light because I had expressed my anger, anxiety, and all kinds of negative emotions fully.

"It sounds interesting! Someday I want to try gibberish. Now, can you talk about your repressed emotions, Uncle Salvatore?"

"Yes, of course. When I was young, due to my Catholic education, I strove to be a good person, generous and pious. I wanted to be a perfect Christian, full of love, compassion, and free from envy and a negative mind. But to do so, I suppressed my real nature. It means that I buried my spontaneous emotions and natural desire to live my life as I wanted. It was as if I acted the role of a good man, a perfect Christian, but that model was not me. Whenever I felt envy toward somebody, I said to myself, 'You must not be envious. It is a sin!' I strove to be unenvious, but my true nature was just the opposite. To be a good Christian, I suppressed my emotions."

"Did gibberish help you to live as you wanted?"

"Yes, gibberish helped me to clean my mind and meet my authentic being. Not only by doing gibberish, but also by studying, traveling, and attending religious meetings, I realized that *what I am* and *how I act* are not the same thing. You can be a good person but sometimes act badly, and vice versa, good actions can come from a wicked person sometimes.

"Therefore, don't try to change your nature, rather change your actions! Accept whoever you are and don't suppress your nature. Instead, try to act well. Your shortcomings are a part of yourself. 'What I am is nothing, what I do is everything,' someone said. What a person is and what a person does can be likened to the fruits of a tree. It is not important that a tree is good or bad, short or tall, upright or bent. What matters is that it brings forth good fruits."

"Your opinion, Uncle Salvatore, doesn't match with Jesus's teachings. According to Matthew's Gospel, it seems to be impossible that a bad tree can produce good fruits, and vice versa. Do you agree with Jesus?"

"Not much. Despite the great love I have for Jesus, I want to keep my opinion intact. On the other hand, all good masters set their disciples free to think in their own way. I think Jesus also allows me to express my opinion."

"So, don't I need to change myself?"

"Don't change yourself, Benedetto! You must accept yourself as you are. A human being is like a beautiful painting with a variety of gradations and a myriad of colors. For instance, if you don't like the color black and cut it off from the painting, it loses its originality and harmony of colors. If you change your nose, teeth, shyness, impulsiveness, and so on, you will be a different person, quite different from the original yourself."

"I think the same goes for society."

"Yes, Benedetto! The world is like a gigantic tapestry. Its weaving shows all the figures existing on Earth. There are vicious and meek animals, all kinds of plants, good and wicked people, and so on. Seen from the sky, the tapestry is fantastic. When you cut out what you dislike, for instance, mice, spiders, wild animals, bad people, and so on, many figures will disappear from the tapestry. It will be a different tapestry and will lose its unique beauty and splendor."

"I definitely agree with you, Uncle Salvatore. But you digress too much. You go off the subject."

"Don't worry. My aim is not to write a bestseller. On the other hand, the title of this chapter is Gibberish, isn't it? Gibberish allows one to express freely whatever one feels. So, let me tell whatever, please!"

"Okay! Do as you like. I'll keep typing."

My uncle took the Bible again and read aloud, 'Do not judge, so you will not be judged. For in the way you judge you will be judged, and in the way you measure you will be measured' (Matt. 7: 1-2).

"What does this passage mean? It means that it is not appropriate to say this person is good or that person is bad. You should say this person acts well or that person acts badly. The interior of a human being can't be judged or condemned. We can't know what happens inside a human being.

"I remember that once I broached the issue of good and evil with a Carmelite monk in a Christian meeting. He was

Father John from Veneto. At that time, Sicily and Veneto were a Carmelite province. He was tall, blond, and athletic with enticing blue eyes. I couldn't make out why such a handsome man left the worldly life to become a monk. But, maybe things are simpler than guesswork. When his talking was over, I asked him, 'Genesis tells us about the tree of good and evil. It is said that man must not know about good and evil, otherwise he will die. Hence, Father John, does God want man to be ignorant?'

"Father John turned to me. Through his smile I could have a look into his great heart. Then he said a few words with a strong Venetian accent. 'Yes, the Bible is right. Man oughtn't to know what is good and what is evil,' he said.

"At first, I couldn't understand his laconic answer. There was a big gap between that great monk and me in regard to theological and spiritual matters. Furthermore, as I was within a group of several people, I didn't want to deepen the discussion lest I monopolize the conversation.

"Then, a very young man intervened. He surprised me, because he was quite educated despite his young age. He sat opposite me. I can't remember his features after so many years have gone by, but his words are still engraved in my memory. 'There are different ways to confront evil. St. Jerome removed a thorn from the paw of a lion, while St. George killed a dragon. The lion and the dragon are just metaphors symbolizing evil. While St. George suppresses evil through violence, St. Jerome dialogues with it. Which way is better? I don't know. However, I can know only my own good and my own evil, not others' good and evil. On the other hand, other people's deeds concern themselves not me. What matters is my good actions regardless of others' deeds. In other words, even though others act badly, I ought to behave well anyway. To love others I don't need to be loved first,' the very young man said.

"I was astonished by his words. I couldn't imagine that he could go so deeply into the topic of good and evil."

"Why were you surprised? Do you think only elders have a philosophical mind? Tell me, what is the difference between elders and youngsters, ancient and modern civilization? For me, man's mind and heart are the same, regardless of age or the epoch in which he has lived."

"If we consider technology development, we are tempted to claim that man has progressed over the centuries, but the progress refers only to scientific discoveries. In regard to morals, philosophy, religion, music, and literature, man has not progressed. The human heart cannot progress. For instance, the Homeric poems or the Greek philosophers who lived thousands of years ago are not out of fashion, for they are beyond space and time."

"Uncle Salvatore, we started from gibberish, but we talked about other topics too much. That's okay. Something has been interesting to me. How about switching to another topic?"

"Okay!"

CHAPTER V
ESOTERICISM

"After I left the theater group, I felt sad. I really had enjoyed that experience, but it was over. Whenever one door closed, life opened a new door to me. It was the mystery of life. One evening, while I was strolling in the street thinking of Pietro and the theater group, Rino, a friend of mine who was also Bruno's friend, pulled his car next to me and motioned me to get in. He was a manager of an important multinational insurance company, one of Bruno's best clients. Over the years, a close friendship arose between them. I had a feeling that both of them belonged to the same Masonic lodge.

"Rino came from a small town near Isola, Rosabianca. The inhabitants of that village had a rough appearance. They all looked like peasants. Even their way of dressing was rustic and outmoded. As for Rino, after spending many years in Isola, his manners became less rough. Although he was very sociable, his tendency to bully led him to lose his friends, even the closest ones. He liked to stand out. To make up for his innate roughness, he used to dress in a unique way. That evening he wore a red leather jacket and a blue bow tie. 'Would you like to participate in an astrology course?' 'What?' I asked with my mouth and eyes wide open. 'I say again, would you like to take part in a series of lessons about astrology?'

"I got into his car, and in doing so, I thought about what to say. Actually, I had no interest in astrology. I didn't believe in it. I was convinced that astrology was based upon a wrong assumption. According to astrologers, it is the sun that rotates around Earth, and not vice versa. For them the sun is a planet. Being based upon an illogical postulate, astrology was irrational, in my opinion.

"Nevertheless, at that time, I was very sad for having cut off my relationship with Pietro and the theater group. Rino's proposal sounded like a diversion from my sad feelings. 'Yes, thank you very much. I'll participate in the course. When does it start?' 'Next Saturday at three o'clock in a nearby city, Capodarso. A friend of mine will host the workshop at her home. It is quite difficult to reach her house, so our meeting place will be at the square in front of the Hotel Vacation Inn at a quarter to three. You can wait inside your car in case someone is late. But usually, all of us are very punctual.' 'Okay, I'll be there at the exact time.' 'Would you mind doing me a favor?' 'No, of course not. What is it?' 'Can you give two friends of mine a ride? One is a doctor and also a good poet. The other is a teacher of classical literature.' 'Sure!' He gave me the telephone numbers of those fellows, and then we parted.

"On Saturday at two o'clock, I pulled up in front of Dr. Giuseppe Musumeci's house. I tooted my horn briefly, and a man came out of the main door of a two-story working-class house. He was about fifty, short, thickset, and sturdy. His long and thick trunk was out of proportion to his short legs, which looked like two logs. His beard, quite long and unkempt, was turning gray. He had the appearance of a blacksmith, not of a doctor.

"The building where Giuseppe and his wife lived was located by the shore of a mythological lake. According to myth, Kore, Jupiter and Demeter's daughter, was abducted by Pluto, the god of Hades, while she was plucking flowers around the lush shore of a lake. After Pluto abducted Kore, Demeter, the goddess of agriculture, looked for her everywhere. She was so furious about having lost her beloved daughter that she made the earth cease to give fruits. All plants began to wither. Finally, Demeter and Pluto reached an agreement. Kore would stay with Pluto in Hades for six months and with her mother on earth for six months. The myth symbolizes the life on this planet with two periods. One is fall and winter, when the earth looks lifeless, and the other is spring and summer, when it wakes up from the winter slumber and plants are luxuriant.

"Seeing me, Giuseppe waved his hand very gladly and got into my car. 'I am Salvatore Gagliano. We both live in the same small town, but we haven't met before.' 'I am Giuseppe Musumeci. I have lived in Isola for fifteen years. I am from Acitrezza, a small village on the east coast of Sicily.' 'Why did you come to Isola? What do you do here?'

"He lifted up his green eyes and then stared at me for an instant. He wanted to make sure I could understand him, and then he began to talk. 'I got a degree in medicine at Catania University and then I came to Isola. I practiced as a medical doctor for a few years. Then I quit my job. I didn't want to be a medical doctor anymore.' 'What do you do to make a living?' 'My family is rich. So I don't need to earn money.'

"The years I had spent as a businessman made me suspect that he wasn't telling the truth. He didn't look like a rich man at all. His jacket was a bit worn. Furthermore, he didn't have a car. But I wanted to be discreet and not to dig further into his privacy. He started talking with an air of a professor. 'I want to devote myself to studying human society and religions. I dream of a new humanism in a society where human beings can live free from religious oppression. I aim at writing a monumental book to prove that the Bible is a trick.'

"Giuseppe talked in a refined language and looked learned, but I sensed that he tended to show off, although he was erudite. He was so involved and excited in his talking that I didn't feel like interrupting him. When he stopped talking, I asked him, 'Why do you think the Bible is a trick?' 'The stories told in the Bible are not original at all. Many religions tell the same stories as those written in the Bible. For instance, the myth of creation in Egyptian mythology is older than that in the Bible by at least fifteen hundred years. According to Jewish tradition, the first book of the Bible, Genesis, was written by Moses when he led his people through the desert. The Exodus from Egypt happened around fifteen hundred BC, while the Egyptian mythology ranges between five thousand BC and three thousand BC.'

"I listened to him silently, and for the first time I had doubts about the originality of the Bible. Even though I was and still I am Catholic, my desire to know the truth was much bigger than my blind faith in the Bible. He went on. 'The myth of the creation of man from clay is in the Egyptian mythology as well. Khnum, the god of creation, was called the Potter God, because he gave life to living beings by shaping clay. The God of the Bible created Adam in the same way. Hence, the Bible is not original. It imitates other religions.'

"His easy and fluent talk was like the rushing of a river. It seemed unstoppable. 'Do you think the Christian religion is original? Not at all! Christianity borrowed its rites from the cult of the god Mithra, who was also born in a cave on December twenty-fifth.'

"I stared into his eyes, and then I raised my voice, 'Tell me! Where did you find such information? Can you prove what you said?' 'Yes. I'll give you written proof, but don't ask me to prove anything else. Everything I say is true. I don't invent anything,' he said severely. Actually, a few days later, he showed me the encyclopedia through which he had learned about the god Mithra.

While I was driving toward downtown Isola, he kept talking about religion. 'The Roman Catholic Church built many cathedrals on god Mithra's temples. Do you want me to give you evidence?' 'Yes, I do!' I answered eagerly. 'Hence, go to Rome and visit the Basilica of San Clemente. It's near the Colosseum and easy to reach. This basilica has one ground floor and two basements. At the entrance, on the ground floor there is the newest church dating back to the twelfth century. If you go down to the first basement, you'll find another church which goes back to the fourth century. On the second basement, you'll find god Mithra's temple. Some people perceive a peculiar energy in the lowest basement, especially when they stand near the water which flows down there. I don't believe in extrasensory energies. I only believe in what I can touch, see, and hear. I am just reporting that somebody feels an arcane energy in the Mithraeum of San Clemente Basilica.'

"Giuseppe was still telling me the story of the god Mithra when we got to Umberto Sabatini's house. Umberto's build was different than Giuseppe's. He was a tall redhead with a more refined way of dressing. Umberto had the air of a teacher, while Giuseppe looked like a blacksmith. Actually, he had been a teacher of Latin and ancient Greek, but he quit his job. Even though he had a degree in classic literature, he wanted to become a municipal policeman. Strangely, although Giuseppe and Umberto had master's degrees, they didn't want to have the job they had studied for. One wanted to be a writer instead of a physician, and the other a municipal policeman instead of a teacher. Two uncommon persons! Like them, maybe many of us would want to be uncommon, to lead a different life, change jobs, move away from our country, city, family, and so on. But we don't do that because we tend to live according to the social patterns that have conditioned us since childhood. Umberto, at a brisk pace, got into my car and sat in the back seat. We introduced ourselves briefly and set off toward Capodarso, which is almost a half hour away from Isola.

"On the road Giuseppe resumed his tirade. 'The Christians changed the figure of Jesus. The Greek word *Christos,* which means anointed, doesn't apply to Jesus. The term was coined later by the early Greek-speaking Christians. Jesus was anticlerical, but the Christians turned him into a priest. Jesus didn't hand over any rite, but the Christians borrowed their rituals from Mithraism, such as baptism, Holy Communion with bread and wine, and so on. The idea that Jesus was born from a virgin was also borrowed from Mithraism. In fact, Mithra was born from the virgin Anahita, who had been inseminated by the god Ariman through a miracle. Like Jesus,

Mithra promised eternal life to his followers and was very popular among the Roman soldiers who could die in battle.'

"Umberto was less talkative than Giuseppe, but from time to time, he broke in on his friend's talking. 'Catholics turned Jesus into an inquisitor monk. You have to know,' Umberto said, meeting my gaze in the rearview mirror, 'that there were two kinds of inquisition. One was the Spanish Inquisition, and the other was the Roman Inquisition. The latter was much worse than the former, more violent and crueler. Pope Paul III created the Roman Inquisition in the sixteenth century. Unlike the Spanish Inquisition, its jurisdiction was restricted to Italy. It was an awful court. It made an index of forbidden books and held trials that in many cases ended with the accused person being burned at the stake. If you go to Rome, visit Campo Dei Fiori, a square near the French Embassy. There, you can see the statue of the philosopher Giordano Bruno, who was burned at the stake due to a verdict of conviction issued by the Tribunal of the Roman Inquisition.' 'Galileo Galilei', added Giuseppe, 'abjured his ideas and discoveries. At the end of the trial against him, Galileo was forced to state that the sun orbits Earth and not vice versa. Otherwise, the Roman Inquisition would have burned him at the stake like Giordano Bruno.'

"Both Giuseppe and Umberto talked convincingly, but I felt that they were prejudiced against the Catholic Church. Their tone burned with hatred against it. However, my two new friends touched my mind. From then on, my way of living with religion changed. I started to consider that truth has many aspects. Since then, I began to study other religions, rites, and cults, trying to approach them freely, without prejudice."

"Abruptly Giuseppe burst out, 'All priests should be sent to the gallows!' I wanted to tell him that my opinion was different from his. Many friends of mine were priests and I respected them much. Furthermore, I was convinced that we should give thanks to priests because without them it would be impossible to celebrate ceremonies and rites that elevate human beings' spirits. Without priests, man would fall into materialism, as happened in Communist countries. I was about to argue with Giuseppe and tell him, 'You are too self-important! You consider yourself a pure being, while priests should be hanged. It is completely wrong, for many priests live holy lives.' But I didn't. Meanwhile, we arrived in Capodarso, where we would meet the rest of the group.

"While we were waiting in the square in front the Hotel Vacation Inn, we talked about astrology. None of us seemed to believe in it. 'I believe only in what I can see, hear, and touch. Astrology is out of my sensorial field,' said Giuseppe. 'Astrology is anachronistic. Nowadays only the credulous believe in it,' added Umberto. 'I wonder why we have come to Capodarso. The meeting is about astrology. Are we here just for fun or curiosity?' I said.

"As if by magic, suddenly the whole square swarmed with cars. The plates showed that they came from all over Sicily, many from Palermo and Catania. Everybody got out of the car and gave one another very friendly kisses. I noticed that their way of greeting and kissing was unusual. It was as if they had a secret sign to recognize and greet one another. If I had seen only a couple of them acting in that way, I would have missed the details. But since all of them kissed one another on the cheeks in the same way, I inferred that there was something unusual in them.

"Uncle Salvatore, can you tell me how they greeted one another? I want to write something about their mysterious secret sign."

"I can't tell you it, Benedetto, because I promised them not to spread any of their rituals. If I told it to you now, I would betray their trust."

"I respect your feelings, but the book would be more attractive if we added something unusual."

"My honor and respect for my friends come first, and then all the rest."

"Okay, go on, Uncle Salvatore. I won't insist anymore."

"I was reluctant to get out of my car. I liked to observe them from my car. Giuseppe was the boldest of us. He went toward them and introduced himself to a man who had the air of a leader. 'My name is Giuseppe. Are you going to the astrology course as well?' 'Yes, I am. My name is Gaetano. Nice to meet you,' answered the fellow, who stood out for his long, white pointed beard.' 'You look like an architect, don't you?' said Giuseppe. 'I am the architect of myself. I work to shape myself into a spiritual being,' Gaetano said to cut his answer short.

"We all waited for Rino, who was the only one who knew where the course would be held. He arrived after a few minutes and waved his hand from his car. All of us followed him with our cars toward a house located on the outskirts of Capodarso. It was surrounded by a garden with luxuriant plants and flowers. At the entrance a nice lady welcomed us. She was about fifty years old and charming. What hit me was her smile. She had slicked-back blond hair. Maybe she dyed it. I'm not sure about that. Her designer red trousers and white silk blouse made her look rich. Overall she looked like a very refined, polite, and educated lady. I felt that she belonged to the old nobility which was once widespread in Sicily. 'My name is Nunziatina. Please come in, and feel at home,' she said, holding out her hand to each of us as we crossed the threshold of her house.

"In the lounge, there were armchairs, chairs, and couches covered with velvet or something similar. Nunziatina had already arranged the sitting places on one side of the large room. On the opposite side she had placed a board with wide paper sheets. In the room was a broad glass door that led to the back of the garden. We all took our places and sat down. Suddenly, a tall and lean black-haired man in his forties wearing a light-colored V-neck sweater over a checked shirt stood up and went to the board. He was the person who would lead the course.

"He introduced himself, 'My name is Giacomo. I am an astrologer, or, more exactly, a person who loves astrology, for I am an attorney.'

"He drew the twelve signs of the zodiac on the board. Then he explained the specifics of each sign. As I had a prejudice against astrology, I didn't follow him. While he was talking, my mind wandered elsewhere. I often turned my eyes to the walls of the room and admired the beautiful paintings hung there. Afterward, he explained the degrees as units of measurement in astrology. He did many complicated calculations, which I couldn't understand. At school, I was not a genius in mathematics.

"He also talked about ephemerides. He said that once there were just seven planets in astrology, but after the new discoveries, now Neptune and Pluto are also considered in astrology. However, their influences are weak, for they complete a revolution round the sun in the course of several years. He also associated metals and colors with planets and zodiac signs.

"Once his talk was over, Giacomo asked the participants to put questions to him. Some wrote the year, month, day, hour, and minute of their birth on a piece of paper and asked Giacomo to figure out their ascendants and give them predictions about their future. They seemed to believe in astrology. Giacomo's calculations to cast a horoscope were so complicated that I diverted my attention from them.

"I wanted to ask him, 'Is astrology based upon the Ptolemaic mistake, or is it something different? Is astrology a science, or not? How can we assess the validity of what astrology tells?' But I didn't want to embarrass the lecturer, nor spoil the cheerful atmosphere in the lounge with my skepticism about astrology.

"When the lecture was over, we tasted biscuits and drinks set on a table covered with a white linen tablecloth. Then, Rino headed for the other side of the lounge. He thanked Giacomo for his learned lecture and said that the next meeting would be held in another house on a different area of Capodarso. 'Next Saturday we will meet at the square on the hill of Capodarso at the same time as today. You can't miss it. It is the only hill in Capodarso. Then, I will lead you to the house.'

"On the way back to Isola, Giuseppe, Umberto, and I exchanged our impressions about the meeting. 'Did you see the way they kissed one another on their cheeks?' I asked. 'No, we didn't,' answered Giuseppe and Umberto with one voice. 'When they kissed, the way they smacked their lips seemed to be pretty unusual.' 'Could you be more specific?' asked Umberto. 'Yes, of course. When they smacked their lips, they made a distinctive sound.' 'I couldn't notice that detail. However, I think we have stumbled across a secret society.'

"His words brought me back to school time. Since then I have been attracted to esotericism. Secret societies like *Carboneria,* a nineteenth century Italian secret republican organization, had an important role in unifying Italy. I had a feeling that the world was ruled by secret societies able to condition politics and even religion."

"In a few churches of Isola, there are some mysterious symbols painted on the walls. For instance, on the ceiling of the Church of San Giovanni is painted a triangle with an eye inside. Do you think this symbol is related to esotericism, Uncle Salvatore?"

"I don't know the symbol you are talking about, Benedetto. However, I think there is no relation between the Catholic Church and esotericism.

"While I was driving to Isola with Giuseppe and Umberto, I tried to learn something more about esotericism. 'What kind of secret society?' I asked them. 'I don't know yet, but the participants in the meetings are an esoteric group. I'm sure about that. Otherwise, it is inexplicable why they come from different, distant parts of Sicily for an astrology course. Moreover, they are very familiar with one another. Therefore, they must be a group or an association,' said Umberto. 'I'll research this at the library. There is a rare book which contains a lot of information about esotericism. I'll try to sort out which esoteric society uses astrology in its practices,' Giuseppe added.

"I drove from Capodarso to Isola slowly. I wanted to make friends with them and know them more deeply. Giuseppe seemed to read my mind. 'I don't practice medicine, and Umberto doesn't teach, but it doesn't mean that we don't work. We have already written a book together, and we are going to write more books in the future.'

"I was surprised at having two writers, two scholars, in my car! 'What is your book about?' 'It is a collection of essays,' answered Umberto. 'But it is very difficult to get our book published by a good publishing house.' 'At my own expense, I have also published a little book of poems about talking with my brother, Satan,' said Giuseppe. 'What? What are you talking about? Is the devil your brother?' I asked, turning my astonished eyes toward him. 'Don't misunderstand me, please! The devil doesn't exist, indeed. The fallen angel is an invention of priests. Satan with horns and cloven feet belongs to iconography.'"

"Uncle Salvatore, I think Giuseppe and Umberto were strange. I can't understand those who quit their jobs and don't try to find a new one. Writing a book is not a job. You can't count on writing a book to make a living. In my opinion, they were just two idle dreamers."

"Benedetto, even though they look like useless idle dreamers to you, the two writers improved my life a lot. They taught me how to write well. Now, let's continue the story."

"Okay!"

"I said to Giuseppe, 'If you claim that Satan doesn't exist, it means that his opposite, God, doesn't exist either.' 'I just want to say that good and evil are not external to man. Wickedness comes from the inside, not from Satan! I call Satan my brother because he doesn't exist outside humans, whom I consider my brothers,' he answered.

"I was touched by Giuseppe's words. He considered all people as his brothers and dreamed of a new humanism. He was a great man!"

"Uncle Salvatore, sometimes you are credulous. Giuseppe wanted to hang all priests. How can he consider all human beings as his brothers? Priests are also humans, indeed. What do you think about Satan? Does he exist or not?"

"Benedetto, if you listen to what I am going to say, you can know something more about this issue."

"Please, go on, Uncle Salvatore!"

"Umberto backed Giuseppe's words. 'Separation between good and evil is a legacy of the Manichaean dualism. The idea of two antagonist forces, good and evil, comes from a philosophical or religious mind. Reality is quite different.' 'Life,' added Giuseppe, 'is neither good nor bad, neither beautiful nor unpleasant. It is just life.' 'What does dualism mean?' I asked. 'It means discrimination between good and evil. Actually, they coexist in every person, for in each of us there is both good and evil. Therefore, Satan, who symbolizes evil, is inside us. He is not an external creature that pushes us to act badly. Only man is responsible for his deeds, not Satan,' answered Giuseppe. 'Is your book available in the bookstores?' 'Sure. You can buy it. But I'll give you one. The ignorant think I am a Satanist. It is wrong. I am not a Satanist. I just want to show that Satan doesn't exist.'

"How strange life is! An astrology meeting brought about an encounter with two writers, I thought.

"I drove Giuseppe to his house near the lake. Then I dropped Umberto in front of his home.

"The following week I worked at the haulage company as usual, but I looked forward to Saturday afternoon. The astrology course and my new friends became part and parcel of my life at that time.

"The meeting house was in the upper part of Capodarso, almost on the top of a green hill. It was a foggy day. While we were waiting for the others, a patrol car with three policemen inside pulled up. 'Show your identity cards, please!' ordered one of the policemen.

"We fumbled in our wallets and took out our identity cards. The three policemen took them, went to their car, and called their headquarters. Then they came back with our ID cards. 'What are you doing in this remote place?' a policeman asked. 'We are waiting for the rest of our group. We're going to an astrology course,' I answered.

"The policeman, who had the air of a chief, looked up at the clouded sky. 'Astrology? With such foggy weather?'

"Policemen are men of force. Sometimes it is not easy to make them understand how things really are. If they suspect something, their minds don't change readily. 'In our course, we don't use a telescope, so we don't need to look at the sky,' I said with a quiet tone. 'Astrology, not astronomy!' Umberto snapped.

"The cop seemed to be embarrassed by Umberto's words. Apparently, he didn't know the difference between astrology and astronomy. Another policeman talked on the telephone in the patrol car. After a few minutes, he came back and said something in the ear of the commander, who saluted us. 'Enjoy your astronomy or astrology course, whatever it is! The operations room said that you had no previous convictions.' He swung about and went back to the patrol car.

"After the cops left, Rino arrived with the rest of the group. 'Let's park the cars in the square and walk for a while. My friend Mario lives nearby,' he said.

"Like Nunziatina, Mario lived in a detached house, but it seemed grim to me. Nunziatina's house was full of flowers and colors. Here, the facade was quite old and blackened by air pollution. At the entrance, a middle-aged fellow welcomed us in a gentlemanlike manner. He seemed to know Rino well, but not the others. His hair was black, straight, and pomaded. He shook hands with the men and bowed to the women to kiss their hands, but he didn't give a direct kiss on the hand. It was just a gesture to greet. His wife looked older than him. She was short and dressed in a simple way. She merely greeted us with a smile from a distance. Obviously, she was not interested in astrology.

"The furniture of the living room was in a classical style, a bit similar to the English style of the early twentieth century. Many portraits of persons in old-fashioned dress were hung on the walls. I don't know whether those paintings were portraits of ancestors or were there just for decoration. What attracted my attention was a round three-legged table. I don't know why, but I associated those portraits with the three-legged table. I sensed that they were there for séances. This house looked sinister!

"Mario had already arranged the basement room for our meeting. We were led underground through a narrow stone staircase that had some niches in the left wall. In one of them I saw a mouse trap. I inferred that there were mice in the house. I feared mice, and the idea of coming across a small rodent made me tense. Both the sides of the underground room were slightly elevated. They were narrower than the central part and filled with tables and chairs. I sat down in the middle of the central row to be far from mice, which usually don't run in the midst of people.

"A very beautiful lady came and sat close to me. Soon all the chairs were occupied, and Giacomo started his astrology lesson. The first part was similar to what he had explained at Nunziatina's home. He talked about astrological houses and their meaning, the zodiac, and the influence of planets upon Earth. 'Let's consider tides,' he said. 'They happen because of the attraction of the moon. It influences life on Earth. Many farmers sow their fields when the moon is waxing for the seeds to grow fast and strongly. If you want to test this theory, cut your hair during the waxing moon. It will grow quickly. We can perceive the influence of the moon more than that of planets because the moon is closer. As a planet gets farther from Earth, its influence decreases.'

"Suddenly, I started in fear. 'What happened?' the lady sitting close to me asked. 'Nothing, but I thought I saw a mouse passing very quickly along the side corridor.' She smiled at me and kept following the lesson."

"Uncle Salvatore, I didn't know you were afraid of mice. It is funny that a strong man like you fears a small rodent."

"Even elephants fear mice. It is normal to have a fear of something. Some people are afraid of geckos, some of snakes, some of toads, and so on. Once I knew a woman who feared birds. Everyone has his own little phobia."

"I don't have any kind of phobia. Now keep telling your story."

"Thank you, Benedetto." Uncle Salvatore smiled mischievously.

"After a while, Giacomo stopped talking about astrology and began to explain symbols. 'The term symbol comes from the Greek word *sunbolon*, which means put together. In ancient times, the *sunbolon* was an identifying token. It was an object split into two halves. Only the individual who possessed one half of the *sunbolon* was allowed to join the group or the tribe that had the other half. These days, the symbol has lost its original function. Now it is just considered as a veiled truth. Esoteric secrets are veiled, but understanding the symbol makes it possible to remove the veil and know the truth. Through the symbol, we can make a synthesis between different levels of existence, spirit and matter, sky and earth, cause and effect, part and whole, et cetera. The sky is the most widespread symbol. All religions associate the sky with the supernatural. Through the symbol the different parts become one. I want to introduce you to the world of symbols. They are not man's creation. You can find the same symbols in different places of the earth, among various tribes and cultures. For instance, the swastika is a very ancient symbol. Hitler borrowed it. The swastika existed in India, Rome, America, and many countries since time immemorial. It was considered as a bearer of good luck, peace, and well-being. Ordinary people can't understand symbols well, for this faculty belongs to mystics, initiates, and heroes.'"

"I don't agree with the lecturer, Uncle Salvatore. If I go to the library, I can find many books about symbols. Do you think the authors of those books were mystics or initiates or heroes? In your opinion, is it needed to enter an esoteric school to know veiled truths?"

"Maybe yes. There are some secret teachings that have been transmitted orally within esoteric schools. Reading books is not enough to broaden your mind. Some secrets are only orally passed on from master to disciple."

"Thank you, Uncle Salvatore. But I am not convinced about that. Let's go on now."

"It was the first time I heard the word 'initiate' inside that group. My suspicions that I came across an esoteric group were about to be confirmed.

"Giacomo went on. 'The pyramid is one of the most famous symbols. If one reproduces a small Pyramid of Cheops in its exact proportions and parameters and then at night he puts a blunt blade into it, the next morning he will be surprised to see that the blunt blade has become sharp overnight. Try it, and then you will see! Inside the Pyramid of Cheops there is the King's Chamber. Even though it is called the King's Chamber, neither a sarcophagus nor mummies were found there. Once a French explorer was visiting the King's Chamber, and he saw a garbage basket on one of the sides of the room. Besides small pieces of fruit and food, there were also little dead mice inside the basket. What surprised him was that the bodies of the small rodents were not in a state of putrefaction and didn't stink at all. The mice were just mummified. It was evident that the pyramid has an effect upon physical processes.'

"The lecture was very interesting and went on until late. That evening there was not much time to ask questions. The next meeting would be held at Nunziatina's home the following Saturday.

"On the way back to Isola we gave a ride to a young lady who taught Latin and Greek in Capodarso. She used to spend weekends at her parents' in Isola. Giuseppe sat in the front of the car, while the lady took her place in the back seat next to Umberto. They had known each other for a long time. They both had degrees in classical literature and had once worked at the same school.

"The young lady looked elegant. She wore a close-fitting black skirt and a red blouse, which almost hid a wide wine birthmark above her collarbone. Her glasses had silver-plated frames, her hair had a pageboy cut, and her eyes were the color of roasted almonds. The thin, silver-framed glasses lent her the air of an intellectual. I had seldom seen a woman so refined. Seen in profile, her face seemed perfect, but her best feature was her voice. She talked the same way as birds chirp."

"Uncle Salvatore, I think you were attracted by that young lady, don't you?"

My uncle flushed. Maybe I touched his buried feelings toward her.

"Benedetto, let's not digress for now. Later I'll talk about that. Let's go back to the scene of my car. 'My name is Maria Paola. Thank you for giving me a ride. I'm sorry to bother you. Usually I go home by bus, but this time I wanted to listen to the lecturer until the end. So I missed the last bus to Isola.' 'Don't worry! It's my pleasure to go to Isola together,' I answered.

"While Giuseppe and Umberto kept silent, I talked with her. 'What do you think about the meeting? Do you really believe that a small reproduction of the Pyramid of Cheops can have an effect on matter? Do you think the process of decay can slow down inside the Pyramid of Cheops?' 'Yes, I think so. Pyramids can influence both organic and inorganic matter. Do you remember what Giacomo said in the second part of the lecture?' 'No, I don't.' 'He said that if you put a blunt blade in the King's Chamber of the Pyramid of Cheops, it will become sharp overnight.'

"Looking at the driving mirror, I saw Umberto stirring restlessly in the back seat. Maybe he wanted to break in on my talking with Maria Paola. 'I agree with Maria Paola,' he said abruptly.

"I felt that he was interested in her. I was happy to travel with three smart persons. Usually it takes thirty minutes for me to drive from Capodarso to Isola, but that night I drove on a country road slowly instead of the usual fast road. After half an hour, we were just halfway. It was quite foggy and drizzling, and the windshield steamed up with the breath of four persons inside the car.

"There were no other cars on the road besides mine. Umberto seemed to want to impress Maria Paola and talked more than usual. 'Everything is energy. We can't perceive immaterial energy with our sensory organs because we can't go beyond our three-dimensional world. Let's take a worm as an example. It can know one dimension, only the dimension of length, not that of width and height, because it moves straight along a plane and can't lift its head upward. The sky, stars, moon, and sun are unknown to it. So are we in regard to immaterial dimensions. If we could develop another organ to perceive intangible energies, we would go beyond our world. For now, we are trapped in our three-dimensional world like worms. Matter doesn't exist. Einstein demonstrated that if we cast a particle of matter at the speed of light, it changes into energy. At the speed of light, space and time are nothing. At a speed proximal to that of light, the material space-time processes undergo mutations. If, for instance, we take two twins, and one of them remains on Earth while the other travels on a spaceship at a speed proximal to that of light, the traveling twin's time passes more slowly. Once he gets back to Earth, he will be much younger that the other.'

"Maria Paola seemed to agree with Umberto and added, 'Matter is made of particles of energy that attract each other. Our soul is not immune from the law of attraction. If we do well, we attract good energy. If our thinking is negative, negative situations will happen to us. For instance, if you worry about something too much, you'll attract negative energy, and the situation you are afraid of will happen to you.'

"Giuseppe reasserted his idea. 'What I can see, touch, and hear through my senses is real, all the rest is fantasy. I believe in what can be tested by scientists. It is impossible that a pyramid can sharpen a blunt blade. No scientific test can prove such an assumption.'

"Maria Paola was a sincere Catholic with different ideas than Giuseppe's. 'I have been leading studies on the Shroud of Turin, and I have concluded that it is authentic. It is the shroud in which Jesus's body was wrapped,' said Maria Paola with her birdlike voice.

"Giuseppe was anticlerical. He was convinced that all relics were tricks to deceive people, so he interrupted Maria Paola. 'Don't be absurd! You must know that some samples of that fabric were cut out from the shroud and sent to three different laboratories in different countries. All three fixed the time when the fabric had been made. The result was that the shroud dated back to about the fourteenth century AD. It means that the Shroud of Turin is a fake.' 'No, it is not a fake!' replied Maria Paola. 'Do you think the Carbon-fourteen test is unreliable?'

"Maria Paola looked upset but tried to control herself. And then, she expressed her opinion calmly. 'I don't want to say that the Carbon-fourteen test is unreliable, but energy can alter matter. At the moment of Jesus's resurrection, the energy was so powerful that all physical laws were upset. Therefore, it is reasonable to infer that the fabric of the Shroud of Turin is beyond time. The Carbon-fourteen test can't work with such an altered material.'

"We got to Isola an hour later. First I dropped off Maria Paola and then Umberto, who lived in the upper town, in front of their homes. Then I drove Giuseppe to his house by the lake. During the short journey from downtown Isola to his house by the lake, I told him that I also wanted to write a book. 'If you want to become a writer, the first thing you have to do is to read a lot. After you have read many books, buy a tape recorder to record your ideas, thoughts, and feelings that you want to express. Then I'll write your book with your recording.'

"I accepted only the first part of his recommendation. I didn't want him to write my book. What for! I bought many books and started training to become a writer, like Giuseppe and Umberto.

"On Saturday at the appointed time, first I picked up Giuseppe and then Umberto. 'Did you find out what kind of esoteric association they belong to?' I asked Giuseppe. 'No, I didn't. I read a lot about esoteric sects at the library, but I couldn't make out which is their sect.' 'This is the second to last lecture. At the end we'll figure out the enigma,' said Umberto.

"When we got to Nunziatina's house, she welcomed us with her usual warmth. Everything had been arranged for the lecture: chairs, couches, a table with beverages and cookies, and the board opposite the audience. At the first lesson, there were many participants in the course, but they decreased little by little. Only Nunziatina, Umberto, Giuseppe, and I remained, besides those who had known one another before the beginning of the course. Maria Paola was absent. Evidently, her strict Catholic creed was incompatible with astrology and, above all, with esotericism.

"Giacomo started his talk. 'Fewer and fewer people have participated in the course until now. Only persons of desire have remained. So, I have reserved a surprise for them at the last lesson.' He overemphasized the expression *person of desire,* making me believe that these words were very important to him in some way. But he didn't explain the meaning.

"At the last lesson, the theme was about dyads, which are elemental couples, for example, heaven-earth, masculine-feminine, and spirit-matter. They form the basis of all religions since unrecorded time. The symbol of the cross expresses the spirit-matter dyad. Its horizontal stem represents the stasis of the matter, while the vertical stem symbolizes the tendency of the spirit to go up to higher spheres.' At last, Giacomo unveiled the mystery underlying the astrology course. 'We are an esoteric group called—'

"Sorry, Uncle Salvatore. I didn't catch the name of the group. Say it again, please."

"I don't want you to write the name of this association, because it is secret."

"Giacomo went on, 'Many of us come from Freemasonry, but we are more spiritual. We devote our meetings and our lives to elevate our spirit. We set two conditions for those who want to join our group. First, they must believe in God, and second, they must believe in the occult. Our order is poor. It means that you don't have to pay to become a member, nor do you have to pay any membership fee. You have to pass through the initiation ceremony. In two weeks, we will have a meeting open to all Sicilian lodges. It will be held at a brother's house at the foot of Mount Etna. That day, if you want, you can come there and become an initiate. During the week before your initiation, don't smoke cigarettes, don't drink coffee, and don't eat meat. When you come, bring a white robe and a black girdle. The robe should be similar to what priests wear.' Giuseppe, Nunziatina, Umberto, and I nodded our heads.

"After I was back home, my first concern was how to get the white robe. In Isola, there were no shops that sold white robes. What to do? I thought about going to a tailor. But if I had asked him to make a white robe for me, he would have asked me, 'Do you want to become an altar boy, Mr.

Salvatore?' Such a question would have embarrassed me. Of course, I couldn't have answered him that I needed the white robe to join an esoteric group. After thinking about what to do for a while, I finally decided to turn to Sister Felicia, who lived at the Franciscan convent near my house. Sometimes I met her at church.

"I rang the doorbell of the convent. An old wizened nun came and opened the door. I knew her. She was Sister Serafina, a nun who loved painting. When she was young, she used to stand in front of a canvas on an easel and paint seascapes or lake landscapes for hours. Her paintings were permeated with peace and tranquility. I still have two small pictures by her which my mother gave me. When I was a child, my mother used to take me to the kindergarten in that convent. Quite often, I left the other children playing in the yard and went into Sister Serafina's room. I sat next to her and watched her painting. 'Good morning, Sister Serafina!' 'Good morning, Salvatore!' 'You still remember my name!' 'How can I forget it! What brought you here?' 'I'd like to talk with Sister Felicia.' 'She teaches mathematics at Santa Chiara Middle School. But you are lucky today. She is here, because today is her day off. I'll call her. Would you like to wait for her in the lounge?'

"Somebody says that monks and nuns live longer than ordinary people. Maybe it depends upon their lifestyle based on the regularity of their awaking, sleeping, praying, and eating. I think that, above all, the spiritual air they breathe contributes to their well-being. The calm, harmonious voice of Sister Serafina touched me like in the old days.

"I sat on one of the couches. The sitting room was wide but without much light. The nuns probably kept it in the half-light purposely. It was full of beautiful plants and flowers. I had hardly seen plant leaves so green, vivid, alive, and clean. Obviously, the nuns dusted off the leaves with a wet cloth. Piano music came from another room. The sound was not continuous. Probably a nun was giving a piano lesson. Even though the sound was discontinuous, it seemed different from the music I had heard in other places. Here, the sound seemed to purify the atmosphere.

"In this Franciscan convent, all the nuns were active. Some gave piano lessons, some tutored, and some made hand-sewn products and embroidery. Sister Felicia was able to repair torn clothes perfectly. You couldn't notice the difference before and after the tear.

"Her habit was as white as snow. Through the veil it was possible to notice her reddish hair that had begun to turn gray. She must have been a beautiful girl when she was young. But the marks of time appeared on her delicate face. Nevertheless, she had not lost the gaiety of youth. She was also witty, and when she spoke, she couldn't stay still. It seemed that the joy of life danced inside her. 'Good morning, Mr. Salvatore! It's an honor for me to meet you here. What can I do for you?' 'I am here because I need a white robe. Can you make one for me?' 'Yes, of course! I'll go get the measuring tape, and I'll take your measurements right away. Do you want a neckband as well?' Her question caught me off guard because I didn't know whether the esoteric group required a robe with a neckband or not. 'I don't know. I have to ask. I'll let you know tomorrow.'

"My answer made Sister Felicia suspicious. Although she was good-hearted, she was as clever as a fox. At my hesitation, she gazed into my face silently for a moment, and then she asked, 'Whom do you have to ask? Do you need the white robe for the church or for something bad?' 'No, Sister Felicia. I don't do bad things with it. You know I am a good man. I'll let you know whether I need the neckband or not.' 'Okay, I won't start the work now. I'll wait for your answer.'

"When I came back home, I called Nunziatina to ask whether we needed a robe with a neckband or not. 'Yes, the neckband is needed. Furthermore, you'll look smart with it,' she said.

"The following day, Sister Felicia started sewing my robe. As she was very precise, she asked me to come for a fitting twice. Finally, she made a superb robe with a perfect neckband. To complete the outfit, I needed a black girdle, which I easily found at a notions store in town.

"The day of our initiation came. The meeting took place in a private house at the foot of Mount Etna. We filed into the meeting room one by one according to the rank each person had. The color of the girdle was not the same for everybody. The lower level girdle was black, the higher grade wore a red girdle, and the top grade wore a white girdle. Before the beginning of the ceremony, the top-grade members performed the rite of purification. Except for them, nobody was allowed to see how the rite of purification happened. The room smelled of incense.

"Lighted candles and many symbols of the order were set on a table. Three top-grade brethren sat behind the table, with the grand master in the middle, who led the ceremony. He asked us would-be initiates first to swear to tell the truth upon our honor and then to answer a few questions. 'Do you believe in God and in the occult?' he began.

"Giving an affirmative answer to this question was basic to be accepted in the order. If our answer had been negative or even doubtful, we would not have been admitted. I was sure that Umberto and Giuseppe were atheists. I didn't know Nunziatina's religious beliefs, yet. As for me, even though I went to Mass every Sunday, I was a searcher for God, not a believer.

"Giuseppe, Umberto, Nunziatina, and I looked at one another with hesitating eyes. But there was no time to hesitate. We had to answer quickly. I thought that if I let Giuseppe give his answer first, he would have answered doubtfully and wouldn't have been admitted in the group. So I answered first, 'Yes, I believe in God and in the occult!'

"Then immediately I turned my eyes to Giuseppe and nodded my head. Although Umberto was smart, he tended to conform to Giuseppe's decisions. I was sure that if Giuseppe gave an affirmative answer, Umberto would do the same.

Things happened like that. 'I believe in God and in the occult,' Giuseppe answered swiftly. I breathed a sigh of relief. After him, Umberto and Nunziatina also answered affirmatively.

"The grand master asked us the next ritual question. 'Do you swear on your honor that you won't divulge our secret rites outside our group?' 'Yes, we do!' Giuseppe, Umberto, Nunziatina, and I answered with one voice.

"The third question was, 'What did you come here for? And what do you want from us?' 'I am here because I want to deepen my spiritual research,' I answered. 'I am here in search of help,' Giuseppe answered. I can't remember what Nunziatina and Umberto said.

"The forth question was, 'What is your void?' At first, I couldn't understand the grand master's question. I mulled it over for a while, and then I realized that my void meant a gap inside myself, or something that bothered me, or even an unresolved problem. Then I decided to open my heart, but I thought that none of them would understand me.

"I answered, 'I can't distinguish dream from reality. Like Chuang-Tzu, last night I dreamed I was a butterfly. Now I don't know whether I was a man dreaming I was a butterfly, or whether I am now a butterfly, dreaming I am a man. I see reality and dream as an indistinct whole. Everything seems confused or unclear to my eyes. I see houses, streets, people, and events as if they were surrounded by a dense fog. This is my void. I want to see people as they are, not through my confused mind or an illusion that distorts my relationships with them. I want to have a clear mind so that I can have self-confidence when I decide to do something. Before making a decision, I often hesitate too long, and then I don't do what I want to do. Sometimes I am like Buridan's donkey, which stood between a haystack on the right and a pail of water on the left. The donkey couldn't decide whether to drink water or to eat hay first. At the end it died of starvation and thirst.'"

"I am interested in your words about void. Do you remember what Giuseppe, Nunziatina, and Umberto answered about their own void?"

"No, Benedetto. At that time I wrote my answer in my diary, but I can't remember the others' answer exactly. It happened a long time ago. Anyway, all of us were admitted.

"The grand master seemed to have understood my words well. He looked pleased with my answer, nodded to me, and went on with his ritual. He put his hands on our heads and recommended us to God and to the deceased grand masters. At that moment, I could feel love in his words. The esoteric group was not something bad. It aimed at the well-being, inner development, and personal growth of all the members.

"In my opinion, Giuseppe and Umberto told the lie about their belief in God because they wanted to publish their book with the help of the esoteric group. They were convinced that secret societies controlled everything in politics, economics, and culture.

"Finally, the grand master asked us to choose our names as initiates. I chose the name Job. He is a biblical figure famous for his patience. I opted for Job because he was a man who never gave up. He wanted to understand why bad people seemed to thrive, while often good people became losers.

"The grand master handed us two booklets with black covers. Then there was a long speech by the grand master and a discussion. He said that his teachings were fundamental for our spiritual growth. At the end of the ceremony, we performed the rite of the chain. Each member held hands with a brother or a sister, making a circle. There was an exchange of energy among us to create *egregore*, also called *egregor*, a group feeling or spirit that arose from the sum of wishes, thoughts, ideals, and feelings of the members. To create *egregore* we had to connect with the deceased grand masters and with one another. While making a chain, we were asked to concentrate and direct our energy into helping a person who was sick or suffering at the moment.

"We should perform a special ritual at home every morning to strengthen *egregore*. I read the instructions and performed the ritual for a few days. The elements of the morning ritual were salt, water, and prayers. I can't say how the ritual was performed because I swore on my honor not to divulge the secrets outside the esoteric group. After a few days, I dropped the morning rituals. I decided to follow the Way of Heart, which also aimed to create *egregore*."

"What is the Way of Heart, Uncle Salvatore?"

"It is the way of feeling friendship, love, and spiritual communion with all the members. I followed this way for two reasons. First, I couldn't understand the rituals well, so it was possible for me to perform them incorrectly. Second, I thought that opening my heart toward the deceased grand masters and all my brethren and sisters was more effective than the ritual to create *egregore*.

"One of the booklets described the morning ritual. The second booklet was a guide to spiritual growth. What touched me was their basic maxim about religion: *There is only one universal religion; the ways of worshiping differ*. Religion is the desire of the individual to be connected to God, while worship is how one expresses one's religious feeling. Denominations and worships differ according to culture or traditions, but religion remains the same for everybody because the universal desire to join God is the same.

"A brother who was sitting next to me whispered in my ear, 'It's like going to Rome. All roads lead to Rome. You can go to the Eternal City by bus, by train, by airplane, on foot, and so on. So are religions. They are different ways that lead to God. You can take the way that suits you.'

"The grand master echoed him. 'No religion can claim to be the best or the only way to God, as all religions are worthy of respect and consideration.'

"Esotericism opened my mind and widened my cultural horizons. The meetings with my brethren and sisters took place at the house of the grand master of the lodge monthly, sometimes in Palermo, sometimes in Catania, and seldom in Syracuse. After some time, Giuseppe and Umberto stopped attending the meetings. Their atheist attitude was obviously an insurmountable wall between them and the other members. Only Nunziatina and I remained in the group.

"When we met in Palermo, we came home very late at night. After the meeting was over, we went to the restaurant. We left Palermo around three in the morning. Nunziatina was at my side in the car. We chatted all the way, but I was very sleepy. We risked an accident. Nunziatina was very attractive, but I didn't want to spoil our friendship by making advances to her.

"Although Giuseppe and Umberto dropped esotericism, I continued to meet them. We strolled in Via Roma talking about religions, the Bible, and Sicily. They had written another book together, but they couldn't find a publishing house to publish their book.

"Actually, it is very difficult to have a book published. The publishing houses don't want to take risks with unknown authors. Even though a manuscript may be a masterpiece, its fortune depends upon the taste of the person that evaluates it. Many employees of publishing houses read manuscripts hastily. In some important publishing houses, hundreds of manuscripts are sent every week, so it is difficult to give them the right evaluation.

"Giuseppe and Umberto looked discouraged, and they had almost given up their hope to be published authors. I continued to attend the esoteric meetings, and through them the horizons of my mind broadened more and more. For the first time, I came into contact with Kabbalah.

"Capodarso and Isola are nearly midway between Catania and Palermo. Nunziatina and I belonged to the lodge of Palermo, but we were allowed to attend meetings wherever we liked. As Nunziatina preferred to go to Catania, sometimes we went there. In Catania the topics we discussed were different from those in Palermo. The latter had a tendency toward general culture, astrology, and philosophy. The former tended to explore themes related to occultism and esoteric disciplines. In Catania, the meetings took place at the grand master's house. Before the beginning of the meeting, usually we chatted with one another for some time. One day I sat on a couch and exchanged some words with a brother of mine. He was a senior official in the municipality of Catania. He looked intelligent. His talk was calm and refined. Looking at his big black eyes, sharp nose, and his pale, bony face, I had the impression that he tended to take things too seriously.

"Suddenly he asked me, 'Do you want to know how you can get supernatural ability?' 'What kind of ability? What do you mean? Supernatural ability?' 'I can move an object from a distance.' 'I don't understand. Could you be more specific?' 'Yes. My wife is from Lampedusa, not far from southern Sicily. From time to time, she goes to her home island for a few days. Last night, when she was in the lounge with her parents, I connected with her and, due to my concentration, the lights of the room blinked. My wife realized it was I who made the lights blink. Immediately she called me from Lampedusa and screamed, 'Don't do that anymore! Otherwise, I will leave you!' For her sake, I didn't try the connection at a distance again. Nevertheless, my study and experiments on occultism go on.'

"Looking at his eyes, I felt creepy. But I strove not to show my embarrassment to him. 'So far, what have you found?' I asked. 'You have to know that there are many angels. They all have names. Some of them can be summoned easily. As for other angels, it is better not to do that, for summoning them may turn very dangerous. Do you want to get acquainted with angels?' 'What can I do for that? I have no skill in this field.' 'Tonight before going to bed, try and visualize a hill and the sun on the top. Close your eyes and keep visualizing both the sun and the hill. This is just the beginning. I'll let you know how to practice more.' I never did the visualization experiment he recommended to me. Considering what would happen later, it was a good choice.

"The grand master and other white girdle brethren purified the meeting room first. Then we entered a large living room. The furniture was old but still had brilliant colors. Couches and armchairs seemed to be as old as the grand master. Maybe they had been purchased when he got married. He was about seventy years old, short, and had a white goatee. The walls were covered with dull yellow wallpaper. There was not much light. In that room I felt as if I were in the waiting room of the kingdom of the dead. On one side of the room was a board with wide sheets of paper, similar to that at Nunziatina's home. The grand master drew a tree, the Sephirot Tree, or the Tree of Life. He drew some circles and linked them with lines. The whole image looked like a tree. I had the impression that the drawing was similar to the Atomium of Brussels, a futuristic structure that represents the atom. Then the grand master wrote a name inside each circle. The upper one was given the name Kether and the lower one the name Malkuth. He said, 'The Sephirot Tree can be likened to Jacob's ladder, which connect earth to heaven.'

"The grand master tried to set out Kabbalah and the Sephirot Tree as clearly and as easily as possible, but as it had happened in regard to astrology before, I couldn't understand him. Although I had read all kinds of books, I couldn't understand this astrology and Kabbalah. When he talked about Sephirot, I was confused and dimwitted.

"One evening while Giuseppe, Umberto, and I were strolling in the street, I heard a nightingale voice in the air: 'Peripatetics, what are you doing?'

"I whirled round and saw a figure that seemed to be a fairy to me. She wore a hat with a broad brim, which is unusual in Isola, a white long skirt, and a green blouse. A gold necklace with a golden small cross adorned her snow-white neck. It was Maria Paola!

"As soon as I saw her, my heart started pounding like a drum. I felt like I couldn't endure so racing a heart. My throat throbbed as well. My heart was about to burst, but I managed to keep calm. 'Hi, Maria Paola,' we all greeted her in one voice. 'Good evening, all of you!'

"Maria Paola looked glad to see us in the street. 'What does Peripatetics mean?" I asked her, while my legs were still trembling with excitement. Umberto looked down at me. 'Don't you know it? 'No, I don't.' I cut short. 'Peripatetics attended the school of Aristotle, who used to teach philosophy while walking. You are strolling now, like them, aren't you?' answered Maria Paola with a mischievous smile.

"I was a bit ashamed that I didn't know Peripatetics in front of Maria Paola. 'We are talking about our book. No publishing house wants to accept it,' said Giuseppe. 'I also have written a book, but I don't even hope to get it published,' said Maria Paola.

"I was surprised at Maria Paola's words. 'Have you written a book? What is it about?' I asked with curiosity. 'It is about Greek mythology.' 'That's very interesting,' I said, trying to please her. 'It tells about Helen of Troy, who never got to Troy.' 'What are you talking about? Helen was Menelaus's wife. She left her husband and fled to Troy with Paris. Don't you know Homer?' said Giuseppe with the air of a pundit.

"Maria Paola didn't care about his acrid remark and went on chirpily. 'According to an unofficial version of the myth told by Euripides, after Paris and Helen ran away from Menelaus's house, they both wandered the seas, drifted and tossed here and there by the currents. Finally they landed in Egypt, where Hermes replaced the true Helen with a simulacrum, unbeknown to Paris. Paris took to Troy just a simulacrum, not the real Helen, who remained in Egypt. In other words, the Achaeans and the Trojans fought for an effigy for ten years. Through this myth, I want to say that reality is not what it appears. We are often misled. We think we are leading our lives for something valuable, but from a different perspective, we realize that we fight battles for nothing. Not only wars break out in vain, but also our daily lives are dotted with nothingness. Many times we think we have found our true love, our soul mate. We would fight for the sake of our lover against anything. But often love is an illusion. Like Helen of Troy, Hermes turns our lover into a simulacrum! Hence, the ultimate nature of all phenomena is emptiness. This is my opinion about life!'

"I was enraptured by her so much so that I stammered, but I strove to control myself and asked her, 'Don't you mind if your book is unpublished? Giuseppe and Umberto are sad because they can't succeed in publishing their book.' 'No, I don't. I will leave my manuscript in the bookcase. Maybe someday some of my descendants will read it and remember me. My heart will remain in my manuscript. The vibrations of my words will resound in the heart of those who will stumble upon my story about Helen of Troy that never went to Troy. The vibrations of my words will last for a long time through my manuscript.'

"Giuseppe was a pragmatic person, so he could hardly understand Maria Paola's words about vibrations. 'You are a dreamer, Maria Paola. You live in the future. What matters is the here and now. I want to be famous now, not after my death, as happened to Vincent van Gogh,' he said. 'We are different, Giuseppe. Sometimes I feel you have no heart,' replied Maria Paola.' 'I just follow my emotions, not my heart. Life is just emotion! If I feel something, I live it, otherwise I don't live it. There is no heart in humans. We are driven by pleasant emotions or unpleasant emotions.' 'Surely, we can't get along. We have different ideas! Now I have to go to church. Today Mass starts at eight o'clock. It is a special day.' 'May I come with you? I'm Catholic,' I asked Maria Paola with my voice still wobbling. 'Sorry, it's not possible. I'm going to meet my parents at church, and then we'll all go home together.'

"That evening Nunziatina called me. She told me that the next meeting would be held in Isola at Rino's home. 'I'll come to Isola by bus,' she said. 'Okay, I'll wait for you at the bus stop.'

"Rino's house was not easy to reach, so everybody met at the main square of Isola. From there I led the line of cars to Rino's house. He lived with his girlfriend in a three-story townhouse. In fact, he had divorced. In his house everything was new, even the saplings in the garden. He had turned the garage in the basement into a recreation room. It was quite large but a bit dark. The stems of the plants were bent toward the light that came from the entrance.

Rino had arranged rows of chairs on one side and a table with three chairs on the other. The grand master sat behind a table with Rino and another brother. The theme was the term initiation.

"The grand master started off, 'Only members of an esoteric group know truths that ordinary people can't know. The initiates live in a higher plane, compared with others.'

"I waited for the conclusion of his speech, and then I raised my hand and objected, 'Many great persons have lived on this earth without having ever been initiated, but they were geniuses, great writers, poets, painters, scientists, artists, musicians, and so on. Do you think we initiates are superior to them?'

"Our host, Rino, went red with embarrassment. He thought my question showed a lack of respect toward the grand master. So he raised his hand to reproach me, but the grand master, who was sitting next to him, held his hand down. 'Let it go! Job is right!'

"Rino calmed down, and then the grand master turned to me. 'Yes, everybody is allowed to know the truth, even those who are not initiates. The main tragedy of humans is the death of the soul. It is possible that the soul dies. In order to prevent such an eventuality, a few beings, over the course of history, in different epochs, came to Earth to save humanity. For that, we had Mohammad, Buddha, Jesus, Krishna, and others. Not everybody can do what they did to save the human soul.'

"I couldn't understand the grand master, or rather I thought he digressed from the point of my question. But, after many years, I understand the meaning of his words. It is true that all human beings can know the truth, but what one can learn in an esoteric school can't be learned through ordinary studies.

"The grand master said that Isola was a special town, full of energy because it was located near the center of Sicily. At that time, I rented a country house with a large living room and a small bathroom on the first floor. On the second floor was another bathroom and a bedroom. A marbled staircase connected upstairs with downstairs. When the meeting at Rino's home was over, I offered my house for the next meeting. It was a remote place. Only one family lived near my house. We shared the yard and the garden. Once in a while the owner came there to garden.

"I hosted the esoteric meeting on the day of the feast of Saint John the Baptist, which falls on the summer solstice. That afternoon my neighbors were at home. Seeing all those cars parked in the yard, they were surprised.

"While the white girdle brethren purified the living room, the others waited on the upper floor. In fact, we were not allowed to see how the purification ritual took place. Rino was one of those who performed the ritual, and later he told me that it was a kind of exorcism.

We burned a lot of incense. Moreover, there were intervals of silence, especially when we did the chain. Surely my neighbors wondered why so many people stayed silent and burned incense. That evening, the grand master talked about solstices, equinoxes, and rites related to those special days.

"He said, 'Equinox and solstice come from the Latin words *aequinoctium* and *solstitium*. Since time immemorial, people have celebrated solstices and equinoxes. The winter solstice is related to Jesus's birth, the summer solstice is related to St. John the Baptist's birth. They were second cousins. The former was the son of Mary and the latter the son of her cousin Elisabeth. The birth of John the Baptist preceded that of Jesus by six months. On the summer solstice, herbs have a special energy. There are many practices related to the magic night of St. John. On that day people start bonfires, which are the symbol of purification, and pluck special herbs, above all, the hypericum also called Saint-John's-wort. Spring equinox is related to Cybele, the goddess mother who symbolizes the earth, and to Attis, her son, who symbolizes the vegetation of the earth.'

"When the meeting was over, everybody left, and I remained alone in the house. That night, when I was about to sleep, I sensed that something was happening downstairs. I felt that there were ghostly presences in the living room. I wanted to go there, but I feared an unpleasant encounter. I got up and headed for the landing of the staircase. I thought I saw a ghostly figure with horns coming toward me. As we met almost face-to-face on the landing, he went back downstairs, and I returned to my bed.

"The next day, while I was walking to my car, the owner of the house was working in the garden. As soon as he saw me, he put aside the hoe. I greeted him. Foreseeing that he would say something about the esoteric meeting, I tried to get to my car as quickly as I could. But he blocked my way and said calmly, 'If you want, you can take all the girls you like into my house. You can also have a lot of parties. But, please, don't hold satanic rites again!'

"Obviously, my neighbors had informed him about the esoteric meeting. I thought it would be difficult to make him understand that our meeting was not satanic but esoteric. 'Okay,' I answered. 'I won't host this kind of meeting anymore.'

"June of that year was unusually cold in Isola. It rained incessantly. One night when I got home and opened the front door, I sniffed a strange smell, but I didn't care about it. I was tired and chilly, so I went to bed. Early in the morning, I got up to go to the bathroom, but I felt faint. It was dark. I went to the bathroom downstairs. I felt that the house would explode when I turned on the light. But it didn't happen, and I felt relieved. I went back upstairs. I couldn't go to work in such a bad physical condition. Maybe opening the window and airing the room will revive me, I thought.

"After some bad weather, fortunately that day the rain and the wind ceased. The sun was rising, and it was natural to open the window in the morning. But, right after, I threw myself onto the bed, almost senseless. I slept for more than three hours, from about six to ten. While sleeping, I first saw something that looked like ghastly geometric figures. They came from underground and tried to pull me downward. Then, those dreadful figures disappeared, and I saw myself in a room full of light. The floor was in terracotta tiles. The room was divided in two by a very subtle diaphragm, and I was on the point of crossing over that diaphragm. Through the window, I could see a small town perched on a high hill or a low mountain. That town was surrounded by walls, and I could see some roundish towers in the town. On the top of those towers were roofs with a conic shape. I was in bliss, and I wished to stay in that state for a long time. I stood by the diaphragm and was about to cross it when I heard the telephone ringing. It rang once, twice, three times, and maybe many times before I reached out and lifted the receiver. 'Hello, who's speaking?' I asked with my mind in the clouds. 'This is your neighbor, Sebastiano, speaking. How are you?' 'I am in very bad condition.' 'Come down immediately and open the door!'

"I went downstairs, following his order mechanically. Walking to the door, I didn't notice the cloud of black smoke which stagnated in the room. I opened the door, and soon I stepped back, swinging like a pendulum from one side of the room to the other. 'What are you doing?' Sebastiano shouted. 'Do you want to die?' 'I don't know what is happening. I feel dizzy.'

"Sebastiano began to cough and didn't dare enter the living room. 'Open all the windows!' I went back, still swinging from side to side, and opened all the windows one by one. I had tremendous difficulty in breathing, moreover, I couldn't stand easily because I continued to swing. 'Do you want me to take you to the hospital?'

"Usually, I was against going to the hospital, but this time I really needed it. 'Yes, take me to the hospital, please.' The doctor inserted two small tubes connected to an oxygen bottle into my nostrils. Breathing oxygen, I felt better, but it was hard when I tried to breathe without the help of the oxygen bottle. Finally, after one hour, I asked the doctor whether I could go back home or not. The doctor didn't allow me to go home, but I signed out under my responsibility.

"On the way back home from the hospital, I considered how it was easy to die. It is like moving from one environment to another. A very subtle diaphragm separates life and death. One step more, we cross over to the other side. What a miracle life is! It is like a spark! The normal condition is death, maybe. We come from nothing and return to nothing after the spark is over, I thought. Once, a doctor of Isola said, 'People should be surprised at being alive, not at dying. The human body is fragile, like glass. Easy to break.'

"While Sebastiano was driving me home, I saw people in the streets who were chatting and walking. I was allowed to live a bit longer on Earth, like them. Additional time on this planet was granted to me, like an oil lamp when the owner revives it by pouring some more oil into it. My neighbor was proud of having saved my life. Actually, his call was providential.

"I couldn't work. I still swung from one side to another like a drunken man who has just finished drinking a bottle of hard liquor.

"My next-door neighbors were good-hearted to me. They were husband and wife and had a little baby. The man, Sebastiano, was a truck driver. As he was powerfully built, he worked as a bouncer at a disco at night on weekends. His wife, Lisa, was tall and slender. She used to wear black leggings over her long legs and a crew neck sweater. They invited me for lunch, and she cooked small pasta soup just for me. When his child slept, she used to teach me physical exercises in the garden.

"It was still cold in the house. I needed a new gas boiler. Sebastiano called a friend of his who was a plumber. 'I wonder how it was possible for you to survive. It is a miracle! Carbon monoxide is deadly. Don't you know that?' he said. 'I think it was methane that poisoned me.' 'No. The electric wires of the boiler burned and emitted carbon monoxide, a lethal gas. He who is poisoned by carbon monoxide first loses consciousness because his brain receives less oxygen, and then he dies from asphyxia.'

"Once I felt better, I went back to work. I bought a new gas-fired boiler and stayed in that house a few months longer. In the evening I used to stroll in the street with Giuseppe and Umberto. 'Have you ever heard about near-death experiences when one comes back to life after a deep coma?' I asked Umberto. 'Yes, Carl Gustav Jung told of his own near-death experience.' 'Some people have reported that they were in the light and felt bliss while they were dying. It is evidence of life after death.' 'No, it isn't. The experience of a near-death happens inside, not in the external world. In other words, you can't declare the existence of life after death on the basis of your dreams, reasoning, and thoughts which are confined inside yourself. I'll give you an example. If you imagine or dream a hippogriff, a mythological creature that is half horse and half griffin, it doesn't mean that hippogriffs really exist. The whole process of imagining or dreaming a hippogriff happens inside yourself. But that creature doesn't exist in reality. The same goes for near-death experiences. The whole experience happens inside the dying man, not outside him. The paradise he thinks he sees outside him may not exist in reality,' Umberto answered coldly.

"I was not convinced about his words and retorted that Descartes, a philosopher, proved the existence of God. But Umberto knew the topic well and answered without getting flustered. 'Yes, you are right, but another philosopher, Emmanuel Kant, confuted Descartes's theory. In Descartes's reasoning, as well as in the reasoning of anyone who wants to prove the existence of God and life after death, there is an inexplicable gap between the logical and the ontological field.' 'Could you speak more plainly so that I can understand?' 'Yes. You can't extrapolate the reality from an idea or reasoning. It is not correct to reason that as there is a creature, then there must be a creator. In fact, reasoning can never give existence to a being in reality. If you dream of being a rich and powerful man, you will discover that you don't have those attributes when you wake up. In your dreams your mind creates objects that will disappear when you awake.'

"Staying at home for one week, I pondered over my dreadful experience. On the day I almost died, the circumstances helped me mysteriously. Isola had unusual bad weather with continual storms in June. If it had been a windy and rainy day, I wouldn't have opened the window of my room. That day the sun was shining with no wind at all. Furthermore, my neighbor couldn't leave with his truck that day early in the morning because of the ice on the road and stayed at home. What a mysterious coincidence!

"I ask myself, 'Is it possible that angels help us in everyday life?' Sometimes I think that my deceased parents and relatives guide me whenever I am in a difficult situation. And does Fate, the mythic Fate that even the almighty Zeus couldn't change, exist? Or is it just a fantasy? In situations that turn out well, all circumstances concur positively from the beginning, while in those that end badly, everything interlaces negatively from the beginning. It seems that events follow a course designed in advance.

"In the late afternoon, I received a call from Nunziatina. She informed me that the grand master of Catania had invited us to a meeting at his house at the foot of Mount Etna next

Sunday. I accepted with pleasure, and on Sunday morning I went to Capodarso and picked up Nunziatina.

"We arrived at the grand master's house before noon. This time, before starting our usual meeting, we entered an annex to the main house. It was big enough to contain at least fifty persons. When we went in, I was surprised to see the grand master wearing the vestments typical of a priest. He looked like a cardinal. Besides the ordinary clergy vestments, he wore a miter. Both the miter and the chasuble were embroidered with gold threads.

"His Mass was not dissimilar to a Catholic Mass. One of the variations was the reading of the Gospel. He read a passage from the Apocryphal Gospel of Thomas. Near the end of the ceremony, he celebrated Holy Communion with bread and wine. I was about to eat the bread when my eyes met those of Nunziatina, who lifted her eyebrows and shook her head. I followed her advice, and I neither ate bread, nor drank wine.

"Over time, I no longer felt like remaining in the esoteric group. Life is also emotion! Sometimes you can't do what you don't feel like doing. My enthusiasm to attend their meetings cooled. I left my esoteric group naturally, like a dead leaf that falls from a tree in late autumn. I still cherish all my brethren and sisters in my heart and have a very good memory of them.

"As for my friends in Isola, bad news came on a sunny day. One night, Umberto felt unwell. He got dressed and tried to reach the hospital on foot, but when he arrived at the entrance, he fell down, struck dead by a heart attack. It was a heavy loss for me.

"Giuseppe returned to his hometown and didn't come to Isola anymore. He had been a good friend to me. Although he was brusque, he broadened my views. The conversations with him were like a mirror to look inside myself.

"Every friend related to the esoteric group faded away like a dream. The grand masters of Palermo and Catania, Nunziatina, Umberto, Rino, Giuseppe, the owner of my rented country house, Sebastiano, and his beautiful long-limbed wife disappeared from the stage of my life. I couldn't see them anymore. Life is transient!" concluded Uncle Salvatore, sighing deeply.

"What happened to Maria Paola? You said that when you met her in the street, your heart was about to burst. Did she also disappear from your life?"

"I loved Maria Paola. I courted her for four years, but at last she opted for someone else. Love is bilateral, not unilateral! Of course, she didn't love me."

"I think, Uncle Salvatore, the readers of your book will wonder when this happened. Did you join the esoteric group after your first wife died?"

"Yes, Benedetto. This happened at that time. Unfortunately, my first wife, Maria, died from an incurable disease before her time. She was like an angel. If paradise exists, she is there. I tried to save her life and did everything I could do for her. A famous doctor from New York came to Isola to cure her. But it was in vain. She died in my arms. I got married to my second wife twenty years later and had two children from her, as you know."

"Now the story is clearer, Uncle Salvatore. Do you have anything else to say about esotericism?"

"No. I told everything I had to say on this subject. Let's start a new chapter, Benedetto."

"Okay!"

CHAPTER VI
MY DAYS IN PUNE

"Near the Church of San Clemente in Rome, which Giuseppe had recommended I visit, I stumbled across a book vendor who sold second-hand books on a cart. He had Indian features, was bald, and wore a long white beard. He looked like a learned person. Some books were written in English. I got near the vendor and had a quick look at the books scattered on the cart. Suddenly, my eyes fell on a book that had a picture on the cover very similar to the face of that street vendor. I gave a start of surprise. 'Are you the author of this book?' 'No, I'm not, but I recommend it to you. It is more precious than a diamond mine.' 'How much is it?' 'Just one thousand lire. It is very cheap.' 'Okay, I'll take it!'

"He wrapped the book in a sheet of newspaper and handed it to me. At home I unwrapped and dusted off the book, which looked new. It was *The Book of Secrets* by Osho. Reading it, I was surprised at the author's ideas. His words vibrated inside me. I was very moved by this book, so I bought more books by the same author. Reading his books, I felt that Osho wanted to spread love all over and help people break their conditioning. His teachings were: 'Be yourself! Don't strive to be different from who you are. Remain in the center of your being. Find your original face, your real being, your nature. Don't suppress your feelings and emotions. You should accept your shortcomings because they are a part of yourself. Love yourself, and then you can love others. Sex is not a sin, for life comes from sex.'

"I was so fascinated by Osho that I talked about him with my friends. One of them was a sannyasin and an Osho disciple. He gave me the necessary information to go to the Osho Ashram in Pune, India. After Osho's death, his disciples changed the name from ashram to meditation resort, because, according to them, an ashram can exist only as long as the master is alive.

"The meditation techniques he invented were different from those I had come across until then. In the Buddhist centers I had visited in Italy, England, and America, meditation was silent. Osho's meditation was innovative. It aimed at eliminating all the garbage we had accumulated inside ourselves in the course of our life conditioned by religion and society.

"In the ashram there were many kinds of meditation, but the most helpful to me was Dynamic Meditation. At six forty-five was the evening meeting called White Robe. All the participants wore white robes. It began with dancing. Then, we did gibberish, speaking out madly in a meaningless language for a few minutes.

"When I was just a boy, coming back home from school, I threw my schoolbag full of books on the floor and uttered incomprehensible words and sounds similar to the howling of a dog or the meowing of a cat. Maybe I wanted to express what I had inside through an unknown inner language. My mother didn't like my gibberish. She told me that our neighbors asked her whether we had a dog at home. Apparently, at that time, I tried to do gibberish instinctively without any idea about it. Due to my mother's scolding, I stifled my tendency to express my nature as I wanted.

"It was not the only suppression of my spontaneity. Since Isola was a provincial city, people liked to meddle in other people's lives. My mother used to say to me, '*Vox populi vox Dei*', the voice of people is the voice of God. I remember one day in early fall. I felt cold and wanted to go to school with my coat on. My father said, 'Do you want to make chickens laugh?

No one wears a coat in this season.' I looked at his stern face and couldn't understand him. When I grew up, I came to know that in Isola we usually put on our winter coats after November second, the Day of the Dead."

"Uncle Salvatore, the same thing happens in the Italian army. The change of uniform from winter to summer happens on June second, Republic Day. They don't consider that there are different climate zones in Italy. The ritual of changing uniform outweighs weather conditions. In military life, rituals are very important to make the military efficient. From the beginning of the day, soldiers perform rituals, starting with the daily ceremony of hoisting the national flag and ending with the trumpet playing 'The Silence' before going to bed. You can't salute as you like, for you have to follow the ritual salute of putting your hand up almost parallel to the tip of your hat. If you are not able to salute properly, you are forced to remain in the barracks and punished."

"I agree with you. We are conditioned by a lot of rituals. For instance, Christmas, New Year's Day, Thanksgiving Day, Black Friday, and so on are rituals. In Isola, there is a proverb that says, 'The best word is the one you don't say.' It means that the less you talk, the better it is. It is related to the famous proverb, 'Silence is golden, speech is silver.'"

"Don't you like these proverbs, Uncle Salvatore? I think they are right. Being silent is better than talking bullshit."

"No, I don't. They are wrong! And I, Salvatore Gagliano, at the age of ninety-two, want to create these new proverbs: 'The best word is the one you say.' 'Speech is golden, silence is silver.' We have to express ourselves anyway."

"Do you want to turn the world upside down, Uncle Salvatore? Proverbs contain the wisdom of ancestors."

"Do you know what the difference is between civilized and uncivilized people?"

"What is it? Tell me, Uncle Salvatore."

"Uncivilized people blindly repeat what their ancestors have taught them. Civilized people, even though they follow and respect their traditions, add something new and innovative to them. This is called progress. In my case, I transformed my father's firm. It was based upon haulage by mule-drawn carts, but I introduced a new kind of business when I bought a new truck."

"Yes, I know. You have already told me about your first SPA truck."

"At the Osho Ashram, when I did Dynamic Meditation, I shouted as loudly as I wanted without risking being sent to a mental hospital. By shouting, I released all the never-said words and unexpressed emotions I had repressed in my life. Little by little, I was getting rid of my conditioning."

"What did you do at the ashram? Can you tell me the kind of meditation you did?"

"Yes, I got up at five twenty in the morning. At six o'clock, I did Dynamic Meditation at the ashram. This meditation was a panacea for me. It consists of five stages and is accompanied by music that changes at every stage except the fourth stage, which is silent.

"In the first stage we have to breathe chaotically through our nostrils as fast as we can in order to stir up anything inside ourselves: pain, sorrow, repressed emotions, negative feelings, old patterns, conditioning, and so on. The first stage is like stirring a pond with a lot of mud underneath. Through breathing fast and chaotically, we stir up all the mud we have accumulated inside ourselves over the years.

"In the second stage, we get crazy. We can explode, shout, cry, roll on the floor, laugh, scream, jump, dance, sing, do gibberish, and whatever we want to do. We can act as if we were mad.

"I found the second stage to be liberating. Many times in my life I wanted to shout as loudly and madly as I could, but obviously it was not possible. If I had shouted like that at home, I would have surprised my neighbors."

"I think, Uncle Salvatore, it is not difficult to behave like a madman, because the boundary between insanity and sanity is like thin paper."

"Yes. The border between sanity and insanity is not based on the quality of abnormal behavior, but rather on the quantity of behavioral abnormalities. In other words, everyone has a certain amount of garbage inside. Madmen have more garbage than those with a normal mind. Neurotics are halfway between sanity and insanity, for they have a lot of garbage inside, but it is not enough to make them cross over the border to madness."

"You say, Uncle Salvatore, that the state of the human mind depends on the quantity of garbage inside. Can you give me an example for me to understand better?"

"Yes, of course. For example, fear is an emotion that can be considered garbage. If you don't have much fear inside, nothing bad happens. But if fear is excessive, it becomes pathological and turns into anxiety or panic attacks."

"Give me one more example, please. This is really interesting."

"The same happens with regard to paranoia. It is just a question of quantity. Let's take a suspicious person as an example. Being distrustful is normal, but when mistrust becomes bigger and bigger, it turns into the belief that others may harm you and, finally, into paranoia. As you know, I love money. I consider it God's blessing. If love for money is not excessive, it is called thriftiness. If greed for money is excessive, it is called miserliness and it is pathological."

"I don't think so, Uncle Salvatore."

"Go ahead!"

"I think the causes of mental diseases lie not only in the amount of garbage inside but also in the quality of the brain. In fact, mental disease often comes from a sick or damaged brain, regardless of the garbage inside."

"Yes, you are right, a sound brain as well as the chemical processes inside the human body are important, but, this is the point, body, brain, and mind are connected. Therefore, if you reduce the quantity of garbage inside your mind, also your brain will benefit from it, and the body's chemical processes will work better."

"According to you, Uncle Salvatore, what causes fear, anxiety, panic attacks, and paranoia?"

"Sometimes we can't control those states. It happens because there is a substratum under the mental condition. What is the basis of neurosis? Can you answer, Benedetto?"

"I think the substratum is our past failures, the emotions we have suppressed over the years, trauma, and, above all, our difficult relationships with others."

"I agree with you, and I can assure you that Dynamic Meditation is helpful because it brings the substratum which gives rise to our fear, anxiety, and all kinds of neuroses, to the surface. As for me, I had the symptoms of anxiety, panic attacks, and paranoia. Actually, I don't know if I was already paranoid at that time. As I said before, the border between abnormality and normality is very subtle. It is very easy for a neurotic to cross over the border to insanity. It is just a question of quantity! Actually, my anxiety was very high, and I was seized by panic attacks quite often. The substratum of both anxiety and panic attacks lay in my difficult relationship with others. When I was at home, I was well. But when I went out, my anxiety arose like an undergrowth of mushrooms after rain. It was evident that my anxiety and panic attacks sprang from the disorder of my relationship with others."

"This affects everybody, Uncle Salvatore, not just you. Without conflict with others, everything runs smoothly like a river that flows quietly. Only when its bed has irregularities, the river becomes rough. What was your main ailment?"

"Whenever I walked in the street, I felt that everybody was staring at me, judging me, and also pitying me. I felt like people talked about me: 'Look at that poor man! Look, how strange he is!' So I didn't look at anybody when I walked in the street. I looked at the ground."

"Uncle Salvatore, you were a businessman. If you had such difficulties in relationships with others, how did you manage your haulage company?"

"Inner self and social self are different. As for me, the gap between the two selves was very big at that time."

"I understand you. Actually, almost all people act in life as if they were actors on the stage. Okay, let's go on."

"To avoid being hurt by others, I decided to protect myself. What did I do? I thought, If I am immersed in my thoughts when I walk, I won't mind others. So I withdrew into myself. My thoughts were an invisible protective shield. By thinking during my strolls, I felt safe like an ostrich that puts its head into the sand when it is attacked and feels safe. I was under the illusion that I was safe with my protective shield, but I dug a deeper and deeper ditch between the world and myself. My thoughts were not my shield, because they couldn't protect me. Furthermore, they made a wall between the others and myself.

"An invisible thread of events led me to Pune. The thread was the vendor I met near the Church of San Clemente, and the meeting with a friend of mine who was a sannyasin and informed me about the Osho Ashram. Without them, I wouldn't have come to India. Is it possible that an angel appeared to me in the guise of that book vendor who sold me *The Book of Secrets*? I have a feeling that a celestial entity sent me to Pune to heal myself through meditation.

"While I was doing Dynamic Meditation, I recalled the religious feast of July second. It is the most important festival in Isola. In ancient times, it was a pagan celebration in honor of the goddess Demeter, the protector of the harvest. On this day, select devotees bear on their shoulders a heavy litter with the wooden statue of Our Lady holding Baby Jesus. Two smaller litters precede that of Our Lady, one with the statue of St. Joseph and the other with St. Michael the Archangel. The latter is carried on kids' shoulders. The wooden statue of St. Michael the Archangel portrays a boy dressed like a Roman soldier with a helmet, a shield, and an unsheathed sword. People crowd the streets to see the procession of the litters.

"Since I was a child, I had suffered from anxiety. It was so much that I couldn't stand in crowded places. My disease is called agoraphobia. The etymology of the word agoraphobia is from Greek. *Agora* means square and *phobia* means fear. So agoraphobia is fear of open spaces and often of any place outside home. The agoraphobic feel comfortable only within their domestic walls. In more serious cases, they can't leave their home.

"Agoraphobia includes fear of traveling. The world is seen as a minefield. One often feels faint while one is outside home. The more the agoraphobic strive to be normal and at ease, the more this effort of will turns into tension, cold perspiration, and accelerated heartbeats. Apparently, behind agoraphobia there is something related to the relationship with others. Conditioning by religion, society, and family is buried deep in the mind, and it generates a permanent conflict between repression and expression of emotions and feelings. I felt my conflict was unbearable. Accordingly, I fled the external world and withdrew to my home and the office of my haulage company to feel better. I was tortured by a huge ambivalence. On the one hand, I wanted to live my life fully, going out and walking freely on the streets, squares, and crowded places. On the other hand, I felt dizzy outside my home and my office, as if I were about to faint.

"Uncle Salvatore, I didn't know about your disease. It looks very serious. How did you overcome your agoraphobia?"

"I was helped by the divinity that sent me persons as healers and teachers. Events don't happen by chance. Our path of life has already been designed by an invisible entity that leads us along the way. An invisible and subtle thread led me to Osho. 'Please, St. Michael the Archangel, help me and make it possible for me to walk the streets without anxiety and panic attacks!' I prayed to St. Michael the Archangel when his statue passed by me during the procession on July second."

"What happened to you afterwards, Uncle Salvatore? Did St. Michael the Archangel answer your prayer?"

"I can just say that from that day on, my life started to change for the better. I met many masters. Little by little, I could get over my anxiety and panic attacks."

"Besides St. Michael the Archangel, have you been helped by other saints?"

"Many holy persons appeared in my life, and they led me toward my spiritual growth. One of them lived in Kamut. He was a young man, called Mario, around thirty years old."

"I didn't know there was a man that looked like an angel in Kamut."

"There was, indeed. I can testify he was a special man. Every year on July eleventh, something mysterious happened at his home. At noon he fell asleep. All his friends gathered around his bed and watched him while he was sleeping.

"On July eleventh, I went to his house in Kamut. At the entrance of the living room was a statue of the Virgin Mary. There was water around the base of the statue. It had the scent of roses. Mario's room was in the loft. There was a blue blanket on the bed and a blue ribbon on his belly. It was similar to the ribbon I had seen on the statue of St. Michael the Archangel. At noon Mario slipped into the sheets. His eyes blinked and then he fell asleep. I sat down on the floor and watched him.

"From time to time, Mario turned his head to the right and then to the left. Sometimes, he smiled. Then, his hands turned reddish. Little by little, red spots appeared on his hands. The spots looked like coagulated blood. Often Mario folded his hands. He tried to say something, but his voice was so low that it was impossible to hear him. One of Mario's friends sat beside the bed, put a microphone near his lips and recorded his words. I heard Mario utter volcano or volcanoes.

"While I was watching Mario, a picture of Mia Martini on the wall caught my attention. She was an Italian singer who committed suicide. Suddenly, the lady sitting at my side started to tell what she heard from Mario. She turned to me and said, 'All convicts will be set free. All bonds will break.' She also uttered a third sentence, but I didn't keep it in mind even for a short while. It was as if I had a sudden lapse of memory.

"I tried to interpret those strange words. I recalled that I caused two tragedies when I was young."

"What happened to you then?"

"Two dramatic, gloomy events were buried in my unconscious. They strove to get out of my unconscious like snails shut in a pot that climb up and try to lift the lid to get out."

"Uncle Salvatore, can you tell me those sad events?"

"Yes. As you know, I was the founder of Gagliano Angelo Haulage Company. After I bought our first SPA truck, our company expanded. Our trucks transported goods from Isola to Catania. At that time, many craftsmen purchased merchandise in Catania. One afternoon a truck of ours had to deliver goods to Catania. The driver told me that a leaf spring was cracked. He didn't want to set off to Catania. I checked the truck, but the leaf spring was not broken, so I ordered the driver to leave for Catania. He followed my order. On the road, he gave a ride to a tailor who needed fabric for his workshop. The truck was carrying iron sheets. Maybe it was overloaded. At a curve, the leaf spring gave way and the truck overturned. The driver was unharmed, but the tailor was crushed to death.

"When I got to the scene of the accident, the tailor was still under the driver's cab. His face was black like coal due to the pressure on his body. This image is still vivid in my memory. I can't forget it. Whenever I met his son, I felt a deep pang of remorse. That boy became a fatherless child because of my fault.

"That year was tragic. The strange thing was that I was presented with a datebook from my bank. At the beginning of it, there was the horoscope for the year. It predicted a bad year for my sign, and it was right with regard to me, oddly.

"I had a girlfriend whose green eyes are still imprinted in my heart. We had been engaged for almost three years. Then I broke off the relationship. She was hurt and decided to put an end to her life. A young bud was cut by the gardener before blooming. All my life I had a guilt complex from these tragedies. The lady's words in Mario's room resounded in my mind and touched my heart. 'All convicts will be set free. All bonds will break.' Hence, I could be forgiven, too! I had considered my two sins unforgivable. Hearing those words, I realized that all sins can be forgiven, even mine.

"In Pune, Dynamic Meditation in the early morning brought what was hidden in the depths of my unconscious to the surface of my conscious.

"I also used to go to the Burning Ghat, a square by the bank of the Mula-Mutha River. Hindus burned the dead bodies of their dear ones in that place. The Burning Ghat was easily accessible from the street with the same name. On the left side of the square was the temple dedicated to Chanchal Das Baba. At the entrance his picture was hung on the wall. In the temple there was also a rectangular pit with ashes and a big log which burned slowly. The person in charge of the temple told me that the fire had been kept lit since Chanchal Das Baba's dead body was burned there. 'What was special about Chanchal Das Baba?' I asked him. 'He was blessed by Lord Shiva. As such, he was very powerful. He used his powers to help the homeless by providing them with food, shelter, and blessings.'

"The temple was austere, with nearly ten small statues of Hindu gods. It looked like a morgue or a place where the dead rest for some time before continuing their journey toward an unknown world. I had seen something similar at Pashupati Temple in Kathmandu where a special indoor area was provided to dying people.

"Outside the temple, an area had been arranged to provide a shelter for the homeless. There were some steps opposite the pits where the dead were placed to be burned. I guessed that the relatives of the dead used to sit on the steps. At night some tramps slept there. In the square, six pits, all of them approximately thirty centimeters deep, were paved with clay bricks and were iron-edged. The square was surrounded by green benches. Some were made of iron and some of cement. At the back of the pits were water taps placed above a tiled washbasin and connected to a tank.

"I don't know why, but I enjoyed staying at the Burning Ghat. I felt comfortable there. I watched corpses burning for hours, contemplated death and where we are going after death."

"Sometimes I can't understand you, Uncle Salvatore. Instead of enjoying the life in the ashram and making friends, you went to the Burning Ghat to watch burning corpses. I have a feeling that you preferred death to life, didn't you?"

"No, I didn't. At that time I speculated about life and death. I tried to see whether the burning bodies released a soul or a kind of energy."

"How can you see the soul with your eyes? It is absurd."

"I don't give up trying until I find the answer to my question. It is my shortcoming and merit too."

"Did you find out anything about life after death at the Burning Ghat?"

"Maybe not, but the horizons of my insight broadened a lot."

"Let me know what you learned at the Burning Ghat, Uncle Salvatore."

"Okay. Usually, after a body has been burned, the ashes and a few bones remain in the pit for one or two days.

Apparently not all the bones burn out. Then the families of the dead person take away both the ashes and the bones.

"One day, I saw a few men set a corpse inside a heap of wood and cowpat chapati in one of the pits of the Burning Ghat. They poured some ghee on the pyre and started the fire in two different spots. A man dressed in white filled an earthenware pot with water and stood in front of the pyre for a few minutes. With a special tool, someone made a hole in the pot, and the water started to come out. While the water was leaking from the pot, the man walked around the pit clockwise. Then a second and a third hole were made in the pot, and the man walked around the pit twice more while the water kept leaking. Finally, he got back to the starting point and dropped the pot. The leftover water spilled from the broken pot. The man dressed in white squatted down and broke the pot into tiny pieces."

"What is the meaning of this ritual, Uncle Salvatore?"

"When the funeral was over, I asked the man dressed in white to explain to me the symbolism of the ritual he had performed. 'I am the eldest son of the dead man. So, it's my duty to pay funeral honors to my father, but don't ask me about the symbolism because I don't know it. I just follow our family tradition. The ritual is transmitted from generation to generation. However, you can ask Rajan, a good friend of mine about it. He is educated and lives just here in the shelter for the homeless,' he answered."

"Uncle Salvatore, can a homeless person be educated? I can't understand why a learned person becomes homeless."

"Sometimes life makes a person fall into the worst situation. Benedetto, you can find a golden ring in the garbage by chance. Although he was homeless, Rajan was smart and extraordinary."

"I am curious to listen to something about him."

"The man dressed in white introduced me to Rajan, a dark-skinned man of medium stature, about forty years old. He had long curly hair down to his shoulders, a black beard and wore very thick glasses. His hair and beard were so long and bushy that they looked whole. I asked him to tell me something about the Indian ceremonies for burning dead bodies. We took a seat on a bench facing the river, and then he started talking: 'On their shoulders, friends and relatives carry the dead body on a bamboo frame. Then, they place the corpse on a first layer of wood and remove the bamboo frame. They also lay incense, dry coconut, and ghee, also called milk butter. Then, they set a second layer of wood and dry cow dung pressed and shaped like chapati and add more ghee and dry coconut, but the face of the dead person should not be covered with anything. At last, one by one, the families pour water of the Ganges River into the mouth of the dead person.'"

"Uncle Salvatore, I wonder how they can have water of the Ganges. India is a large country. I think it is not easy to have it."

"I asked Rajan the same question. He answered promptly: 'In many Hindu houses, there is Ganges water. It is collected when a family goes on a pilgrimage to the Ganges, usually to Varanasi. This water is considered holy, and it cleanses people of their sins. After every member of the family has poured water into the mouth of the dead person, his face is covered with dry cowpat. At this point, the eldest son, freshly shaven and wearing a traditional Indian kurta pajama, starts the fire in the pyre, fills an earthenware pot with water, stands before the pyre holding the pot on his shoulders, and walks around the dead person three times, as you saw. Finally, he takes a bath in a place near the pyre and puts on new clothes. Sometimes, those who come to the funeral say the funeral oration. The families fix the day and time for taking away the bones and ashes, usually after one or two days. They collect ashes and bones separately. They scatter the ashes on the river. They take the bones to a holy place, usually where two rivers join, and throw them into the water.' 'Where's this holy river?' 'It's two or three kilometers away. The river is called Mula-Mutha because it originated from the confluence of the Mula and Mutha Rivers. One is an Arabic name and the other is an Indian name. It is the same river in front of us. The families throw the bones at the exact point where Mula and Mutha join. Sometimes, the bones are taken to a town called Allahabad, where the Yamuna and the Ganges join, and sometimes they are thrown into the ocean.'

"Rajan didn't look like a homeless man when he spoke, but his clothes and sandals were old and dirty. His hands and feet were quite dirty, too. Obviously, he couldn't wash himself well. 'How can the homeless manage to live? You neither work nor beg!' 'Sometimes there is social distribution to the poor. In the temple they give food, too. Nevertheless, we do some kinds of social work. Can you see Vijay?' Rajan pointed his finger at another homeless man who was sitting on the nearby bench. 'Vijay sets the wood for burning corpses, and he gets small donations every time. Sometimes he makes graves for children in the nearby cemetery. He also collects the ashes and the bones, and then he hands them to the families. Most of the bones become ashes, but a few remain unburned,' Rajan answered."

"Uncle Salvatore, I don't think there is social distribution in India. There are too many homeless and poor people and even many beggars. The government can't afford to feed all of them. If so, it would go bankrupt. What kind of social work did Rajan do? I think he hid something from you. Don't you think so?"

"Yes, I do. I had the same doubt as yours. So, one day I asked Vijay how Rajan could make a living. He answered that his families came to the Burning Ghat every week and gave him some money. I don't know what kind of social work he did."

"Anyway, he was a lucky homeless man, Uncle Salvatore."

"I don't think he was a lucky man. He was a loser! Feeling that Rajan was learned, I began to ask him more deep questions: 'What does it mean that the eldest son walks three times around the pyre and spills water?' 'In every culture water is a symbol of purification. In this case, water purifies the dead person.' I said, 'Once I was at the Hindu temple of Pashupati in Kathmandu. It is a holy place for all Hindus. While I was standing there, I watched a body on the pyre by the bank of the river. The eldest son also performed the ritual of turning around the pyre three times.' 'In Hinduism, the rituals are similar, indeed,' Rajan answered. 'Yes, but the ritual performed here differs from that in Kathmandu. The eldest son put some fire into the mouth of his dead parent there. At that time, I asked a person who was sitting close to me why the eldest son put fire into the mouth of the corpse. He answered that all impurities come out of the mouth through the words one says. Bad words are impure. For that reason, it was necessary to purify the mouth of the dead person. Why in Pune don't you purify the mouth of the dead person, too?' Rayan answered, 'We do it! The ritual is the same. In Nepal they use fire to purify the mouth, while in Pune we use water. The element is different, but the symbolic meaning doesn't differ.'

"I was eager to know more about Rajan and Hindu culture. So I kept asking him questions. 'Are you Hindu?' 'No. I am Christian, though I know the Hindu religion well.' 'Can you tell me more about Hindu funeral ceremonies?' 'Yes. Besides children and enlightened persons, we don't burn the bodies of the unmarried because we consider them incomplete.' 'I haven't seen any women in a funeral ceremony. Is it just a coincidence, or aren't women allowed to attend funerals?' 'Usually, women don't go to funerals because they are more sensitive than men. They can be pregnant, and the evil influences from the corpse may affect the fetus.'

"Then I asked Rajan, 'What kind of social work do you do? You told me about Vijay's work, not about yours.' 'Work is related to time. God is timeless. By meditating, I want to reach the state of timelessness.' 'How can you meditate in such a crowded place?' 'I have to get into silence.' 'Where?' 'The place of meditation doesn't matter. It is important for the mind to be silent. When I meditate, my body and mind become more sensitive and my awareness increases. Then, I can go into myself to find the answer I seek. If I work, I can't clear my mind. In fact, while working, many thoughts come and go in the mind.' 'Only for meditation you don't work?' 'Maybe yes.' 'Thank you, Rajan. Thanks to you, now I know something more about Hindu funerals. I hope to see you again.'

"I had already begun to learn the piano in Isola, but with the frequent interruptions from my traveling, I couldn't improve. I needed to practice the piano as much as possible. So in Pune I tried to find a music academy. I asked rickshaw men who knew everything about Pune, but they didn't know where a music academy was. Then I asked the owner of a bookshop near Koreagon Park whether he knew anybody that could give piano lessons. 'No, I don't, but on that wall is a poster about lessons of Indian classical music and the sitar. There is the telephone number of the teacher. You can ask him,' he answered.

"I dialed the number and arranged a meeting with the man who answered the phone. A few hours later I met him. His name was Ravi. He was about thirty years old, with an olive complexion and a bristly, well-kept beard. He had a skeletal look as if he were sick. 'I am looking for a piano teacher. Do you know one?' 'No, I don't. But a friend of mine who is in Bombay at the moment will be here in two days. He plays at the Osho Ashram during the evening meetings. He can teach you to play the piano.'

"We met at Ravi's friend's home three days later. I couldn't spot any piano in his apartment. I was sure that I had seen him in a white robe with his head covered with a white foulard in the Temple of Chanchal Das Baba on the previous night. He sang, and a man in an orange robe played the harmonium. 'What can I do for you?' he asked. 'I'm looking for a piano teacher.' 'I'm not a piano teacher. My specialty is the guitar.'

"I looked at Ravi. I wanted to say, 'Why did we come here? He is not a piano teacher.' But I kept silent. Ravi didn't seem to be embarrassed and asked his friend, 'Do you know where

Salvatore can learn the piano?' Ravi's friend showed him a newspaper with an advertisement for a music academy. Ravi phoned for information, and we went there by rickshaw. Later Ravi became my good friend."

"Apparently you could make friends easily, Uncle Salvatore. Listening to you, I sense that you felt in India as comfortable as in your own country."

"Benedetto, my country is the world. My hometown is the place where I am at the moment. In other words, if I am in New York, my hometown is New York, if I am in Moscow, my hometown is Moscow, if I am in Addis Ababa, my hometown is Addis Ababa, and so on."

"I think you were lucky to find a piano academy in India. They play other instruments in Indian music such as sitar or harmonium."

"Yes, I was lucky. But the academy was different from that in Isola. As soon as I entered there, I saw several musical instruments in one room. I couldn't expect that they gave lessons for the violin, guitar, keyboard, and piano simultaneously. When I went to the academy for my first lesson two days later, two students were playing the violin, one the guitar, two the piano, and one the drums in the adjacent room. All those sounds didn't annoy me. On the contrary, there was a delightful harmony of noisy sounds.

"The teacher was a young woman called Swara. She was quite fat, with long wavy black hair down to her shoulders. If she had been less fat, she would have been a beautiful woman, but her fatness made her body look like a wine bag.

"I sat down at a black upright piano and started playing by reading the score on the piano. Now and then, the teacher came and checked my practice. If my playing was acceptable, she turned the page of the piano book to a new page.

"At that time, I wondered whether this was useless work. I was too old to learn a musical instrument. But I felt that playing the piano was like a kind of meditation that made me a less cerebral person.

"After I finished the piano lesson at the music academy, I went to Ravi's home. He showed me his favorite musical instrument, the sitar. 'The sitar is an Indian string musical instrument used in classical music. The sound box is made from a pumpkin. The strings are supported by two ivory bridges. Sometimes in the cheaper sitars, they use bones of a camel as bridges. The number of the strings ranges from eighteen to nineteen. There are two rows of strings, seven on the upper part of the sitar and twelve on the lower part,' Ravi explained like a teacher."

"Uncle Salvatore, it seems that the sitar is similar to *the viola d'amore*. You've already talked about this musical instrument when you met the lawyer Bruno."

"They are not similar, Benedetto. The *viola d'amore* looks like a violin or a cello. The sitar looks like a guitar. However, the common thing of these musical instruments is that some strings vibrate though they are untouched. It was the first time that I saw a sitar.

"Ravi went on, 'When two strings are tuned in the same frequency, it doesn't matter if the string is in the upper part or in the lower part, whenever you pluck one of them, the other string vibrates.' 'Some time ago I heard about vibrations from a friend of mine in my hometown. He said that everything vibrates in the universe. Do you agree with him?' 'Yes, I do. Everything in the universe has its own frequency. The frequencies are measured in hertz. For instance, if the frequency of the glass I am holding in my hand now is x hertz, when you produce the sound of x hertz, both frequencies are the same and the glass vibrates. Everything vibrates, both organic and inorganic matter, both material and immaterial. That's why when beautiful music is played, our whole body vibrates. Our bodies are made of many particles that react to the various sounds.' 'Do you believe in the existence of the soul, Ravi? If yes, I want to know whether the soul can vibrate as well,' I asked Ravi."

"Uncle Salvatore, I want to know whether you believe in the soul or not."

"I don't know, Benedetto. I'm not sure about that.

"Ravi said, 'The world is made of energy. When a musical instrument is played and you feel well, it happens because the sound contains positive energy. On the contrary, when you hear the noise of the cars and horns in the street, you are stressed. There are two kinds of energy. One is good, and the other is bad. The world is ruled by two opposite energies. Everything is energy, and Einstein proved it by the well-known formula, $E=mc^2$. It means that energy can change into matter and matter into energy.' 'Is the soul energy?' I asked.

"Ravi lit a candle. Then he went on. 'The human body and the soul are similar to a candle. When the human candle is burned out, it can't contain the soul, which leaves the body. Stones are also energy, for they are not dead. There are souls in the universe when an embryo enters the womb. It attracts a soul with the same frequency. When you work under pressure or have pain, your body loses its natural positive frequency. That's why you need good music to harmonize your body. The soul can feel vibrations as well. Body and soul are connected, and both vibrate. Words and thoughts have vibrations, too. If we say something or think of something, our words or thoughts create vibrations. Do you know why we met? It happened because we have the same frequencies. We both love music. If we had had different frequencies, our meeting wouldn't have been possible. People attract one another according to their frequencies. Among millions of people in the world, you can attract your soul mate who has a frequency similar to yours. It is like playing the sitar. The string that vibrates in resonance must have the same frequency as the string you pluck.' 'What is the difference between frequency and vibration?' 'Frequency is the number of vibrations in a second. It is measured in hertz. Hertz are the number of vibrations. In other words, one hertz is one vibration, two hertz are two vibrations, and so on.'

"In the afternoon, I went to the Burning Ghat. Rajan came up to me with another man. He looked different than Rajan. His complexion was less dark, and his black hair was combed well. If I had met him in Isola, I would have thought he was an Italian not an Indian. He sat on his white scooter and wore a well-ironed checkered shirt. He didn't look like a homeless man.

"He watched the river and then turned to me. 'What a beautiful landscape! Once people used to come here and walk along the bank of the river until late at night. Now this river is full of garbage. It flows into another river called Krishna. It is the only river of India flowing eastward before arriving in the Bay of Bengal.' 'What is your job?' I asked. 'I am a yoga teacher, now! I was rich at one time. Then I lost all my money at the stock market. I just followed the advice of the managers of the bank, but things didn't go well.'

"I didn't have any reason to doubt his words. Maybe he was rich at one time. Who knows! It is not unusual to fall from riches to rags. As he said that he was a yoga teacher, I thought he knew something about the relationship between body and soul. So I asked him, 'Do you think there is life after death?' 'After death there is a mutation. It happens because the frequency changes and the wavelength changes, too. Then, resonance takes place according to the whole cosmos. Resonance is everywhere. It can be chaotic or smooth. Human intelligence has to learn to accept the polarity of destruction and creativity, which is one infinite energy. These days women can't resonate due to the education system. The male scientific mutation dominates the feminine resonance, so we are proceeding toward a global suicide,' he answered."

"This person's words sound quite strange, Uncle Salvatore. I can't understand him. What does it mean, 'The male scientific mutation dominates the feminine resonance, so we are proceeding toward a global suicide'? I can't trust him. Was he really a yoga teacher?"

"I couldn't understand him, either. I couldn't know about his reality. But I kept talking with him. 'I think women can express themselves very well in Western countries nowadays. Why do you talk like that?' 'In Western countries, women imitate men. Men smoke, and women smoke. Men enroll in the army, and women enroll in the army, too. It is imitation, not real freedom.'

"His talking became more and more complicated. 'The meaning of God is the perfect synchronicity between resonance and mutation, society and individuality, male and female, the new generation and the old generation, and so on. In a perfect society, everybody concurs to a global government that works out of love, without a professional money-minded hierarchy and without a grudge against society. Patriotic countries, wars, diseases, which are all psychosomatic, fear of death, suicides, murders, stealing, rapes, drug addiction, sexism, mechanical sex without love are all pieces of evidence of imbalance between male and female synchronicity. All the enlightened ones, Jesus Christ, Krishna, Kabir, Muhammad, Buddha, Mahavira, Guru Nanak, Paramahansa Yogananda, Ramana Maharshi, and other masters are examples of perfect resonance and mutation. They really worked hard to achieve meditation, godliness,' he said confusedly."

"What is he talking about? According to him, meditation is an achievement! Meditation is done to achieve a peaceful mind. Do you agree with me, Uncle Salvatore?"

"Yes, I do. However, I let him talk, though I couldn't understand him well. 'Techniques of meditation are made to achieve the state of meditation which is to stop the mind and to discover the heart and the infinite expansion.' 'What is the soul?' I asked. 'The soul is atomic super intelligence inside the body in synchronicity with the outside.' 'Are the mind and the soul different?' 'Yes, they are. The mind is different from the soul. The mind is thinking and dreaming. The thinking mind creates science, which is male. The heart is a pure feeling that helps discover the soul. The soul is the original female religion,' he said."

"If you continue to tell his nonsense words, I won't keep typing, Uncle Salvatore. I can't understand his ideas about soul and female religion. His words seem to be bullshit to me."

"Calm down, Benedetto. I wasn't convinced by his words, either. So I asked him, 'If the soul is a religion, who are we? And where is our individuality?' 'Our individuality is just pure feeling. If we meditate on this feeling, we will discover atoms inside our feeling. We will find out the super intelligence inside the soul, which is you, me, and everything. Everything is mutation of wholeness,' he answered."

"Did you ask his name, Uncle Salvatore?"

"Yes, I did. 'My name is Prem. I had my first death experience at the age of eighteen. The second experience came through pranayama, yoga, and long-time vipassana, or cosmic self-love. I was dying during my prayers. My mind stopped slowly, and my body also stopped. No breath, only awareness and cosmic vibrations. Peace, oneness, feeling of being drunk in bliss, freedom, and being in the now and here, no future, no past.' 'You said that everything is mutation of wholeness. Trees, animals, stars, the moon, human beings, and so on are mutations. Is wholeness God?' 'I don't use the word God, I use the word godliness. God is a noun, while godliness expresses action, creativity, and quality,' he answered.

"I wanted to stop the conversation with him. But I continued to talk because I didn't want to hurt him. So I asked him, 'Are people with a low intelligence a mutation of godliness?' 'They are a mutation of our retarded social system.' 'Is our retarded social system a mutation of godliness?' 'It is a mutation of the animal kingdom.' 'But the animal kingdom is also a mutation of God!' 'Look! There are three things: pain, pleasure, and transcendence of both. If there is no pain, there is no pleasure and no transcendence. Godliness means all three: animal, human, and superhuman.

Being human means that through the right effort man can transform the inner animal into a superhuman being. If we don't try to transcend instinct, we are not human beings, yet. We are just animals with contracted hearts or maybe without hearts. We are just robots that act mechanically. Our scientific inventions created by our animal minds are of no avail to go beyond animality.' 'Does evil come from godliness?' 'Evil means a closed and contracted heart. Good means an open and expanded heart. It depends upon us and our educational system.'"

"This time I agree with him, Uncle Salvatore. His idea about good and evil is unique. Yes, if our heart is closed and contracted, we can be evil, while good is an expression of an open and expanded heart."

"Yes, once in a while, he said something interesting. I asked him, 'There are narrow-minded people. How can we have relations with them?' 'Pain and fear are the best teachers. Through them we understand life well. The pseudo-male lesbian scientists are trying to control mutations, resonances, time, space, and changes, but they can't control their own minds, their own restlessness, loneliness, inferior egotism, fear, pain, and sense of separation. On the other hand, religion doesn't want to control anything. Ordinary religious people just want to control their own minds in the right sequence. They want to find the ultimate super special sequence to live life in total awareness.'

"I couldn't endure the conversation with him anymore. 'Okay, Prem, it's enough for today.' Before we parted, he said, 'If someday you mention our conversation to others, please don't change my words.' 'Okay, I see.'

"Then Prem took me to the house, or, rather, the room where his daughter lived. 'My daughter works at a call center and sometimes performs fire dance for weddings or other events.' His daughter was a typical Indian beauty. But her face was pale and two dark circles shadowed her black eyes. She looked tired. She prepared some Indian tea for us. We drank it silently. I felt that the milk in the tea was sour, but I drank it to the end. Then Prem led me to a park. We sat on a bench for a few minutes. 'This is my bed,' said Prem. I opened my eyes wide. 'Don't you sleep at home? Are you homeless, like Rajan?' 'Yes, I am. I sleep outside. I can't live in a room. I need open space, indeed.' 'But it's very cold in Pune at night in this season. How can you stand the cold, lying on this iron bench?' 'I wear many layers under my shirt. But sometimes it's really cold.'

"Often the scene of Prem sleeping on the bench in the park in the cold night occurred to my mind when I lay in my warm bed. I wished to be an angel and cover Prem with a thick woolen blanket while he was sleeping there at night. The condition of human beings differs from one another. When the end of my life arrives and God asks me what wish I want to come true, I already have an answer. I'll ask God to make me a guardian angel of the homeless to provide them with warm blankets on cold winter nights."

"Uncle Salvatore, why are you so touched by the homeless?"

"Because some of them are extraordinary. We don't know what is hidden inside them. The Burning Ghat was the place where Rajan and Prem hung out. They were homeless but also two learned and sensitive men. They could be likened to Odysseus of the Homeric poems who landed on his island of Ithaca after long peregrinations. With the help of Athena, he assumed the shape of an old, weak man to avoid recognition by his enemies. He looked old and weak, but inside he had the spirit of the great warrior. My two homeless friends looked weak, but maybe they also had a strong spirit inside.

"One day I asked Rajan, 'Can you tell me something about yourself?' He answered, 'I was Christian. For the time being, I am not a Christian, and I am open to all religions because I don't know the truth. When I was a child, half of my family was atheistic. The other half was Christian. As I grew up, I wanted to know the truth. First, I studied a lot, and then I dropped everything to search for the truth.' 'What did you drop?' 'I quit my job. I was a teacher of business management.' 'Why did you quit your job?' 'I couldn't do two things together, working and searching for God, truth, and love. I had to choose one of the two,' he answered."

"Uncle Salvatore, this Rajan looks more strange than Giuseppe and Umberto. They also quit their jobs, but at least they had a home to live in."

"We don't know the ultimate truth, Benedetto. I felt that Rajan was an unlucky man. 'Where did you work?' 'I was a teacher at Neville Wadia Institute of Management Studies and Research, which is a branch of Pune University.' 'How long did you teach?' 'For three years.' 'Do you have a degree or qualification?' 'Yes, I am a graduate electrical engineer with a master's degree in human resources management, production management, and computer management. My approach to my spiritual search was scientific. My first issue was about God. Is there God? Or is there no God? If there is no God, it doesn't matter how I live my life. If there is God, I have to live a disciplined life. I made the assumption that there is God. On this earth we have many religions, some right and others wrong. Now I have to find the true religion,' he concluded."

"Uncle Salvatore, it seems that religion leads people astray. Both Giuseppe and Rajan quit their jobs because of religion. The former wanted to write a monumental book against the Bible, the latter aimed at finding his true religion. In my opinion, the world would be more peaceful without religions. They trigger hatred, wars, and destruction. 'Religion is the opium of the masses,' Karl Marx said. I agree with him. We don't need priests or monks in our way to God. They can't be mediators between God and us. We can find God by ourselves, inside ourselves, and through life. Living a meaningful life is the best way to God." I got excited and spoke up, "Religion controls human life!"

My uncle was shocked at my words, but he kept calm. "Since the beginning of human history, there has been religion. You can't drive it out. As for me, I can't live without religion. It is like the air I breathe. We have different minds, Benedetto. I can't agree with you. Religion is good. At that time, I had a feeling that Rajan quit his job because of another reason, not because of religion. Maybe he had a heartbreaking hurt that he couldn't tell me about. Sometimes, some persons become tramps after a heavy failure, frustration, or difficulties in life. No, I don't think Rajan became homeless to search for God."

"Even though we are different, I respect your opinion about religion, Uncle Salvatore."

"Okay, let's go on with our story. I asked Rajan, 'How do you determine which religion is right or wrong?' 'I feel that most religions are good because they aim at elevating the human spirit. They have succeeded to a certain degree in this respect. When the religious foundation was solid, society progressed. When in certain areas religion tottered, civilization suffered a setback. Religion makes society progress. Look at Western societies. When they had a strong Christian faith, they progressed. But when Christian and family values were neglected, civilization faded,' he answered."

"Uncle Salvatore, what Rajan said is wrong. Even though there are a lot of religions, nowadays human spirit degrades. Religion has nothing to do with elevating human spirit, I think."

"I don't think so, Benedetto. Religion did a lot for the progress of society. The first university in Italy was started in Bologna in the eleventh century. It was a Catholic university. Not everybody knows that it was just the pope who financed, supported, and encouraged Galileo Galilei. Later, Galileo Galilei attacked the pope without an apparent reason, and they fought. Read history! Therefore, religion is not a synonym of obscurantism. As for Rajan, I found his talking a bit contradictory, but I didn't want to debate about religion with him. So I went on with my questions. 'You said that it was not possible for you both to work and to search for God. I think we can do both. In my case I work, and I search for God, too. Life is an organic unity. You can't split material and spiritual. If you live in this way, you can't live your life fully. In other words, everything is a projection of God. Money is also a projection of God, and work is also a projection of God. So why do you have to give up your work to search for God?'

"I felt that I had hurt his pride. He winced and answered quietly, 'I live my life. I do my regular things.' 'What things?' 'Eating food and sleeping.' 'Just eating and sleeping? I don't think it is enough in life. There are moments of life that you can't live, such as traveling, dancing, working, drinking a glass of beer at a pub, loving a woman, and so on.'

"My remark was too obvious, so he couldn't help agreeing with me. 'Yes, you are right. But I want to focus on a particular job, a search for God. For the sake of my quest, I gave up certain aspects of life.' 'How do you lead your search?' 'Mostly, studying and learning from the environment and life itself, not from books. The most important aspect of the environment is people. A person's behavior is different when he works.' 'Rajan, I think if you want to study people when they don't work, you will always meet people like you. There are some groups of people that you can't analyze. So there will be something missing in your quest.'

"I didn't feel like continuing to talk about his private life. So I diverted the discussion to another topic. 'Rajan, have you ever watched a burning corpse?' 'Yes, many times. I came here fourteen years ago. I sleep here in the shed provided for the homeless.' 'Have you ever asked yourself what will happen after death while watching a burning corpse?' 'Yes.' 'And what is your conclusion? Does life after death exist?' I asked him at that time, and still now I ask myself the same question."

"Uncle Salvatore, still you wonder whether there is life after death or not? You have sifted this topic for a long time! You couldn't find an answer, and you won't find it as long as you are alive. After you die, you'll be able to know the truth!"

"Benedetto, I have to search for an answer while I am alive. When I am dead, I can't do anything."

"I hope you can succeed. Now let's go on."

"Rajan answered, 'Man gets many chances to purify his soul during his life. The Christians believe that they will go to heaven. Eastern religions believe that man will become one with God. Does life after death exist? Yes. Life is indestructible from alpha to omega, from beginning to end. No destruction. We are all children of God. He appears in human form to purify himself. He wants to separate good and evil, light and darkness.'

"Uncle Salvatore, God is perfect. He doesn't need to get purified. It's the first time that I've heard such a completely ridiculous statement. It is absurd what Rajan told you. Don't you think so?"

"Yes, I do. But Rajan seemed to be sure about his ideas. He said, 'I believe that God and Satan are the same being. In every man good and evil coexist. The creation was made to separate Satan from God.' 'How can you prove this assumption?' 'I can't prove anything. This is just my insight, my intuition. It comes from my inner world.' 'How can you know whether your insight is right or not? It may be wrong and lead you astray,' I said."

"Uncle Salvatore, only you could lend your ear to that homeless man. Is it possible that God and Satan are the same being? Of course not. They are different."

"Benedetto, I am open to all ideas. However, I, too, have some doubts about the oneness of God and Satan, or no separation between them. I have read Job's story in the Bible. God conversed with Satan, as if they were sitting at the same table. They were discussing Job's destiny!"

"It is interesting! I didn't know about this passage of the Bible."

"Rajan kept talking and asked me, 'In the Bible it is written that God created the stars, the earth, the universe, and everything. Who created Satan? Tell me.' I answered, 'Satan was an angel of God. Later he betrayed God.' 'There is no mention in the Bible about Satan as an angel that betrayed God.' 'Are you sure?' 'Yes, I am one hundred percent sure! I have read the Bible, and I can assert that there is no mention about Satan as an angel in the Bible.'

"The long conversation with Rajan made me recall the days I had spent in studying the issue of good and evil. Many times, broaching this difficult topic, I had the insight that good and evil may come from the same source. Anyway, having an open mind and respecting others' ideas are my strong points.

"Prem introduced me to a friend of his. According to him, he was an exceptional man. Unlike Prem and Rajan, who wore Western style clothes, he wore Indian white clothes. He held his hand out to me and introduced himself. 'I am a naturopath. My name is Hari. I live in a mountain of the Himalayas. My village is located three thousand meters high.' 'What is naturopathy?' I asked. 'Naturopathy is body treatment through the five elements: water, earth, air, fire, and void.' 'Is void an element? Doesn't void mean nothingness?' 'No, it is not nothingness. Void means nothing and everything at the same time,' Hari answered."

"Uncle Salvatore, this third man you met at the Burning Ghat, seems to be a bit more learned than the other two. But I can't understand his words. What does it mean, nothing and everything simultaneously?"

"He said, 'Earth, stars, trees, rivers, and everything emerge and submerge in the void. Everything appears and disappears.' 'How does the process of emersion and submersion happen? What is the meaning of appearing and disappearing in the void?' I asked. 'It is beyond the mind. Nobody can explain it.' 'Do I have to believe blindly? Or is there something rational that I can understand?' 'Yes, there is something rational. Where does this tree come from? And where does this tree go? How does our body survive, and where does it go after death? This is the void,' he concluded."

"Uncle Salvatore, I sense that the void is like a stage. Actors can't act without a stage. They come on stage, and then they make an exit. The void is like that, I think."

"You are very smart, Benedetto. I am proud of you!"

"Then I asked him, 'Is man a fruit of evolution, or a creature of God?' 'A human being is made of developed particles. God didn't create the world. God created only one thing, the first big blast, and then his work was over. After the big blast, there has been the evolution of particles. 'How did evolution set groups of well-disposed and homogeneous cells and give rise to intelligence? Did it happen by chance?' 'Not by chance! Bacteria come from the earth. We eat food, and after digestion we excrete. The excretion produces worms, insects, and then bigger insects, likewise, intelligence develops more and more to create self-consciousness. If you look at a leaf through a microscope, you'll see the particles moving. This is called chemical resonance, which causes further evolution. Resonance is the movement inside the particles. All particles vibrate. The entire universe vibrates. Okay, now I have to go,' said Hari."

"Uncle Salvatore, this man Hari looks quite sure about his theory of evolution, but it is his truth, not the truth. As for me, like Socrates, I just know that I don't know. I just discuss with others to get my own idea."

"Good! We have many things in common, Benedetto. Now let's go on with the story."

"I am ready!"

"One day, Ravi and his girlfriend invited a Taiwanese lady called Savita and me to their home. He tuned his sitar by using a harmonium. Then he started to play. The sound of the sitar was melodious and emitted good vibrations. I felt relaxed while I was listening to the music. 'Now I'll play a piece of Indian classical music named *raga*. Some *ragas* have healing powers. For example, *raga bhoopali* is good for lowering high blood pressure. Physicians have measured blood pressure before and while listening to *raga bhoopali*. Blood pressure lowered while a person was listening to r*aga bhoopali*. The C-sharp in the harmonium is attuned to the sound OM. Singing OM with a musical instrument has healing power,' Ravi said."

"Uncle Salvatore, Ravi looks like a high spirit, even though he is a young man. I can imagine him as a distinguished gentleman who speaks in a calm, warm voice."

"Yes, he was a pure spirit who loved music. I asked him, 'I want to know something more about the sound OM.' He answered, 'AUM, pronounced OM, is the basic sound of life. When you utter OM, your energy level increases. The sound OM creates silence. It's not a common sound. It's the sound of silence. When you are listening to good music, it takes you to silence because you feel relaxed. It seems a paradox, but the sound of music takes you to silence. In India, people believe that the sound OM already exists in the universe. You can hear it when you are silent.'

"I asked him, 'You said that if you tune the C-sharp of the harmonium to OM, the effect is increased when you sing it. Is it right?' 'You can use any note, but the lower notes like the C-sharp are better. If you sing the mantra OM every day, you'll feel energetic and get into silence. When you are silent, you can get rid of what disturbs your mind, and then you can think more clearly. If you are not silent, the clouds and the garbage keep moving in your mind and you can't think or act properly. First, you have to throw out your inner garbage, and then you can get peace of mind. My teacher who taught me to play the sitar is eighty-two years old, but he looks young and his face radiates good energy, for he plays music every day. If you play music, your heart never gets old.' Before we parted, Ravi invited Savita and me to a meditation meeting at his home at ten o'clock the next Sunday.

"During the week I used to go to the Burning Ghat area. I enjoyed staying in that place and wanted to explore it more. One day I came across the man in charge of Chanchal Das Baba Temple. I wanted to ask him something about the Hindu religion, but he couldn't speak English at all. At that time

Rajan came to us to translate his words into English for me, but as soon as I asked him a question, the man slipped into the temple. 'Who is that man?' I asked Rajan. 'He is a Hindu priest. He has studied the Vedas for a long time. A Hindu priest celebrates Hindu ceremonies and temple rituals such as weddings and naming newborn babies, which is similar to Christian baptism. Moreover, he performs daily rituals and prayers in the temple. His income comes from donations, but maybe this priest gets some salary, for this temple is private property.'

"I asked Rajan, 'Are the Vedas written in Sanskrit? Do you know what a mantra is?' 'Yes, the Vedas are written in Sanskrit. As for a mantra, it consists of a few words in Sanskrit. It has healing power. All diseases are caused by distorted frequencies in the body and mind. Certain mantras can reset the inner, unbalanced vibrations. If one recites a special mantra continuously, he will restore the natural frequencies in his body and mind.' 'Do mantras have a meaning?' I asked. 'Sometimes they have a meaning, sometimes they have no meaning. There are also mantras made by only one word, such as the mantra OM.' 'Has the effectiveness of mantras ever been proved?' 'In India, many people have been cured by reciting mantras. This can be considered a piece of evidence that a mantra produces special vibrations,' Rajan said."

"Uncle Salvatore, maybe healing through the repetition of a mantra is due to autosuggestion. What do you think about my idea?"

"Benedetto, many mantras have no meaning, so autosuggestion can be ruled out."

"I don't think so. You can be autosuggested by everything, although you don't know the meaning. For instance, if you think a medicine is good for you, it will create a positive effect on you, though it is not a real medicine but just a placebo. The same goes for mantras. Mantras can heal us because we think they have healing power, but actually they are just empty words. They are a kind of illusion. They are like lullabies, who knows!"

"Benedetto, how can we know the difference between reality and illusion? Possibly our whole life is illusion. It may be just a dream. At our death the dream will be over, and we'll awake in another dimension. Only there, we'll be able to discern the difference between reality and illusion, between dream and waking."

"Great, Uncle Salvatore! You are like a poet."

"Thank you. Everybody can be a poet if he opens his heart. Most people can't find their treasure inside. Benedetto, try and find your treasure inside yourself. It is the way of living your own life without following others.

"Before parting with him, I asked Rajan my fundamental question one more time. 'After we die, will we disappear into thin air or will something of us survive? Whenever I watch a body burning on the pyre, I sense that everything of that person vanishes. What do you think about my idea?' 'The soul is eternal. Death is just the transformation of matter into energy. This energy will turn into matter again by entering another body.' 'How do you know it?' 'A few enlightened beings have related that they can remember their past lives. This is a proof of reincarnation. The soul can't die.' 'Except a few enlightened beings, when the soul is reincarnated, it loses the memory of its past lives. This is like dying. Our individuality, our self-awareness is lost. In other words, with death the individual, Salvatore, or the individual, Rajan, will never appear again on the stage of their life. How about my opinion?' Rajan kept silent."

"Uncle Salvatore, do you believe in reincarnation or not?"

"I am not a believer. I don't know about this. How can I know? I am still a searcher for the truth, not a believer."

"On Sunday at ten o'clock, I rang the bell of Ravi's apartment. Marga opened the door. She was the owner of the apartment. Ravi and his girlfriend, Marie, just rented one of the rooms of the apartment. Marga was tall, dark-skinned, and very beautiful. She took me to Ravi's room, where he and his girlfriend had already set two harmoniums and one sitar on the bed. The room was very small. So we all sat on the bed. Marga seemed to be the leader of the meditation that day.

"She said, 'We'll practice gibberish for ten minutes. Do you know what it is?' 'Sure! But it seems to me that there is not much difference between gibberish and the second stage of Dynamic Meditation,' I answered. 'Gibberish is different. In the second stage of Dynamic Meditation, you are allowed to utter whatever word you want, any words. In gibberish, you can't pronounce words that belong to languages you know. You can only utter unknown and meaningless words. You can move, cry, laugh, shout, and so on.' I asked her, 'Why do you do gibberish?' She answered, 'When you walk in the streets, you can see that people talk to themselves. There is a continuous soliloquy inside a person. Gibberish breaks the internal soliloquy and allows the mind to rest.'

"We did gibberish for ten minutes by speaking in a meaningless language. In my opinion, gibberish is like beating all the keys of a piano randomly and loudly, hitting the unused ones and clearing away all the dust in the hammers inside the piano. There is a lot of garbage inside us, and by doing gibberish we can throw it away and cleanse our mind.

"Marga said, 'When your mind stops wandering, then you can do Samadhi. It means sitting silently.' 'Hence, Samadhi is the same as Vipassana?' 'No, Vipassana is different. When you do Vipassana, you sit silently and watch your breathing. When you do Samadhi, you should not watch anything except absolute emptiness.' I was not convinced about her explanation of Samadhi. For me it was the ultimate state of meditation, not doing meditation. But I didn't want to discuss this with her at that time. We did Samadhi for five minutes and then we chanted the mantra OM with the accompaniment of the harmoniums. 'We must chant the mantra OM seven times,' said Marga. Yes, this is also seven times! Magic number seven! I thought.

"The music of the harmoniums and the mantra OM vibrated and echoed in our hearts. Then, keeping our eyes closed, we rocked slightly from left to right. When we rocked to one side, we pronounced the mantra SO, and when we rocked to the other side, we pronounced the mantra HAA. Then we formed a chain holding our hands, a chain similar to the one in the esoteric group. At the end, Ravi played his favorite musical instrument, and the sound of his sitar ended our Sunday morning meditation.

"Before leaving Pune, I went to the Burning Ghat again. There was a pyre. This time women were also present at the funeral. They stayed at a certain distance from the pyre except the wife of the dead man, who stood closer. She broke her bangle with a stone. There was also red powder scattered on the ground. 'Why did she break her bangle?' I asked a man next to me. 'From now on, she won't wear either bangles or colored saris. Moreover, she won't put the *sindoor* on her forehead. It is the spot of red powder on the forehead of Indian married women,' he answered. 'What color should her sari be?' 'It should be white.'

"At that moment, I recalled my grandmother who had worn black clothes since her husband's death. In India, it was the same. The color was different, white in India and black in Sicily, but the essence of the love toward their husbands didn't differ."

"Uncle Salvatore, it seems that your various travels and experiences had been led by the circumstances, by the weaving of events. In fact, your interest in theater, music, and gibberish sprang from the accidental meeting with Pietro. Your meeting with Rino led you to esotericism. And finally, thanks to the book vendors in Rome and your sannyasin friend in Isola, you could travel to Pune in India."

"Yes, you hit the mark! I have followed the flow of life like water birds that follow the flow of rivers."

"Uncle Salvatore, have you ever done anything in your own way with your free will, without following the chain of events?"

"Yes, indeed! There was one thing I had wished to do, and finally I did. It was my travel to Israel."

"Let's start a new chapter, Uncle Salvatore."

"First I have to read my journal. At that time, I recorded everything about my travel to Israel. Now I want to summarize it. So, let's meet tomorrow evening. During the day, I'll select some episodes of my travel to Israel.

"Okay. Let's go home together. Let's turn off the lights of the kitchen and lock the door."

CHAPTER VII

WHAT I LEARNED IN ISRAEL

"Many times I tried to volunteer in Israel, but I met with difficulties whenever I applied for a position. Most of the obstacles were caused by my age. Organizations didn't accept volunteers over the age of forty. In my case, I was over seventy, almost seventy-three."

"You are still healthy at the age of ninety-two. I think you were like a young man twenty years ago."

"Yes, I was in good health, but regulations are always strict. So my application to volunteer in Israel was rejected repeatedly. As I told you before, I have never planned my travels. I have followed a long thread of events which led me here and there. But for my trip to Israel I tried and tried to get a volunteer job."

"Why did you need a volunteer job? You could go to Israel on your own, or you could visit the holy places by package vacation. You were rich at that time."

"Benedetto, I want you to understand that I was not an ordinary tourist who visited the places superficially and took photos of monuments and landscapes. When I went to a new country, I wanted to meet new people and learn something about their way of living, their culture and traditions. To do that, I needed to stay there with the locals for some time. At last, my firm determination overcame the obstacles. I found an organization that looked for volunteers for an ecological project. There was also an age limit, but I applied for it. Miraculously, the recruitment clerk didn't turn down my application, and finally I was admitted to volunteer for eight weeks in Israel!"

"At the time, you were very lucky!"

"Yes, I was, but I am convinced that God gave me a chance to travel to Israel through the clerk's miraculous decision."

"I don't think so. It was just coincidence and good luck. Anyway, your travel to Israel sounds interesting from the beginning. Let's go on."

"My departure from Isola to the airport of Catania was scheduled at eleven fifteen by bus. I had enough time to go to the cemetery and say goodbye to my dead parents. The cemetery of Isola was like a small town, and the tombs looked like houses where the dead rested."

"Do you often go to the cemetery, Uncle Salvatore?"

"Not often. I seldom go to the cemetery because it's a place of death. Life is to spend time with the living, not with the dead. But that day I had enough time at my disposal. So I visited my parents' tombs before my departure.

"I arrived at Ben Gurion Airport around two o'clock in the afternoon. From there, I took a shared taxi, and one hour later I was in Jerusalem. I had a quick shower, went out of the hotel and walked on Jaffa Street. A lady was walking in the same direction. I asked her where the ancient town was. 'Come with me. Let's cross Jaffa Gate,' she said.

"Without planning it, I was heading for the Holy Sepulcher, guided by a lady from New Zealand, as she said. After a few minutes we arrived at the Holy Sepulcher. Then, the New Zealander said goodbye to me, while another lady from Eastern Europe led me to the back of the Holy Sepulcher to buy a candle. Pointing her finger at a stone, she said, 'This is the spot where the Angel Gabriel stood when he announced to the women that Jesus had resurrected.'

"Then, I entered the sepulcher chamber. Kneeling in front of the tomb, I kissed the base where Jesus's dead body had been laid, according to many Christians. I wanted to stay there a bit longer, but the Orthodox priest in charge of the Holy Sepulcher asked me to go out quickly. So I went out of the chamber. And then, a few minutes later, I met him again and asked him, 'How can we be sure that this is the real spot where Jesus was buried?' He stared at me with fiery eyes and said a few words in a language that sounded like Greek. I couldn't understand him. Maybe he was angry with me. The Eastern European lady led me to Golgotha and showed me the place of the Deposition from the Cross, where Jesus's dead body had been oiled before being placed into the tomb. It was halfway between Golgotha and the Sepulcher. I felt that Jesus's tomb was too close to the place of the crucifixion. For me it couldn't be possible.

"At the orientation meeting, I was given information about my volunteer work and how to visit the Mount of Olives. Between the Mount of Olives and Jerusalem was a valley called the Valley of Jehoshaphat. The Jewish cemetery was located along the slope. The walls of Jerusalem and the Temple Mount with its amazing gilded dome stood out, and the valley resounded with the melodious voice of the muezzin who announced the prayer.

"I spotted the Golden Gate. It is said that Jesus passed through this gate when he triumphantly entered Jerusalem. But Jewish tradition is different. They say that when the Messiah comes, he will pass through the Golden Gate. Fearing it might happen, the Turks blocked it. So, now the Golden Gate is not a real gate. It was blocked with stones and turned into a wall. According to another tradition, which interests Muslims, Jews, and Christians, the area around the Golden Gate will be the place of the Last Judgment. In Hebrew, Jehoshaphat means the place where God will judge. Watching the valley, I imagined a tremendous number of souls from all over the world. They stood fearfully near the Golden Gate, waiting for the judgment of God. In that area there were many graves, both Jewish and Muslim. They believe that on the Last Day, those who are buried in the valley will be resurrected first.

Muslims, Jews, and Christians adopt the same burial system, for all of them believe in the resurrection."

"You're behind the times, Uncle Salvatore!"

"What are you talking about, Benedetto?"

"These days the Christians cremate corpses, too. More and more Catholics opt to be cremated. The funeral rites of cremation are similar to those of burial. An urn with the ashes is brought into the church instead of a coffin with a dead body. Mass is the same. As far as the grave is concerned, there is no difference between them. Usually, the urn with the ashes is buried in the same way as a coffin."

"Yes, you are right, Benedetto. Just now I recall seeing a particular funeral while I was touring Canada. At my age it is difficult to remember something well! Do you know how old I am?"

"Yes, I know. It's possible. Anyway, Uncle Salvatore, you don't need to hurry. Close your eyes, take a deep breath. Sift through your memories, open your eyes again, and then tell me what happened to you in Canada." I felt that my uncle was rewinding the film of his life until a clear scene appeared before his eyes.

"I remember I wrote what I saw there in my diary. In the upper drawer of the cupboard are a few notebooks. Each of them has a title. Please bring me the one with the title North America."

"Okay, Uncle Salvatore." I took the notebook from the drawer and handed it to him. He leafed through the pages, stopped on one of them, and read it. And then he told me what he saw one day in Canada.

"I was walking along the Red River in the countryside near Winnipeg when I heard melodious singing coming from somewhere nearby. I followed the sound until it became distinct. It came from a small chapel. I entered it. The ceiling was covered with wooden planks. On one side of a rectangular table in front of the altar was a small cream-colored box containing ashes, similar to a cookie box. On the other side was a large photo of a woman dressed in violet, with gray hair. I couldn't see her features clearly, because the photo was enlarged, and I was far from it. About one hundred people stood in the shape of an amphitheater opposite the table. They sang with the sound of the organ. Then a lady with a guitar came in. Her singing mixed with the others'. In Sicily, we don't sing during funerals. The funeral rites consist of a stereotyped religious function. No songs at all. But in that small Canadian Catholic church, things went differently. The singing of those who stood facing the cinerary urn sounded like a joyous farewell to the dead woman who was about to leave for another place. It vibrated and resonated in the air like sound waves that would carry the dead woman's soul toward another world. Mass went on. When it was over, a tall and slender young man dressed in white and wearing a black tie took the little box with his hands and headed for the exit of the chapel. All the others followed him. There was a lawn near the church. A hole had already been dug. The young man laid the small box into the little pit while the priest was blessing the grave. Someone took a handful of soil from the ground and threw it onto the little box. One by one, everybody left the graveyard except for four persons who seemed to be the family. An old man with shaved hair and green eyes held a shovel in his hand and waited until the families left. Then, he filled the hole with soil and made a little mound over it. Finally, he also left, carrying the shovel on his shoulder. Everything was over. Yes, one life finished like that."

"I think, Uncle Salvatore, there are countless burial rites in the world according to culture, custom, ethnic groups, historical periods, and so on. Last year I visited Korea with my father. I saw many rounded mounds in a mountain. They were graves shaped like maternal wombs. Somebody said that the womb-shaped grave completes the cycle of life. There are two wombs, the womb of the mother and the womb of the earth."

"There are people that practice neither burial nor cremation. For instance, in Tibet dead bodies are dissected and thrown to vultures. Buddhist tradition gives less importance to the body, which is considered as a mere container of the soul. For the Buddhists, what matters is the soul, a continuum without beginning and end, not the body. But for the Christians, the body will be resurrected on the Last Day. So, it is important."

"Supposing that the body will be resurrected, I don't think the new body will be the same as it was before death. It may be a body of light, ethereal and subtle."

"Yes, I think so. All four Evangelists are unanimous in admitting that Jesus resurrected, but his body was not the same as it was before death. Even the Apostles couldn't recognize the risen Christ at first glance."

"Uncle Salvatore, I want to be cremated after I die. I read somewhere that a few body functions continue for some time after death, for instance, nails and hair keep growing. It would be hideous to feel still alive while you are being buried. What about you? What do you think about the cremation of your body?"

"I don't want to be cremated after I die. I will follow my family tradition. I'll ask to be buried. The most important thing is God's help. It's not important which funeral rites you choose."

"We've talked enough about death in this book. Now let's talk about life. Let's go on with the story, Uncle Salvatore."

"Yes, I understand you. You are young, so you feel that death is far from you. But we can't change the subject right now, Benedetto. In fact, walking along the Mount of Olives, I arrived at an ancient necropolis. A long time ago, the dead were set into a cave for eleven months in Israel. Afterward, they were moved into a common family plot. Later, the custom changed. After nine months inside a cave, the bones were put into a box.

"On the foothill of the Mount of Olives, there is Mary's tomb. According to tradition, Mary didn't die. She fell asleep and the angels took her to heaven."

"What are you talking about, Uncle Salvatore? Don't you know that Mary spent the last part of her life with John in Ephesus? It's impossible that she died in Jerusalem. Mary's tomb can't be there. Probably Mary was buried in Ephesus."

"You may be right, Benedetto. There is no evidence to prove that the holy places were located properly. Then, I crossed the Valley of Jehoshaphat on foot."

"Was it a long way, Uncle Salvatore?"

"Not long. Maybe two or three kilometers. While walking the winding uphill road, I saw an expanse of Jewish tombs on the side of the Mount of Olives. They were made of limestone. It seemed that each tomb was occupied by only one body. In the case of the family tombs of Isola, all the passed away families rest in the same tomb.

"After walking for some time, I spotted an Islamic cemetery on my left. There were armed guards at the entrance, but I was allowed in. Here, the color of the stone was a bit darker than that of the Jewish tombs. Maybe, due to a different orientation there was less light in this cemetery.

"As I kept walking, I caught sight of two armed guards in front of a building. I went in their direction. Pretending indifference, I tried to pass beyond them. But they stopped me. 'You can't get in!' 'Why not?' I asked with eyes full of surprise. 'You can't enter if you are not Muslim.' 'I am Muslim. Including Islam, I follow many religions, therefore, I have the right to pass.' 'You must prove us that you are Muslim. Show us your passport, so we can see what your religion is.' 'In Italy, where I come from, we don't declare our religion on our passport, but I've read the Holy Koran. I've been to the mosque of Catania twice, to the mosque of London once, and I can say the last surah of the Koran entitled 'The Men.'

"I recited the last surah, which I loved. On listening to me, one of the guards seemed to be convinced. He was about to let me pass. But the other intervened. 'Show us how Muslims pray.' At that point I gave up entering because I didn't know how Muslims pray. 'If you want, you can come here from seven to eleven o'clock in the morning. You can visit the Esplanade, but you can't go inside the Dome of the Rock. This is the third holiest place of Islam after Mecca and Medina,' one of the guards said."

"Uncle Salvatore, I want to know the last surah of the Koran. It must be very beautiful if one of the armed guards was about to let you in after listening to it."

"Yes, Benedetto, I learned that surah by heart. Here it is: 'In the name of compassionate and merciful God, say I seek refuge in the Lord of humans, the King of humans, the God of humans; from the evil of the whisperer, who slinks off, who whispers into the hearts of humans; from jinn and men!' Can you understand?"

"No. What does it mean?"

"It means, seek refuge in God whenever the devil comes into your heart and pushes you to be a bad man. When the devil blandishes you and pushes you in the wrong direction, invoke God, and then the devil will become smaller and smaller."

"Good!"

"The whole Koran is a wonderful prayer book. Now let's go back to the story.

"I left the guards and kept walking toward Jaffa Gate. After a while, on my left I saw more armed guards. I went toward them, but they stopped me again. In fact, they kept guard over another entrance to the Dome of the Rock. I turned back and kept walking.

"Not far from there, on my left I saw another checkpoint. It had a metal detector. I thought it was one of the many entrances to the Al-Aqsa Mosque. I was about to leave that area, but my instinctive curiosity prevailed. So I walked to the door with the metal detector. The guards looked at me. I was sure they would stop me, but this time they didn't. I passed through the metal detector, and to my surprise I caught sight of the Wailing Wall in the distance. I didn't have a map with me at that time. But I was attracted by some kind of energy, and naturally I arrived at the square in front of the Western Wall, which was the holiest place for the Jews. It was a supporting wall. On the upper side of the wall was the Esplanade of the Mosques.

"The Western Wall, also called the Wailing Wall, is what remains of the Temple of Solomon. The first temple was built by King Solomon in the tenth century BC, but it was destroyed by the Babylonians in 586 BC. Then, it was rebuilt when the Jews returned from the Babylonian exile. This second temple was remodeled and enlarged by King Herod, and finally it was destroyed by the Romans in 70 AD.

"In front of the Western Wall was a wide square. The combination of wall and square was unique. The houses which looked onto the square didn't spoil the environment. They fit in the urban context. Everything was white, from the wall to the limestone of the houses. Entering the square, I saw a fountain with many water taps. Plastic jars were tied to each faucet with a string. At first, I thought it was drinking water, but then I saw people washing their hands there. In fact, they filled the jars and poured the water on their hands before and after they touched the Wailing Wall. I also poured a jar of water on my hands and washed them.

"Some bushes of wild herbs were here and there on the external part of the wall. They looked like capers. I saw only men praying in front of the wall. While they were praying, they shook their bodies back and forth, bending their heads. On the left side near the wall was a wide table with many books on it. Besides shaking their bodies, the Orthodox Jews uttered a kind of gibberish while they were reading the books. But this gibberish was different from those of the Osho Ashram in Pune and of the Protestant church in Isola. It sounded shriller.

"The square was divided into two by a barrier. I peeped through a gap in the barrier and saw women praying. The part of the square reserved for them was smaller, so they crowded in front of the wall.

"On the right side of the square, not far from the Wailing Wall, was a stand. A man sitting behind a table lent me a white-colored kippah. He said to me, 'Talk with God! Confine yourself to talking with God!'

"I wore the kippah and headed for the wall. I took a seat on one of the many white chairs in the square, raised my head, and admired that majestic wall that seemed to touch the sky. I thought of its history and pictured the Temple of Solomon in my mind. How gorgeous it was! It had been built to house the Ark of the Covenant.

"People prayed with one arm against the wall and their head against their arm. They were talking with God. I also stood up, put my arm against the wall, and set my head against my arm according to the Jewish custom. I told God everything I wanted to say at that moment. I loved that kind of prayer. Talking with the divinity is more sincere than reciting an absentminded prayer."

"You wore a kippah? What did you say to God at that time?"

"I wore a kippah for the first time in my life. I liked it. About the prayer? It was related to my basic question, is there life after death?"

"Uncle Salvatore, aren't you sick and tired of your question about life after death? Okay, now let's continue the main story."

"No, I'm not. I will ask this question until I find the answer. Yes, let's go on. On the right side of the Wailing Wall was an inner domed space. I entered there and saw the original foundations of the Temple of Solomon through a glass floor. There were plenty of books on many shelves in that domed space.

"I went out and headed for the man who had lent me the kippah to give it back to him. He asked me to put a leather black strap with a small leather black box in the middle of it on my arm. 'What is this for?' I asked him. 'Oh, you aren't Jewish. You can't!'

"I washed my hands once more at the fountain and left the square for Jaffa Gate. As soon as I arrived at the hotel, I met a German lady in the lounge. We exchanged a few words. That day seemed to be the longest day in my life. I asked her to have dinner together at the restaurant. She accepted it."

"Usually you traveled alone, Uncle Salvatore. But it seems that you were never alone. How was it possible?"

"The secret is to have an open heart. When your heart is open, all people are your friends. You don't need to strive to socialize, because it happens naturally."

"When you are in Isola, you are different. I seldom see you at the restaurant. Here in Isola, you don't have many friends. It seems that you have two different personalities. You are reserved and introverted in Isola, but you are open and extroverted when you travel abroad. I feel that you traveled so often to flee from something, from Isola, from your fellow citizens, didn't you?" I asked him what I felt honestly. My uncle flushed. Maybe there was some truth in what I said. He avoided answering my question about his two different personalities.

"Benedetto, all my friends already died. So I don't go to the restaurant nowadays. Anyway, keep in mind that you will never know that the sea exists if you spend your whole life only in Isola, a city located near the center of Sicily. Do you agree?"

"Yes, I do."

"I travel to explore new seas, new lands, to come across new people and spiritual masters who can teach me something helpful to my life and can give me a concrete hope that the soul can't die. And also I travel to know myself better and grow my spirituality."

"Sorry for the interruption. Keep telling me about your trip, Uncle Salvatore."

"That's okay. You can ask me whatever freely. The next day, I left Jerusalem for Nazareth. I arrived there at six thirty in the evening. I got off the bus near the Basilica of Annunciation, and from there I walked through the souk, the traditional Arab marketplace, trying to spot the sign for my hostel. At that time, few people were in the lanes, which looked deserted. I saw some boys sitting on a step and asked them where my hostel was. They knew the place and walked me there. I thanked them, pushed the street door of the hostel, which was kept open, and crossed the doorstep. The boys lingered by the street door and held out their hands. They wanted me to give them some money, but I didn't. After all, they had just given information to a foreigner.

"Later, I came across those boys again while I was walking toward the Basilica of the Annunciation. They threatened and tried to attack me. They wanted money because they had given me information. I was ready to react, but I passed by them silently and went on my way.

"To return to my hostel, I had to pass the lane where those boys hung around. I was ready to defend myself, but I guessed that maybe there was another way to my hostel. After a few attempts, finally I found it.

"I had the alternative of walking the previous lane, facing those boys, or taking another way, passing for a coward. Here in Nazareth, Jesus offered me his first teaching: *Whenever you meet two lanes, one that leads to peace and the other that leads to war, choose the former.* From that day on, when I walked through the souk, I avoided taking the lane where I could meet those boys.

"I worked for six hours a day as a volunteer at the hostel, and I had two days off a week. I worked at the reception, welcoming the new guests, offering glasses of cold water and some cake, and guiding them to their rooms.

"On my first day off, I visited the Basilica of the Annunciation. It was a big two-storied church which had been built on an ancient house that belonged to Mary's parents. I walked the nave and sat facing the crypt, which had a room and a staircase that looked similar to the one in my grandmother's house. The shape of the staircase was the same, but at my grandmother's house it was longer and darker, for it led to the stable.

"Almost every evening I went to the basilica. Often, I was the only person in the church. I just watched the room and the stairs inside the cave for a short time. In fact, I felt that if I kept watching them for a long time, Mary would appear, and the apparition would upset my life.

"While I was watching Mary's parents' house, a doubt occurred to me: How can we be sure that this ancient house in the crypt of the basilica was really Mary's parents' house? Do we have to believe in it on faith? Is doubting a sin? One evening, I saw a Franciscan monk talking in Italian with a guy in the courtyard of the basilica. I stood nearby and waited until their conversation was over.

"I scrutinized the monk from head to toe. Like many monks he was a bit plump. Perhaps their sedentary life and the plentiful food to make up for sexual abstinence make them a little fat. He wore a brown frock and a white girdle with three knots to symbolize his three main vows: poverty, chastity, and obedience. I approached him with reverence. 'Excuse me, Father. I hope you'll not get angry, but I want to ask you a question.' 'If I know the proper answer, I'll tell it to you,' said the monk with a candid smile. 'I'd like to know what criteria were used to determine that this was Mary's parents' ancient house,' I asked."

"Uncle Salvatore, you doubted many things at that time. If everybody doubted like you, it would be useless to write history books. When we read a history book, we just trust the author."

"Benedetto, history doesn't always tell the truth. Sometimes facts are distorted for various reasons. As far as the location of the places related to Jesus's or Mary's life is concerned, we can't exclude that the early Christians invented these places of worship to make a myth of Jesus or Mary. After listening to my question, the monk looked reassured. He knew the topic well.

"He answered, 'The places related to Jesus's or Mary's life are just four: the Basilica of the Nativity in Bethlehem, the Basilica of the Holy Sepulcher in Jerusalem, the Basilica of the Annunciation in Nazareth, and the House of Peter in Capernaum. All the other places are approximate.'

"The father's answer cleared away some of my doubts, but I still wasn't convinced. So I asked him, 'Once I visited Lumbini, the town where Buddha was born, according to many. In a room in the ruins of the royal palace, I saw a sign to show the exact spot of Buddha's birth. In the Basilica of the Nativity of Bethlehem, I saw a silver star indicating the exact spot where Jesus was born. Hence, Father, I ask you how is it possible to locate the exact spot of an event that happened two millennia ago? When Jesus was born, only Mary and Joseph were there. The shepherds and the others came there later. So there were no witnesses except Mary and Joseph. I think the spot marked with a silver star is merely symbolic, for nobody can know the exact spot of Jesus's birth.'

"This time the monk didn't seem to be self-confident. He changed the subject of my question. He answered, 'The silver star you saw in the crypt of the Basilica of the Nativity is a copy. In fact, the original was stolen. As I mentioned before, the four places related to Mary's and Jesus's life were located precisely. Here in Nazareth, archeologists found columns of the second century AD with inscriptions about an ancient worship of the Virgin Mary. There is also historical evidence for the other three holy places.' Thanks to his answer, my doubts about Mary's parents' house in the Basilica of the Annunciation in Nazareth diminished a little."

"Uncle Salvatore, sometimes religion becomes business. Almost all the holy places of Mary's apparition attract pilgrims and tourists. Hotels, shops, vendors of holy items, restaurants, travel agencies, and so on make big business thanks to the apparition of Mary. Once I heard of a statue of Mary that wept tears in Capodarso. I was curious about that weeping statue, so I went there with my friends. The statue was inside a small cave. There was a small iron gate at the entrance, so it was not possible to have a close look at the statue. The lights in the cave made the face of the statue glimmer. I watched the statue carefully. I couldn't see any tear. Then we went to a restaurant near the cave. It was crowded with people. Karl Marx was right. He wrote that the greed for money clouds all human feelings. What do you think about?"

"I don't know, Benedetto. Maybe some people use religion to earn money. What to do! That evening, after talking with the Franciscan monk, I walked the streets of Nazareth and pondered over intolerance and persecutions. Often we can't tolerate someone who interferes with our ideas, our way of living, or our economic interests. For instance, if one stood in the square in front of the Basilica of the Nativity in Bethlehem holding a placard that said the silver star inside the crypt is false, he wouldn't be breaking the law, but many people wouldn't tolerate his action. Cab drivers, storekeepers, vendors, priests, pilgrims, et cetera would curse him.

"The intolerant tend to remove obstacles in their way instead of being open to dialogue with the obstacles. The intolerant sweep away whatever doesn't correspond with their ideas. Herodias, a Judaic princess who abandoned her husband to live with her brother-in-law, Herod Antipas, is an example of intolerance. St. John the Baptist condemned her behavior, but her intolerance or tendency to remove the obstacle to her happiness led her to get rid of her critic bloodily. Intolerance was the cause of the death sentence on Jesus and the persecutions against the Christians, Jews, and pagans.

"Intolerance can happen within a family, when parents force a child to conform to their ideas. There is intolerance even at school. Once, in Isola, a teacher forced a schoolboy to have his hair cut, for she didn't allow longhairs.

"If we leaf through the pages of history, we can meet with many cases of persecution, some well-known, like the persecutions against the Jews and the Christians, and some not well-known, like the Christians' persecution against the pagans or the persecution against the Jehovah's Witnesses."

"Uncle Salvatore, it's the first time that I have heard about Christians who persecuted the heathens. Are you sure about that? I thought the heathens persecuted the Christians under the Roman Empire."

"Yes, I am. The pagans were persecuted, too. After the Edict of Constantine in 313 AD, all religions were admitted in the Roman Empire. The Christians were not persecuted anymore. And then they started to show intolerance against the pagans. Little by little, they destroyed the pagan temples. Afterward, mainly for economic reasons, they converted the pagan temples into Christian churches. In Syracuse, the hometown of Santa Lucia, the temple dedicated to the goddess Athena was converted into the Catholic Cathedral of that city. It stands on the island of Ortygia. As soon as you enter the church, you can see the former pagan temple with its well-preserved Dorian columns."

"Also in Isola, Uncle Salvatore, paganism merged with Christianity. In fact, in our town the cult of Demeter was replaced with the worship of Our Lady. Deep down, nothing changes. Religious faith remains unaltered over the eras."

"Yes, it is as you said. After the Edict of Constantine, many pagans were persecuted and killed by the Christians. Apparently, the Christians lost the spirit of nonviolence and love taught by Jesus. They persecuted the pagans, showed intolerance against the heretics, and burned them at the stake.

"One of the cruelest cases of persecution against the pagans was the murder of Hypatia, a martyr and a symbol of freedom of thought. She was a pagan scientist, philosopher and mathematician from Alexandria in Egypt. The Christians killed her during the persecutions against the pagans.

"A persecution that has fallen into oblivion is that against the Jehovah's Witnesses. They have been persecuted not only in Germany. Not long ago, they were sent to jail because they refused to serve in the army. For the Jehovah's Witnesses, the principle of neutrality is at the basis of their creed. In the case of war, they don't take sides for or against belligerents. They don't vote at political elections. But they are viewed with suspicion by many people and are often marginalized. In Germany during Nazism, they were regarded as an obstacle to remove. Their pacifism and internationalism were incompatible with the nationalism and the militarism of the Nazi regime. Almost twenty-five thousand Jehovah's Witnesses were sent into concentration camps, and many of them died there. It was possible to distinguish them from the other prisoners because they were made to wear a violet triangle on their clothes.

"Persecutions and discrimination can affect not only ethnic or religious groups but also social classes. The disabled have been the object of intolerance over the centuries. In the ancient Greek city of Sparta, newborns with a physical defect were thrown from Mount Taygetos. In Italy, some lidos didn't allow kids with heavy physical disabilities to enter.

"Recently, in the United States and in Italy, the device that kept two vegetative patients alive was unplugged. Consequently, they died. In my opinion, this is a case of intolerance. When I volunteered at a center in England that provided holidays for the disabled, I looked after a young man who was completely paralyzed except he was able to move his eyes. He lay on a stretcher. I still remember his name, Neil. I asked the nurse how to feed him. The nurse answered, 'You have to spoon-feed him as if he were a little bird. When he wants to say yes, he raises his eyes, and when he wants to say no, he lowers his eyes. It's easy.' I did like that. At the beginning, the spoonful I gave him was too much. He couldn't swallow the food and coughed. By and by, I found the proper mouthful, and he ate quietly. He couldn't smile, for every part of his body was paralyzed. But looking at his eyes, I felt that he was happy while I was feeding him.

"Some say that the heavily disabled like Neil are better off dead because they suffer so much. This opinion comes from an incorrect idea of happiness. They think that only good fitness brings happiness. This assumption is a kind of prejudice. There is a soul inside a body. The soul can be happy even in a disabled body, like Neil's body."

"Uncle Salvatore, maybe some kinds of life are useless. People who are alive but show no sign of brain activity don't feel anything and can't move. Don't you think it would be better to put an end to their life?"

"I don't think so. I am favorable to all kinds of life. We don't know what will happen after death. Who knows, maybe we'll disappear forever. Therefore, between to be and not to be, I'll choose to be, regardless of the form of life, healthy or unhealthy, normal or disabled, happy or unhappy.

"One day, when I was on duty at the hostel, I met an Italian guy from Naples. He was an engineer. His features were typical Italian. He wore a black mustache. His hair was so curly that it looked like the head of a ram. We talked for a while, and then I asked him the same question that I had asked the Franciscan monk. 'How can we be sure that the locations related to Jesus's presence are real?' He answered, 'My mother is a teacher of classical language and literature. She has been to Israel many times. She advised me to visit the stairs of the Temple of Solomon. Jesus certainly had been there. Do you remember the passage of the Gospel in which Jesus chased away the merchants from the Temple of Solomon?' 'Yes, I do.'

"That guy looked well-informed about Israel and the holy places. I asked him, 'How can I go to the stairs of the Temple of Solomon? It was destroyed by the Romans. Nothing of it remains except the Western Wall. 'No, it's not like that. The stairs are still there. Just walk down the right side of the Wailing Wall. You'll find the stairs to the Temple of Solomon definitely.' 'What else can you advise me to visit in Jerusalem?' 'The Tower of David, the Chapel of Flagellation, the Esplanade of the Mosques, Mount Zion with the Tomb of King David, the Chapel of the Last Supper, and the Church of the Dormition. Moreover, you can visit the Holocaust Museum.' I noted those places on a piece of paper and planned to visit them, starting with the stairs of the Temple of Solomon.

"That very evening, while I was sitting in front of Mary's parents' house in the Basilica of the Annunciation, a doubt arose in me: In Jerusalem I saw Mary's parents' house, and here I am sitting in front of another Mary's parents' house. How is it possible?

"I asked this question to the first priest who passed by me. He was a monk and answered my question in Italian with a heavy Portuguese accent. He answered, 'There is no contradiction. Joachim, Mary's father, was a priest, and as a priest he moved from one place to another.' This answer comforted me. In fact, I came to Israel because of my love for Jesus, not to lose my faith.

"Nazareth is an Arab city. Sixty percent of the population is Muslim, the others are Christian. Both religions coexist without rivalry. Mosques and churches, both Catholic and Orthodox, thrive next to one another. I couldn't see a synagogue. The population of Nazareth is one hundred percent Arab. One of the reasons I came to Israel was to study the Jewish religion which Jesus practiced.

"The hostel manager, Mary, was a very beautiful, lively brunette Arab. Sometimes she came to the hostel wearing a breathtaking miniskirt. I turned to her to have some information about Judaism. 'Do you know a Jew that can teach me something about his religion?' 'Yes, I do,' she replied with her bewitching smile. 'I'm Christian, but I live in Nazareth Illit, where most of the residents are Jewish. I'll ask one of my neighbors if he wouldn't mind teaching you something about Judaism.'

"The next day the telephone of the hostel rang. Another volunteer called my name. There was a person on the phone who asked for me. I ran to answer. A man on the other side of the phone said, 'This is Daniel. Your hostel manager told me that you wanted to talk with me. So, shall we meet in front of the Hotel Plaza in Nazareth Illit at four o'clock in the afternoon? Does it suit you?' 'Yes, thank you very much. I'll be there at five to four.'

"I was very happy. I couldn't believe my ears. For the first time in my life I had the chance to meet an authentic Jew who would teach me Judaism. I thought I shouldn't waste this chance by asking him questions randomly. So I took pen and paper and wrote down my questions to ask him.

"He was short, had a gray beard, and wore a black kippah. Some threads dangled from his shirt. At first, I thought those threads were frayed parts of his shirt, but looking at them carefully, I realized that they were independent threads. We sat at a table in the hall of the Hotel Plaza, and he ordered drinks for us. Then he stared at my eyes. At that moment, I felt like I was a journalist who was about to interview an important person. Instead, he started to talk. 'Why do you travel, and why are you interested in religions?'

"I didn't expect such a question and was caught off guard. I had a list of questions to ask him, instead, he asked me a question. 'I travel to many countries and study religions to know whether everything ends or something of us remains after we die. I want to know whether there is life after death or not. By the way, what is the opinion of the Jews about the afterlife? What will happen after we die?' I asked."

"Uncle Salvatore, your question about life after death is useless and boring to me. It is your obsession. I can understand you, but, in my opinion, the book will be too heavy for the readers. They want to read something cheerful. Please, let's skip this topic of life after death."

My uncle shook his head with a faint smile.

"Sorry, Benedetto. But life can't avoid death. And also, I don't have much time to know the truth. I hope you'll understand me. Now, I'll continue my story. Daniel answered, 'At our death, there is a trial. It is similar to a normal trial in a court of law. We are brought to trial for the actions we have performed in our lives. If the judgment is positive, the soul will go to heaven. Otherwise, it will go to a place of purification where it will stay for eleven months.' 'Eleven months? Why eleven months?' 'I don't know why. But it is written somewhere in the Jewish doctrine.'

"I wanted to know his opinion about good and evil, but I had many questions to ask about Judaism. So I skipped over this."

"Uncle Salvatore, you did well. We've talked about it many times in this book."

"I asked Daniel, 'When I was standing by the Wailing Wall, I saw some Jews with books in their hands. While they were reading, their heads and bodies swung. It was a kind of shaking. Can you tell me what this swinging or shaking body means?' 'Yes. It happens because they feel God inside themselves. There are also people who dance. It is due to the presence of God inside them.'

"I went on with my questions. 'In the hall on the left side of the Wailing Wall was a table with many books on it. Some Jews dressed in traditional clothes uttered a kind of shrill gibberish while they were saying their prayers. Why did they do so?' 'Due to the same reason I told you before. They felt the presence of God inside themselves. Through the gibberish, they expressed what they felt,' Daniel answered."

"Uncle Salvatore, did you ask how to become Jewish? Is it possible to convert to Judaism?"

"Yes, I did. Daniel answered that the conversion to Judaism was possible. In fact, his wife, who was Canadian, converted to Judaism. He said that it was difficult to become Jewish, and one needed to study a lot. He said, 'Generally speaking, one is Jewish if one's mother is Jewish. We don't consider fatherhood for Jewishness.'

"I asked Daniel, 'What is Kabbalah?' 'Kabbalah is the power of words. Words have vibrations. Through a word, you can even create things or life. Jesus was a great Kabbalist. He could perform all those miracles because he knew Kabbalah well,' he answered."

"Uncle Salvatore, it sounds strange to my ears that a person can perform miracles if he knows a secret. How can one create things or life by knowing the power of some words? It is absurd! If it is true, I want to learn Kabbalah."

"Benedetto, to learn Kabbalah well, you have to know Hebrew first. A word in the original language has a different meaning than a word translated into another language. Nevertheless, I've never studied Kabbalah, so I can't answer your question properly.

"I asked Daniel, 'What are the threads dangling from your shirt?' He looked at the threads, put his hand on them, and showed some knots to me. 'These are called tzitzit. They symbolize the word of God. As you see, there are knots along the tzitzit. The knots mean that you have to hold on to the word of God, you shouldn't let it go away.'

"I asked, 'How do you pray in the synagogue? Can I visit a synagogue on the Sabbath?' 'Unfortunately, I can't go to the Synagogue of Nazareth Illit because I believe that Yeshua or Jesus was the real Messiah. In the synagogue, they don't approve of my point of view. A short time ago, they damaged my car. So I go to the Synagogue of Afula, a town near Nazareth. There are Messianic Jews throughout the world and also in Israel, even though they are a minority, who believe that Jesus was the Messiah. You can come to the Synagogue of Afula, if you don't mind. But I don't think the Sabbath is right for you. The ceremony is too long. It takes almost three hours. Do you want to visit my house?' 'Sure!'

"While we were walking to his home, he showed me some houses that had been abandoned by the Jews as soon as some

Arab families had settled in the area. The Jews didn't like to live flank and flank with the Palestinians."

"Do you think the Jews are racist, Uncle Salvatore?"

"I don't think so. If they don't want to live next door to the non-Jews, they have the right to do so. Individuals have freedom to stay with whomever they want. In Isola, the Jehovah's Witnesses marry within their religious group. They can't marry those who have a different religion from theirs. In society it happens the same. The rich tend to live next door to those of the same social class, and the poor next door to the poor. This is the landscape of the world.

"Daniel's house was not big. I felt it was a bit grim. There was an old black upright piano. 'Who plays the piano?' I asked. 'None of us. This is a rented house. The piano belongs to the owner.'

"I glanced around the walls and saw some pictures of their children, two girls and one boy, dressed in Jewish garb. Opposite the main door, a lectern stood close to the wall. 'We pray here. We put our holy books on the lectern and read them aloud.'

"His wife offered me a drink and some cookies. Then I said goodbye to her and headed for the bus stop with Daniel. While we were walking, he kept talking about Judaism. 'For you, it is very easy to travel, but for us it is not easy. Whenever we go abroad, big problems arise. There are many foods that we Jews should not eat. The list of prohibited foods is long. We can't eat all kinds of vegetables, meat, and fish like you. For instance, it is absolutely forbidden to eat squid and octopus.' The bus arrived. I thanked Daniel with a smile and waved goodbye until he disappeared from my sight.

"At the reception of the hostel my attention was caught by a brochure whose heading was *The Jesus Trail*. It was supposed to be the trail that Jesus followed when he left Nazareth for his mission. In some ways it was similar to the renowned Camino of Santiago de Compostela, but it was shorter, just forty miles long. There was a map with the stages of the trail inside the brochure. It took about five days to complete the journey on foot. Because of my work as a volunteer, I couldn't stay away from the hostel for more than two days a week. So I decided to cover the distance in another way. Not only by bus and by hitchhiking but also on foot when I couldn't reach the places by transportation.

"The Jesus Trail started in Nazareth and ended at Mount of the Precipice near Nazareth. I started my journey from the last stage, Mount of the Precipice, also called Mount of the Leap. It isn't far from downtown Nazareth. That afternoon, fortunately, it was not too hot. I crossed over a very traffic-congested road and entered a half-open gate, which seemed to belong to a builder's yard. I got in, but I felt that someone would stop me. Nobody did, so I kept going uphill. Now and then, I rested for a few minutes under a tree. The hill was not high, and soon I arrived at the top. Actually, I didn't reach Mount of the Precipice but a hill near it where, according to tradition, Mary watched the scene of the people of Nazareth that wanted to push Jesus down the cliff. All the area was barren. I saw a small altar that looked like a tomb. It had a marble slab on the top, with an Arabic inscription on it.

"There was also a Greek Orthodox chapel. It was closed. At the rear was some shade. I leaned against the wall. In the cool of the shade, I watched the valley and Nazareth. At that moment I thought of Jesus. I considered Jesus a teacher similar to the good teachers I had when I was a student. In my career as a student, I esteemed only three or four teachers at most. In that barren place near Mount of the Precipice, I thought of Jesus as one of my best teachers.

"Nobody was there. The place was isolated, and I felt like Jesus or the Virgin Mary would appear to me suddenly. But I asked them not to do so, for I would be very scared.

"I kept watching the valley and recalled the passage of the Gospel of Luke about the angry mob of Nazareth who wanted to push Jesus down from the cliff. But Jesus walked through the mob and went on his way.

"If Jesus wanted, he could escape death. More than once he used his power to avoid dying or being arrested. Why did he give himself to his executioner to be crucified? What's the point of such behavior? Jesus could have handed down his teachings to the world without being crucified. Why did he want to die? I tried to figure out an answer about his death. Maybe Jesus and the Apostles were hunted to be arrested and executed. Then, there was a pact between Jesus and the Jews. Jesus gave himself to his executioners in exchange for the salvation of the Apostles, and Judas was not a real traitor but the one who negotiated with the Jews. But I had a feeling that such a guess was unsatisfactory. There should be something deeper about Jesus's death, I thought.

"After I left the hill near Mount of the Precipice, I went to the Basilica of the Annunciation to look for the Italian Franciscan friar I had met before. I couldn't see him in the courtyard in front of the basilica, so I went inside, sat on a chair in the central nave in front of Mary's parents' house, and waited for him for one hour. I wanted to ask him why Jesus's death was necessary for the salvation of humanity. After a while, a monk appeared from a side door, but he was not the one I was looking for. So I kept waiting."

"Uncle Salvatore, what is your birth sign?"

"I am an Archer. Why?"

"Because you are single-minded, like most Archers. When you decide to do something, you stop doing everything else and go straight to your aim. You wanted to solve the mystery of Jesus's death quickly. To know the truth you would have spent the whole night waiting for the Italian Franciscan monk, wouldn't you?"

"Yes, I would. However, I don't believe in astrology. After almost fifteen minutes, two monks entered through the front door, and fortunately one of them was the Italian Franciscan monk. He was in a hurry, but I wanted to talk with him anyway. So I stopped him, 'Good evening, Father.' 'Good evening,' he answered, smiling from ear to ear. 'I'd like to know why Jesus's death was necessary for the salvation of humanity. Is it possible that God is so cruel as to demand the crucifixion of his son to save humanity?' 'It is a mystery for me, too. Anyway, Jesus died because of love for us.' 'I can't accept your answer, Father. It is too indefinite. Would you like to think about it and answer me later?' 'Yes, let's meet at the courtyard of the basilica after the Rosary.'

"I waited in the church until the Rosary was over, and then I headed for the courtyard of the basilica. When we met, he looked more tranquil. He was not in a hurry as before. He said, 'Your question can be answered in the light of four thousand years of biblical history. Man parted from God. In order to establish a new alliance between God and humanity, a sacrifice was needed. I know it is difficult to explain and to understand this concept. Furthermore, I haven't studied theology yet.' 'Aren't you a priest?' 'Not yet. I'll become a priest in three years. I took my vows late, at the age of thirty-eight.' 'Do you study in Rome?' 'No, in Bari.'

"I said goodbye to the monk. Still I was not convinced by his talk, so I elaborated my personal idea about Jesus's death. When one is born on planet Earth, death is implicit. It's not possible for a human being to live eternally. When Jesus came to earth, he knew he would die because he had accepted the human condition. The only problem was when to die, either when he was young or when the candle of his life had burned all its wax. Death is just a question of early or late. But why did Jesus accept such a horrible death and tremendous suffering? I pondered on my life and realized that suffering had been necessary for my spiritual growth. In our life, we often confront crossroads. Two ways open in front of us, one is easy and wide, but it doesn't lead us to spiritual growth. The other is hard and narrow, but it takes us to the ultimate freedom. Jesus's message is still alive because of his death and resurrection. 'Without resurrection, our faith would have been in vain!' said Saint Paul. Through his horrible death, Jesus pointed out to us the way of love, which is the only way to God. Love entails everything for the good of the loved ones, even personal sacrifice, torture, and death.

"I did the last stage of the Jesus Trail because it was near Nazareth. But then I wanted to start the trail from the first stage, which was Cana. On my day off, in the early morning I took a bus to Cana, where Jesus performed his first miracle, the conversion of water into wine, according to John's Gospel. From there, I went to Mashhad on foot. It was the town where the prophet Jonah was born. I asked two or three passersby I met in the street where the church dedicated to Jonah was. Unfortunately, few people in that town understood English, so I tried to communicate by gestures. Finally, I entered a fruit shop with four or five women inside, all dressed in traditional Arab clothes. They wore white robes to their feet and veils over their hair. They frowned at me and seemed not to understand both my words and my body language. Suddenly, a fat, young man came from the rear of the store. His eyes looked threatening. 'What do you want?' 'I am looking for the Church of Jonah.' 'The church is up there.' 'Is it far from here?' 'It is near. Go,' he said, pointing his hand toward the door of the shop."

"Uncle Salvatore, maybe in that Arab town they mistook you for a Jew. There is still bad blood between Jews and Palestinians, though they live in the same country."

"I think so. However, I followed his information. So I walked uphill about one hundred meters and then I caught sight of a mosque. It was a quarter to one, and the voice of the muezzin was announcing the time of prayer. I entered the mosque, took off my shoes, and went to the upper floor. I saw a few people standing. One of them came up to me and asked me what I was looking for. 'I am here to pray,' I answered. 'Okay, you can stay here, but sit on the sofa for now,' he said."

"How strange the fruit seller was! You asked him how to go to the church, but he showed you the way to a mosque."

"Benedetto, I didn't care about that. I enjoyed the mosque, too. I sat close to two old men who were reading a book.

There were also a few boys who glanced at me and giggled. While I was sitting, I thought that if there is an upper spiritual sphere where souls live after the body's death, all the great men, saints, prophets, and enlightened men stay together harmoniously and peacefully. I imagined Mohammed, Krishna, Buddha, and Jesus strolling and chatting together. They wondered why humans were so divided and fought one another because of them.

"All the people inside the mosque moved ahead and stood facing the imam. The person who previously asked me to sit down told me to move forward. He set me at the center of a carpet, and then following the words of the imam, we all bowed in Muslim style several times. After the ceremony was over, I headed for Zippori, the town where Mary's family came from.

"That day it was very hot. Walking downhill, I saw a stall and two men selling prickly pears. I stopped there with a sigh of relief and they asked me to sit down. A lady came and offered me a glass of cool orange juice. They peeled the prickly fruit for me. Then I asked for the bill. 'You can go. It's free,' one of the men answered.

"I thanked them and kept walking to Zippori. I took the way the fruit vendors had shown me and arrived at a crossroads. I didn't know which direction to go. The sun was getting hotter and hotter. A few cars passed by. Whenever I raised my arm to ask how to get to Zippori, they didn't stop. Finally, a car pulled in. The driver had a friendly look. 'Excuse me. Do you know the way to Zippori?' I asked. 'This is Zippori.' 'Isn't Zippori a town? This is countryside.'

"I showed him my map of the Jesus Trail, putting my head and trunk into the car to avoid the scorching sun. While he was scanning my map, I eagerly hoped that he would give me a ride. 'Come with me,' he said suddenly. How lucky I was!

"To get to the village of Zippori, he drove for about fifteen minutes. Before I met him, I had been walking in the opposite direction to Zippori. In the meantime, we exchanged a few words. 'Are you Jewish?' I asked. 'No. I am Christian. My mother is Christian, and my father is Jewish. I have followed my mother's religion. My parents had lived in Russia for a long time, but I was born in Israel.' I asked, 'When I was at the Wailing Wall in Jerusalem, a man wanted to give me a kind of black leather strap and a leather box. But when he realized that I wasn't Jewish, he took them back. Do you know what they are?' 'Yes, these are tefillin or phylacteries. The Jews in their prayer wrap one tefillah around their arm and the other around their head. Inside the leather box they put passages of the Torah,' he answered. 'In Jerusalem, I saw a van with a man inside. He was sitting behind a table on which there were many tefillin. Do you know why there were so many tefillin on the table and the man was sitting in the van?' 'Yes, I know. He is one who gives people tefillin so that they can talk with God.' Soon we arrived in Zippori, and he dropped me off with a piece of advice, 'Don't be shy. If you need, try and hitchhike.'

"I walked uphill. Zippori seemed to be a quiet countryside village. It had nothing special to my eyes. So I left the town and I walked on the main road that skirted the national park. I tried to hitchhike, and a car which was going in the opposite direction pulled in. I asked the driver, 'Could you tell me the way to Nazareth, please?' 'This is the right road. I am coming back in seven minutes. If I find you on my way back, I'll drive you to Nazareth.'

"That place was shady, so I decided to wait for him there. After about ten minutes, the man came back. He pulled the car onto the right and opened the door. 'Come in,' he said smiling. As soon as I got in the car, he asked me, 'Have you ever seen Mary's well?' 'Yes, I've already seen Mary's well in Nazareth.' 'Here, there is another Mary's well. This is the real Mary's well. In fact, Mary was from this area.'

"Hearing his words, I hesitated about going to Nazareth with him or going to see this Mary's well. The latter alternative prevailed. 'Yes, I want to visit Mary's well. Where is it? 'It's just three hundred meters away. Cross over that field, and you'll find it. Good luck! After you see the well, you can take a bus to Nazareth. The bus stop is across the road.'

"I walked in the countryside, but I couldn't find the well. I asked a man on the way. 'Yes, it is down there. Some people drink the water of the well, but I've never done that,' he answered.

"After passing by a garbage heap, finally I found the well! I got near to it and was welcomed by the warm greetings of several children. 'Shalom! Shalom! Shalom!' they all sang in one voice. 'Shalom!' I answered with a big smile.

"The children were splashing in the pool, jumping up and down. Actually, the well was a pool. The water had a bluish hue, which degraded into light blue and ended in whitish colorlessness by the edge where I was standing. At first, I guessed that the light blue color of the water was caused by the reflection of the blue sky. But soon I realized that the pool was too small and shallow to reflect the blue sky. The water didn't seem to be stirred up by the children who splashed continuously. Its preternatural blue color remained unaltered.

"I took off my shoes and tried to keep my balance while I was walking on uneven, pointed stones. I sat on the edge of the pool and dipped my feet into the cool water. Then I washed my face and my head. There was an ancient wall on one side of the pool. A small blue rivulet fed the pool. I had never found any mark about this Mary's well on the map. Nevertheless, I visited the well by chance. The sky blue color of the water and its atmosphere enchanted me. When I stepped out of the well, the children performed a Hebraic dance for me. I was happy to see their dance. I waved goodbye to them, smiling. Then I walked to the bus stop.

"At the hostel, two employees alternated at the reception. One was Samuel, an olive-skinned man like most Palestinians. Despite being over fifty, he was unmarried. He dressed like a hippie. He was quite lean, with straight hair in a ponytail and a golden earring in his right ear. When new guests came in, he greeted them with a bright smile. Then he took out a map from the drawer of the counter and showed the new guests the tourist attractions to visit in Nazareth, marking the sites with a round circle. Then he gave them the map. He was very talkative, maybe too much. But guests didn't seem to get vexed with his talking. On the contrary, they listened to him with interest.

"Aisha, the other receptionist, was a woman. She was a traditionalist Palestinian, as I could see from the way she dressed. She used to wear long robes of various colors. Her forehead and head were wrapped up like a nun. But she was married and had two children. Like Samuel, she welcomed the new guests of the hostel warmly. She also showed them the map with the places worth visiting in Nazareth, but she was less talkative than Samuel.

"One of the managers of the hostel was Jewish. His name was too long and difficult for me to remember. He didn't come to the hostel often, but I felt that he was the mastermind behind the hostel. He didn't buy the hostel not to have political problems, for Nazareth was 100 percent Arab. A Jewish ownership in an Arab city would have stirred up unrest. He was good and smart enough to create good harmony among Palestinians, Christians, Muslims, and Jews. I can't forget his smile. He talked, always smiling.

"One evening, while I was sitting in the empty Basilica of the Annunciation watching Mary's parents' house, I heard footsteps echoing in the church. It was Samuel, the receptionist, who walked to me briskly. 'I was sure I would meet you here,' he said. 'What's the matter?' 'I'm giving a dinner at my mother's house. I want you to come and join us. A Venetian lady also will come. She comes to Nazareth quite often. She will be happy to meet you. There will be a few friends of mine and a couple, husband and wife, from Germany. Do you want to come?' 'Of course! Thank you.' 'Let's go. The Venetian lady and the German couple are waiting for us in my car,' Samuel said."

"Uncle Salvatore, you are welcomed wherever you go. How lucky you are! Samuel invited you to his home as if you were an old friend of his."

"You are right. Although I am a bit introverted, people like me. I don't know why. When I traveled, many people opened the door of their house to me. Samuel and I walked to his car nearby. When I got in the car, Frederick was sitting in the front. I sat in the back seat. 'This is my friend, Salvatore. He is from Italy, like you, Giovanna. These are Frederick and Natasha,' said Samuel. 'I am from Russia, but I have lived in Germany for a long time,' said Natasha.

"Soon I felt comfortable with all of them, as if we were old friends. I liked both Giovanna and the German couple straightaway.

"From her complexion and features Giovanna looked like a woman from southern Italy. She was short and a bit dark-skinned, but her accent and family name were typically Venetian. She was a tour guide in Venice and knew everything about the history and monuments of her unique city. In Nazareth, she stayed in a convent. Maybe she was a religious woman.

"The German couple looked close-knit. They smiled at each other often. Natasha was a high-spirited woman and talkative. Like Giovanna, she was a bit short, but her hair and complexion were fair. Her husband stayed silent, and he seemed to enjoy listening to his wife.

"On the way to his home, Samuel drove us round Nazareth. Seen from below at night, Nazareth looked like a Sicilian traditional nativity scene. Samuel's apartment was nice, with a large terrace and a wonderful view of Nazareth. His mother, who looked like the female version of him, just about twenty years older, had prepared many kinds of Middle Eastern food for us. The table was so full of serving dishes that it was difficult to set our plates on it. She explained all the courses one by one, telling us the name of each dish. She looked proud of her cooking. I can remember the name of only one dish, hummus, which was made of ground chickpeas. I sat between Giovanna and Natasha.

"Giovanna began to talk about the political issues in Israel and the relations between the Palestinians and the Israelis. But I diverted the talk from politics to religious themes. I don't like politicians. I prefer to talk about individuals and personal interactions, no matter what country, religion, lineage, or political color one belongs to. 'Have you visited the Holy Sepulcher in Jerusalem?' I asked Natasha. 'Yes, I have. I've already visited the Holy Sepulcher inside the Orthodox basilica and also another Holy Sepulcher called Garden Tomb that was discovered by the British commander Charles George Gordon in the second half of the nineteenth century. He located a tomb and a cliff very similar to a skull in its shape outside the walls of Jerusalem. The place is near Damascus Gate. It's a center of pilgrimage for many Protestants. The Gospels say that Jesus was crucified in a place called Cranium, which means a skull. In that place, besides a tomb, a winemaking press was also found.'

"Frederick broke in on his wife. 'I felt a particular energy at the Garden Tomb. I think this is the real place of Jesus's crucifixion, deposition, and burial.'

"Giovanna was a sincere Catholic. Hearing about the existence of a nonofficial Holy Sepulcher, she was furious. She couldn't stand the discussion about Gordon's discovery anymore and exploded like a volcano. 'The place of the Holy Sepulcher in the Orthodox basilica is absolutely certain. Its location is based upon uncontroversial historical proofs, which come from non-Christian sources, too. Emperor Adrian destroyed the holy places in Jerusalem, and then he built pagan temples on the places where Jesus was worshiped. The temple of Aphrodite was built in the same area of the Holy Sepulcher. Later, when Emperor Constantine converted to Christianity, he ordered the building of a church dedicated to the Holy Sepulcher in the same place where the temple of Aphrodite had been built. The walls of Jerusalem were widened after Jesus's death. At that time, the Holy Sepulcher was outside the walls. Lastly, you have to know that the Byzantines were very precise in locating the holy places.'

"Frederick didn't retort. He wasn't talkative and probably he didn't want to argue with Giovanna. A doubt arose in my mind. I turned to Giovanna. 'You said that the temple of Aphrodite was built in the place where the Holy Sepulcher was worshipped. Who told the Romans the exact place of the Holy Sepulcher? Worshipping Jesus was secret, for the Christians were persecuted. Therefore, the Romans couldn't know where the Christians worshipped Jesus.' Giovanna didn't answer my question. Obviously, she didn't want to discuss this kind of issue while we were eating dinner joyfully.

"Then I turned to Frederick. 'When I visit a real holy place, I feel a kind of energy. It happened to me when I visited the tomb of San Francis of Assisi. Recently, I've been to Venice. I just strolled around in the city, but I was led to the tomb of Santa Lucia by a stream of energy unconsciously. It wasn't a real tomb, for the dead and dried body of Santa Lucia was kept inside a glass box. As for the official Holy Sepulcher in the Orthodox Basilica, I couldn't feel any energy when I entered there,' I said."

"Uncle Salvatore, I want to visit the church where Santa Lucia's body rests when I go to Venice. Do you know the location of the church?"

"I don't know exactly where it is. But you'll find that church easily. Just ask the locals."

"Natasha was also curious about Santa Lucia's incorrupt body. 'I'll visit Santa Lucia's church. I live not far from Venice.' 'Sicily wanted the body of Santa Lucia back, because she was from Syracuse, but the pope said no,' said Giovanna.

"We dropped the discussion about the Garden Tomb. But I didn't drop this nonofficial Holy Sepulcher from my mind. I decided to visit the Garden Tomb, also called Gordon's Calvary. I wanted to verify everything with my own eyes and brain.

"All of a sudden, Natasha introduced a new topic. 'Have you ever heard about voodoo?' she asked me. 'Yes, but I've never done anything like that,' I answered. 'And what about shamanism?' 'I shiver with fear at the thought of doing a shamanistic ritual. But I'd like to know more about the Australian Aboriginals. It is said that they have special powers.'

"Natasha went on, 'Did you study only the Catholic religion, or did you experience other religions?' 'I've studied many religions, from the mainstream to the small ones. At the moment, I am studying Scientology and a religion called Eckankar. The latter practices spiritual exercises by uttering the word HU, an ancient name of God.' 'I don't know Eckankar. I attended a Buddhist center where we chanted mantras. What changed my life was an experience I had in Amsterdam one day. At that time, my mother was in hospital. It was a difficult moment in my life. A friend of mine asked me to go to Amsterdam with her. That travel was the turning point in my life.'

"I stopped eating and turned to Natasha with increasing interest. She continued, 'When I arrived in Amsterdam, I called the hospital and asked about my mother. Everything was okay. Then, my friend took me to a place where almost three hundred people were participating in a kind of ritual. In the middle of the room was a table on which the Seal of Solomon was drawn. A cross was on the Seal of Solomon. Some persons from the Amazon rainforest came in with a drink. We chanted and prayed for a good while. Then I drank the beverage they handed to me. Soon after drinking it, I felt like dying. Everything became dark. Suddenly, many doors appeared in front of me, and the name of a religion was written on each door: Christians, Buddhists, Hindus, and so on. I entered the door of the Christians. I followed a dark tunnel for a while, and then a great light appeared. All the symbols of religions disappeared, and I saw Jesus standing in front of me. I looked at him and stood in awe of him. Afterward, I opened my mouth. I am Jewish, I said. Why are you worried? I am Jewish too, Jesus answered. From that day on, I went to Amsterdam many times to attend the meetings. Once more Jesus appeared to me and said: Why do you come here? It's enough for you to observe the seven sacraments. Hearing Jesus's words, I realized that I ought to follow another way, but which? My lineage was Jewish. I wanted to be Christian. But which branch? Orthodox, Catholic, or Protestant? I had also the option to practice Judaism, for my parents were both Jewish.'

"Hearing that Natasha's parents were Jewish, I inferred that she was well-informed about this religion. So I asked her some questions about Judaism. 'In Judaism, are people baptized?' 'No, they aren't. They just have circumcision eight days after birth.' 'Are both males and females circumcised?' 'Only males. Girls at the age of twelve have their initiation called a *bat mitzvah*, while boys have their initiation at the age of thirteen. It is called a *bar mitzvah*.' 'Is circumcision still practiced?' 'Yes, it is. It is a biblical commandment. The prepuce is the only part of the body that can be removed without being considered a mutilation, which is forbidden by God.' 'How can one become a Jew?' 'Normally, one is Jewish if one's mother is Jewish. And also, one can become Jewish through conversion, but it is quite difficult,' Natasha said."

"Uncle Salvatore, you already asked this last question of Daniel, the Jewish man you met at the Hotel Plaza in Nazareth Illit. Did you forget it?"

"No, I didn't. But I wanted to make sure about the criteria to become a Jew. In Christianity it is different. The Christians don't consider either parents' religion or conversion. The only way to become a Christian is to be baptized.

"Giovanna wanted Natasha to continue to tell about her experience in Amsterdam. So she asked Natasha, 'What happened when Jesus said to you that the seven sacraments were enough? Which was your choice?' 'I opted for the Catholic religion and was baptized.' 'I want to know something about the religious group you met in Amsterdam.

You said that it changed your life. Does this religion still exist?' I asked Natasha. 'Yes, it does. It is illegal in many countries. Many trials are under way. But in Holland it is legal,' Natasha answered."

"Uncle Salvatore, it seems that there is a kind of persecution against this religion. It is anachronistic nowadays, isn't it?"

"No. There is no persecution. Natasha said that the problems arose from the compound of the holy beverage she drank. In Holland it was analyzed. They found a small amount of hallucinogen in the drink. The judgment was pro the religious group. In other countries, like Germany and Italy, the trials were in progress. 'What is the name of this religion?' I asked her. 'I can tell you the name. It is Santo Daime. It is widespread. You have it in Italy, too. A lady who had been diagnosed with brain cancer brought this religion to Holland. According to the doctors, she had only two months left to live. She went to Brazil and met the Santo Daime group in the forest. She stayed with them there for some time. When she returned to Holland, the cancer had already disappeared. The government of Brazil sent fifty special experts to the forest to study the Santo Daime phenomenon. When they wrote their report, they couldn't find anything bad, and even they became involved in the religious practices of the Santo Daime.'

"After finishing dinner, we left the table and took seats on the sofas. A Mexican lady and a friend of Samuel's sat next to me. The Mexican lady, Maritza, had thick black eyebrows, like Frida Kahlo, and was long-necked and light-complexioned. Samuel's friend Yasser was a bit fat and bold. He dressed in hippy style like Samuel. I felt that he had participated in the student protest movement of the late sixties. He took out a picture from his wallet, showed it to us, and said, 'I painted it. It is a small copy of a painting I have at home.'

"Samuel and his mother came to us. He put his hand on Yasser's shoulder and asked us, 'Did you enjoy dinner?' 'Yes!' We three answered with one voice. His mother's face brightened at our answer. She was happy that her son's friends had enjoyed her food. Samuel was happy, too. Looking at his friend Yasser with tender eyes, he said, 'My friend is a great artist! His house is full of his beautiful paintings. It looks like an art gallery. Now and then, somebody asks him to sell a painting, but Yasser turns down every offer.'

"I looked at the small picture carefully. It was a painting of a storm. At the center was a cloud, red like blood. Yasser turned that picture up, down, left, and right. Every time he moved the small painting, it took a different shape. 'Can you find the point of balance?' Yasser asked us.

"I didn't answer him. Actually, I couldn't understand the question. But Maritza talked with him about that small picture for almost ten minutes. Then Yasser turned to me. 'When you write, you use only one pen. Instead, when you paint, you use hundreds of pens. Once, a young painter showed me one of his creations. I looked at it carefully, and then I told him, 'Beautiful! But it's not yours! You've copied from many painters. Your painting looks gorgeous, but it is lifeless. When you paint next time, don't copy anymore! Your own painting may not be beautiful, but surely it will be alive,' Yasser said."

"Uncle Salvatore, we also shouldn't copy others' lives. When I was younger, I had a tendency to imitate my friends who were smart and good-looking. One day I realized that it was ridiculous. Now I just live my own life as I want. I don't follow others. Every life has its uniqueness." My uncle nodded to me with a pleased smile. Then he continued his story.

"Suddenly Maritza asked me, 'Who is your favorite artist?' 'Vincent van Gogh. Usually I don't care about the artist's name when I look at paintings. I like the paintings in which I can feel the painter's spirit. A good painting is, above all, a projection of an inner landscape, not just technique. I felt van Gogh's spirit when I looked at his paintings.'

"It was a beautiful night that I wouldn't forget. I learned new things about religion and life. I learned a good lesson about the importance of not copying from others – at school, in writing, in painting, and in life. Being spontaneous and original makes us express our creativity and can add something to human progress. If you copy, you can't add anything to it. You are just a follower.

"The next places of the Jesus Trail marked on my map with the numbers from five to eight were the Horns of Hattin, Nebi Shu'eb, Arbel, and Migdal. I took the bus from Nazareth to Migdal, which is the hometown of St. Mary Magdalene. The bus dropped me off in the road. I walked to the town, but I couldn't find anything related to the life of the saint. So I went to Nebi Shu'eb, a holy place to the Druses.

"I had never heard about the Druses. Inside the temple was a hall with many carpets on the floor. On the right side, I saw a tomb covered with a multi-colored cloth. Somebody said that each color had a meaning. People prayed and kissed the cloth. I did the same.

"Opposite the entrance of the hall were two footprints left by a Drusian saint. A woman kissed the footprints, rubbed her hands on the footprints, and then passed her hands over her face. I did the same. When she went out of the hall, she didn't turn her back to the tomb. I did the same.

"I went downstairs and took a seat on a bench close to some Druses and monks. 'How do you pray?' I asked a lay Druse. 'We're not allowed to pray. Only monks can pray, for only they know the secret prayers.' 'If you don't pray, what are you doing here?' 'We lay Druses just ask graces.' 'I didn't know about your religion.' 'Actually it's not widespread. Almost one thousand years ago, the acceptance of new followers was closed. From then on, only children of Druses can follow their parents' religion.' I came across a closed religion which doesn't accept new followers.

"I left that holy place and tried to reach the Horns of Hattin where a big battle had taken place between the Crusaders and the Muslims. The Crusaders were defeated by the army led by Caliph Saladin. I met two Druses in Israeli military uniform and asked them, 'Do you know where the battlefield of the

Horns of Hattin is?' 'The place isn't far from here, but we advise you not to go there, for you have to walk under the scorching sun. You should go there in the early morning or at sunset. It is cooler, and you can have a complete view of the battlefield and also of the Sea of Galilee. However, the whole area was a battlefield, even this place where we are standing now.'

"I looked at the uneven ground in front of me and recalled the history of the Crusades. It is common knowledge that the Crusaders were driven by economic and political interests, but it was not like that. What should a person do when he's not allowed to enter his place of worship? There's no choice but to fight. It happened when the first Crusade began. The Caliph Al-Hakim had ordered the destruction of the Holy Sepulcher in Jerusalem. Without this intolerant act, the Crusades wouldn't have been proclaimed.

"In front of my eyes, the view of the battlefield with cliffs and plains unfolded. The ground still seemed to be impregnated with the blood of the warriors. I imagined the armies facing each other, clashing furiously, and in the end, victory smiling on Saladin.

"The next place of the Jesus Trail on the map was Ginosar, a village by the shore of the Sea of Galilee. I entered a small museum where an ancient boat was exhibited. I observed it carefully. It could date back to Jesus's time. I recalled one of the most beautiful passages of the Gospel. Jesus was standing surrounded by the crowd who wanted to be taught by him on the shore. To be seen and heard by everybody, Jesus stepped aboard Peter's boat and moved a bit away from the shore. Standing on the boat, he spoke to the crowd. While I was watching the boat, I thought about Peter's noble soul. He offered Jesus his house, his boat, and everything he owned. Peter's love for his friend and master Jesus was amazing!

"I kept following the Jesus Trail map and moved to Capernaum. The bus dropped me off on the road, so I walked for a while until I spotted the signpost of the Church of the

Primacy of St. Peter. It had an amphitheater and an altar to celebrate Mass outdoors by the lake.

"At that moment, a group of French-speaking tourists came to attend Mass. I sat down on a step and watched the lake beyond the altar. Just then, suddenly Mario's third sentence that I couldn't memorize occurred to my mind" 'All sinners will be forgiven.' Yes, all sinners, including me, will be forgiven! So I felt free, thinking of Mario's words.

"One of the stopping places on the Jesus Trail map was Yardenit on the banks of the Jordan River, where it is believed that Jesus was baptized by Saint John the Baptist. I took a bus from Nazareth to Tiberias, and then a shared taxi to Kinneret.

The water of the Jordan River was calm and green due to the reflection of the green of the eucalyptus trees that bordered the bank. The place was peaceful. There were many beavers and big fish. People enjoyed feeding them. Both fish and beavers ate the food without fighting with one another. From time to time, some turtledoves joined the beavers and ate with them.

"I left the River Jordan to go back to Tiberias. There was no shade at the bus stop. So I tried to hitchhike. After many attempts, a car pulled in. A Jewish couple was inside. The man wore a kippah, and his wife wore a foulard over her head, yet it couldn't hide a straw-colored hair extension braided on the back side of her head. I sat in the backseat. There was a mess of various objects both on the backseat and under my feet. Looking at the mess under my feet, I spotted a ten-shekel coin. I was tempted to pick up that coin and put it into my pocket, but immediately the temptation faded away."

"Uncle Salvatore, I wonder how you, a rich man, could be tempted to put such a coin into your pocket. At that time you were greedy for money, weren't you?"

"Benedetto, as I told you before, it is not important what I was at that time. It is important what I did. I was greedy, it is true, but I acted as a generous and honest man. You have to judge me for what I did, not for what I was."

"Okay, now I can understand you."

"I showed the ten-shekel coin to the man and handed it to him. 'I found this coin on the floor of your car. Today you are lucky. You've found your lost coin!' He and his wife looked at each other and smiled.

"The husband asked me, 'Do you know why today is a special day in Israel?' 'Yes, I do. Someone told me that August nine is the anniversary of the destruction of the Temple of Solomon by the Romans. I also heard that the date is different every year on the Gregorian calendar, while the commemoration falls on the same fixed day on the Jewish calendar.' 'On this day, we don't eat or drink all day long. It is a mourning day, like a funeral day. After sunset, we can eat and drink. Anyway, it's an honor for us that you are here today. You are welcome, even though you are Italian, a descendant of the ancient Romans.' 'I am from Sicily. The Romans didn't consider Sicily part of Italy. In fact, Sicily was a Roman colony, like Judea. We were ruled by a Roman governor like you. You had Pontius Pilate, and we had Verres, who was so brutal that he stripped the Sicilian temples of the golden statues. In my hometown he couldn't steal the statue of Demeter because it was too big, but he snatched away the statue of Victory which Demeter held in her hand,' I said."

"Uncle Salvatore. Don't you think that still now there are differences and misunderstanding between Sicily and Italy? I have a feeling that they are two different nations. As for me, I consider myself as a Sicilian rather than an Italian. What about you?"

"Benedetto, I am a citizen of the world, as you know. So I don't feel like being Italian or Sicilian. My country is the world. Garibaldi unified Italy politically, but he couldn't make one nation with the many small countries that preexisted Italy, because all of them had different history, traditions, and their uniqueness.

"The husband didn't intend to embarrass me by talking about the Romans that destroyed the Temple of Solomon. So he softened his voice. 'The destruction of our temple wasn't caused by the Romans but by the divisions within the Jewish people. We hated each other. We fought one another. Because of that, our temple was destroyed.' I said, 'In my opinion, all people are the same. If the soul exists, it is the same in all human beings. It can't be different. I'd love to go to a synagogue and attend the ceremony on the Sabbath, but I think it is impossible, for I'm not Jewish and I won't be allowed in.' 'No, it is not impossible. Now we'll go together to see a Jewish temple, but only for a few minutes, because I have to take my car to the mechanic.'

"He parked his car in a large square. On the left side of the square the light of a lot of candles looked like a fire. Books and religious items were displayed on a stall. We entered a lobby of a low building. Without a kippah I couldn't stay there. So the husband got one kippah for me. Then we entered a room divided into two by a black curtain, one side for men and the other for women. At the end of the room was a tomb. The black curtain started from the middle of the tomb to allow both men and women to touch the tomb and pray beside it. Some people prayed leaning against the tomb. I prayed like them, too. I saw many small paper notes pushed into the gaps of the tomb. I kissed the tomb like the others. While the husband kept standing by the tomb, I lounged about and had a look at some books on a table, which were all written in Hebrew except for one, in French. I just started leafing through it when the husband came up to me. I averted my eyes from the book and looked at his face. He was taller than me, his beard was maintained well, and there was a slight gap between his two front teeth. His face was bright. He had an extraordinary resemblance to Jesus in the traditional iconography. 'The book you are holding in your hands talks about speech. It tells the importance of not speaking ill of others. You can't go to heaven if you backbite.'

"We went out of the room and I gave the kippah back. Then I asked the husband to write down the name of the holy person whose tomb we had just visited. He wrote Rabbi Meir

Val Baal Hanes, and said that the rabbi was a Roman who had converted to Judaism.

"Before we parted, he and his wife invited me to visit their kibbutz, which was not far from the place where Jesus had been baptized. I asked him to write the name of the kibbutz, his telephone number, and his name. In the end, I came to know his name, Erez.

"That very evening, I called him from Nazareth. He answered on the phone, 'Unfortunately, tomorrow I work in the morning, but you can come to my house after four or five in the afternoon.'

"I took a bus from Nazareth to Tiberias, and there I waited for another bus to the kibbutz. While I was waiting for the bus, men in traditional Jewish garb caught my attention. 'I just can see black hats on their heads. Why don't they wear a kippah?' I asked a girl who was also waiting for a bus next to me. 'They wear a kippah under their hats. Their wives wear a head cloth called *pea.*' 'Why are those men dressed in black except for their white shirt? Why do they wear jackets and hats in such hot weather?' 'We call those people *Haredim*. They are ultra-traditionalist. *Haredim* women wear long skirts and long-sleeved blouses. 'Why do the men have long curls? Is it real hair or just hair extensions?' 'They are real curls. They have curls because the Bible enjoins males not to shave the corners of their head, that is the parts between the ears and the temples.'

"The bus came and took me to an area with many kibbutzim. The driver named each of them in a loud voice. Erez was waiting for me at his kibbutz. 'Welcome to my home! If you like, you can spend the night here. We have rented a new apartment where you can sleep,' Erez said warmly."

"Uncle Salvatore, I would never ever invite a hitchhiker to whom I've just given a ride to spend the night at my home. I think you have a special radiance. Otherwise, it wouldn't be possible to fraternize so easily with those who you come across. Tell me, what is the secret to open others' hearts?"

"There is no secret. It depends on the law of attraction. We're attracted by those who have the same frequency. The similar join the similar. This is a universal law.

"I smiled at Erez with my heart and accepted his invitation for one night at his apartment. While we were walking to his home, I asked him, 'Is a kibbutz a place like a commune? Is it a kind of communism?' 'No, it isn't. In this kibbutz I am just a renter. We heard that someone wanted to buy this whole area to build new apartment blocks. Once, kibbutzim had a special function, but nowadays they have no meaning. When newcomers to Israel had to bring the desert under cultivation and confront many difficulties, it was much better to stay together and form a commune. But now there is no reason to live like that, so kibbutzim don't make much sense.'

"His house didn't seem to be big. The kitchen was before the entrance to his house. His wife was cooking something at the stove. Her name was Noah. Now she didn't have a hair extension, and a headscarf covered all her head. Her complexion was olive. She was tall and slender, taller than her husband. She introduced me to two friends, Maoz and Shulamit, who were sitting in the lounge. They were husband and wife, both with olive complexion and short. The man had a short beard and curls. After putting a tray with coffee and cookies on the small table of the lounge for us, Noah went back to the kitchen.

"As usual, my curiosity and desire to know more about Judaism pushed me to ask questions to Maoz and Erez. 'You have curls!' I said to Maoz. 'Yes, but they are not long. They are just a symbol.' 'Do you trim your beard with scissors?' I asked Erez. He nodded.

"Shulamit, Maoz's wife, sat next to us and said, 'When a woman is married, she has to keep her hair covered because there are hormones in the hair. Woman's beauty lies in her hair. She has to reserve her beauty only for her husband.'

"Abruptly, Maoz got up and left the room. 'He's going to pray,' Erez whispered in my ear. I asked him, 'Do you pray often?' 'We pray three times a day. Our religion gives us many tasks. Non-Jews have to observe seven precepts, but we Jews have to observe six hundred thirteen precepts!'

"I looked at Erez with astonishment. He stood up and took out a pen and a sheet of paper from the drawer of the desk. 'Now, hold this pen in your hand and write down the seven precepts that non-Jews have to observe. Do not kill. Do not steal. Do not have sex with your family members. Do not have sex with animals. Do not eat parts of animals that are still alive. Do not worship other gods but God. Do not worship idols. Do not curse the name of God. Build law courts in your country,' Erez said."

"Uncle Salvatore, the precepts are nine not seven. Why did Erez say seven precepts?"

"I guess that the precepts that had similar contents, that is, those regarding God, were grouped into one. At that time I didn't notice how many they were."

"After writing down the seven precepts, I was doubtful about the seventh precept. 'I think law courts are places where people quarrel. In the courts of law there are arguments, anger, and hatred. Attorneys argue with each other, and there is also acrimony against the judge whenever one feels that his verdict is unfair. So why should we build new law courts? Instead, they should be abolished,' I said. 'No. It's not like that. It is necessary that a third person judges. If law courts didn't exist, people would kill one another, for everybody would think he is right. Without law and judges, humanity wouldn't progress and people couldn't settle their quarrels. To these seven precepts I want to add one special precept for you.'

"I listened to Erez and was enchanted by him. His hair and beard were dark chestnut, and his face resembled Jesus's more and more. Then he spoke, 'Listen to this eighth precept carefully. It is never to say bad words about anybody when they are absent and can't defend themselves. Your words, both spoken and written, should be positive, not destructive or defamatory. I emphasize the importance of this eighth precept, for words contain vibrations and have consequences all the time.'

"I was curious to know the meaning of one of the seven precepts Erez had mentioned, so I didn't take heed of the eighth precept about the vibrations of words. I asked Erez, 'What does it mean, do not eat parts of animals that are still alive?' 'It means that you have to kill the animal before eating it. For instance, you shouldn't eat a thigh of an animal while it is alive,' he answered."

"Uncle Salvatore, this precept is absurd. Who can ever eat just a part of an animal while it is alive? Nobody is so cruel. Can you eat a thigh of a chicken or of a lamb or of whatever animal while it is still alive? For me it is an abstract idea that can't happen in reality."

"If Erez talked to me about this precept, there was a reason. Once I heard about fishermen that cut off the fin of big fish, I don't remember which fish, and then they threw the fish still alive into the sea. Apparently, they were interested in eating only that part of the fish. But I don't know why they did that. Anyway, I also didn't understand this precept at that time.

"In the meantime, Maoz came back from prayer. I wanted to talk with him about Hebraism. 'The number seven is recurrent in life. The days of the week are seven, the notes in music seven, the colors of the rainbow seven, and the precepts that non-Jews have to follow also seven,' I said, turning to Maoz. 'Chakras of the body are seven, too,' Maoz added. 'I heard about chakras in a meditation center in India,' I said. 'In Judaism, we also have chakras, but we give them different names. We call them *Sephiroth*. The Sephiroth tree is made by ten *Sephirah*, three of them are on a very high level and seven are on the level of human beings. The *Sephiroth* tree shows a microcosm and has a corresponding macrocosm.'

"Maoz drew ten small circles and united them with lines. Then he wrote a name beside each circle, starting from the upper one, which he called *Crown*. He named *Understanding* and *Wisdom* the two circles below *Crown*. Between *Understanding* and *Wisdom* he drew a smaller circle and united it to them with two lines. 'This smaller circle,' he said, 'is the result of *Understanding* and *Wisdom*.' He also named the seven lower circles, *Abram, Isaac, Jacob, Aaron, Moses, Joseph, and Messiah King David*. 'And also it is possible to give different names to the Sephiroth, *Kether*. . .'

"Erez broke in on Maoz. 'Leave aside the *Sephiroth* tree,' said Erez, turning to me. 'What matters is that you have to keep in mind the eight precepts I gave you, and above all, live according to the eighth precept: *Don't speak ill of others.* Keep in mind that all of the Torah can be summarized in only a few words: *Love your neighbor as you love yourself.*' 'These are Jesus's words,' I said. 'The precept, *Love your neighbor as you love yourself,* existed before Jesus.' Erez's voice became solemn as he kept talking. 'The Temple of Solomon has already been built in heaven. At the right moment it will be set on Earth. It is the third temple. It stands over the city of Jerusalem. The Torah teaches that every action has a corresponding reaction. It is important to perform good actions, for they trigger a chain reaction, which has a positive effect on the environment. Perhaps the third temple will be set on Jerusalem. It depends upon our actions. Whenever you express a thought, teaching, opinion, or idea that is not yours, you have to mention the source or the author.'

"Erez was trying to teach me as much as possible. At that time, I wanted my brain to be a hard disk of a computer in order to memorize his words completely. Above all, Erez wanted me to know how to speak and write in a correct, honest, and creative way. The teachings he gave me are now part and parcel of my life.

"Dinner was ready. Noah put a big bowl of soup on the table first and then a tray with bread, hummus, and other Middle Eastern special food.

"Before eating, Maoz said prayers. Then he read a passage from a Jewish book. He read it in Hebrew, but Erez translated it into English for me. It told about a few laborers in a wagon that was conveying a cask of Hungarian red wine. The owner allowed the laborers to try a few glasses of wine. Its flavor was unique. After some time, one of those laborers happened to be in a square where someone was selling Hungarian red wine. He tasted it and, turning to the seller, exclaimed, 'You can't cheat me, for I know Hungarian red wine. This is just common wine with a different flavor and taste from real Hungarian red wine.' That laborer already knew the taste of the wine and couldn't be deceived. The meaning of the story is that if you know the truth, nobody can trick you and you'll recognize the true Messiah when he comes."

"Uncle Salvatore, I'm not convinced about the allegory of Hungarian red wine. You said that the laborers could know the taste of real Hungarian red wine only after having tasted it, so we can recognize the real Messiah only after we have tasted the truth. But the Messiah is the truth or, at least, the one who takes us to the truth. When Pontius Pilate wanted to know the truth from Jesus, he didn't answer him. Jesus kept silent, because the truth was just Jesus himself. Why do you need to search or wait for the truth if you already know the truth? In other words, if you know the truth, you don't need the Messiah anymore. How about my opinion?"

"Benedetto, your opinion about the truth is very sharp. But the allegory meant that if you know the truth inside yourself, you can recognize the truth outside yourself. Otherwise you can't discriminate between truth and fake. However, I think the true Messiah is inside us. If we know ourselves truly, we'll know the truth! We don't need to look for an external Messiah. The opinion of the Jews on this topic is different than ours. For the Jews the Messiah is an external Messiah, I think."

"When dinner was over, I asked Maoz to tell me something about Kabbalah. He answered that Kabbalah is the power of words."

"Uncle Salvatore, how was dinner at Erez's house? What did you eat? Was it delicious?"

"Unfortunately, I didn't write about that dinner in my journal. Now I can't remember it well. Many years have passed."

"Why didn't you write anything about it?"

"Because mainly I was interested in Judaism. So my attention was focused on religious topics."

"Okay, let's go on with the story."

"Erez took a book from the table and showed me two pages. 'Look at these pages. They contain explanations for just four single words. Hebrew is not like Italian, in which usually one word has one meaning. In our language, one word has many meanings. Once in Prague, there was a rabbi who laid some soil on a table and then with the soil he created a man with flesh but without a soul. He made that soulless man to protect the Jewish community of Prague. This kind of creature was called the Golem. By words he activated the Golem, and by words he deactivated it. The rabbi of Prague created the Golem through Hebraic words. Afterward, the emperor ordered him to kill the Golem because it became too violent. So the rabbi deactivated the Golem using different Hebraic words. You can't imagine how powerful the word is. Words can create life, events, and actions. Therefore, your word should always be good and creative, not defamatory and destructive,' said Erez, looking into my eyes.

"Noah and Shulamit danced an impromptu Jewish dance for me. They seemed to be happy to be with me. 'The day we met, the anniversary of the destruction of the Temple of Solomon, was a mourning day for us, but today is different. Today is the day of love. It is a special day for the Jews to enjoy dancing and celebration. Tonight we'll have a party on the beach with some friends of us who live in the kibbutz. Would you like to join us?' Erez asked me. 'Sure! I'd love to.'

"The shore of the Sea of Galilee was not far from his house. We walked a trail flanked with reeds. On the shore was a group of almost ten people. They had already lit a bonfire and were cooking meat and potatoes wrapped in tin foil. A big watermelon had been cut into slices. Erez played a soft song with his guitar. They were very composed in celebrating their party.

"A lady had a swim in the warm water of the lake. If I had had my swimming suit, I would have joined her. Instead, I just dipped my feet into the water. I imagined that once Jesus had done the same, and the lake still remembered his presence.

"I stood by the lakeside and admired that fantastic landscape. Behind me there were the Golan Heights. The city of Tiberias was opposite me beyond the lake. Lighted houses studded the hills. The night had no wind, and the clear sky was embroidered with stars. Erez came over to me. 'Tiberias is one of the four holy cities in Israel. It represents the element water. The other three holy cities are Tsfat, the element air, Hebron, the element earth, and Jerusalem, the element fire.'

"After a few hours, Erez, his wife, and I left the party. On the way back, Erez picked up a stone and cast it against the trunk of a tree. 'Look at this stone. First it hits the tree, then it bounces and strikes the grass, and finally it lands on the ground. Three effects derive from one action. When words are said or written, things happen in the same way. Words have vibrations. They trigger a chain reaction, passing from mouth to mouth. Words have an effect on the environment. Therefore, you have to be alert when you speak or write. Sometimes we speak negative words unconsciously. If your words are fair and plain, they will cleanse not only the atmosphere around you but also yourself. The same goes when you write something. Written words have vibrations, too. A book can change the world for the worse or for the better.'

"I was surprised at how Erez seized every opportunity to teach me the importance of using simple, straightforward, and pure words. Gossiping, maligning, and backbiting may kill the soul, while words of love and peace make the soul grow.

"When we were near his house, Erez pointed out a pomegranate tree to me. 'It is one of seven holy plants for the Jews. In this case also the number seven is recurrent. The other six plants are wheat, barley, vine, olive tree, fig tree, and date palm. Man can survive by eating just the fruits of these seven holy plants.'

"He told me that his wife, Noah, was once deaf. She had been healed by a rabbi who lived in a town named Kiriat Tevon. It was halfway between Nazareth and Haifa. He gave me the rabbi's telephone number. 'You'd better meet him. He is a holy man.' 'Okay, I will.'

"I slept in his apartment peacefully. In the early morning I took a walk along the trail that we had walked the night before. The reeds were waving in a light breeze. At the lakeside Erez's friends were still sleeping in their sleeping bags. Their white shepherd dog kept guard over them. It barked at me and didn't allow me to get near the lake. Coming back to the apartment, I saw Erez standing near the kitchen of his house. I walked to him. 'I have to go to work. If you want, you can stay here,' Erez said. 'Thank you for your kindness, Erez. I'll go back to Nazareth.' 'I'll walk you up to the gate.' We walked together to the main entrance to the kibbutz. I had no words to say to him except, 'Erez, thank you for your hospitality!' At the gate I hugged him warmly. I didn't want to part from him. His teaching marked a turning point in my life. I followed him with my eyes until he disappeared beyond the hedgerow, and then I headed for the bus stop."

"Uncle Salvatore, I feel that the meeting with Erez was very impressive and extraordinary to you. It happened by chance, but I think it was due to attraction of energy. At that time maybe you needed Erez's teaching, the vibrations of words. It is the mystery and miracle of life, isn't it?"

"Yes, it really is! You caught the point well. You are very smart, Benedetto. Thanks to our conversation, my book will be more interesting. Okay, now I'll continue my story. As soon as I arrived in Nazareth, I went to the tourist office. The man at the information desk was very kind to me. Not only did he show me the best way to go to Kiriat Tevon, but also he called the rabbi and arranged an appointment with me for the next day.

"The bus dropped me off on the road to Haifa, so I walked toward the rabbi's house. Many people in the yard were waiting to talk with him. One of the rabbi's secretaries asked me to fill a form by writing down my name, my mother's name, and two questions to ask the rabbi.

"I filled the form, writing my questions. First, I asked the rabbi to help my children, second to give an answer to my question, is there life after death?

"The rabbi was about fifty years old with a rosy complexion and a round face. I couldn't see his hair because he wore a white shawl with black stripes over his head and shoulders. I had the feeling that it was for his protection. As soon as I entered his room, he asked me to sit down. His secretary stood behind him and seemed to be impatient. Apparently, he wanted a quick end to my conversation with the rabbi because many people were waiting in the yard. But the rabbi didn't seem to want to finish our meeting quickly. He looked curious and also glad to talk with a non-Jewish man.

"He said, 'I couldn't understand your written questions. Would you mind telling them to me again?' 'Of course not. One of them is about my two children. I am worried about them. The elder one always stays at home. The other is very shy. I want you to help them.' 'Just a moment. I have to ask,' said the Rabbi.

"He lowered his eyes toward something under the desk, it could have been a book or a notebook or something else, I don't know. Then he spoke, 'Don't worry about your children. They are okay. Nevertheless, you are the support of your family. So try and help them as much as you can.'

"The secretary grew more impatient. He looked at his watch repeatedly and beckoned the rabbi to get me out of the room. Nevertheless, the rabbi didn't care about his haste. 'I'll give you something special both for you and for your children.'

"I looked at his rosy-cheeked face, which seemed to be full of light at that moment. 'Thank you very much, indeed!' I said, smiling and expressing my gratitude delightedly.

"The rabbi asked the secretary to open a cabinet and get something from there. He brought two small pieces of paper and handed them to the rabbi, who drew something on them and then gave them to me. 'Always keep them with you. Remember, I will be always with you!'

"I slipped the rabbi's gifts into my trouser pocket and thanked him. I wanted to ask him something about my second question, but there were many people standing in the yard and waiting to talk with him. I couldn't stay there any longer. So I said goodbye to the rabbi and to the secretary as well."

"Do you still have those small pieces of paper, Uncle Salvatore?"

"Of course! I keep them in my drawer."

"Do you mind if I see them?"

"No, I don't. I'll show them to you."

He got up and took out two small pieces of paper from one of the drawers of the cupboard, but they looked too thick to be paper.

"They are not like paper."

"They look like parchment, but I don't know," said my uncle.

I took one of them in my hands and observed it carefully. There was a small drawing on it. It was what the rabbi had drawn for my uncle's children. There was a heart with three dots vertically above it and a dot on the right of the heart which was joined to another side dot with a line. Below the dot on the right of the heart was a letter similar to S, and below the side dot was a letter similar to A. In each of the four corners of the small parchment were six small dots.

"This is difficult for me to understand. Let me see the other one, Uncle Salvatore."

"Come here, Benedetto. Let's see it together because I have to explain something about it. This was drawn for me, even though I hadn't asked anything for myself. Can you see something similar to a house whose shape is cylindrical? I felt strange when I first saw this drawing at the rabbi's house, for it had the same shape as the towers I had dreamed of when I was dying from the poisonous fumes of carbon monoxide. This house has a conic roof and two windows, one of them looks like an eye and the other looks like a mouth. Can you see two pairs of parallel lines that seem to be two paths to reach or to leave the house and six small circles, three over the house and three around the paths?"

"Yes. These two drawings look like amulets. Do you think they are esoteric symbols? In other words, is there a meaning hidden deep in these drawings?"

"I don't know the meaning. But I feel the rabbi's love for me through them. It's enough for me. Okay, I'll continue my story. After visiting the mountain where Jesus's Transfiguration happened, I completed the Jesus Trail in the end.

"After a few days, I went to Jerusalem to see the places that Natasha and the Neapolitan engineer had mentioned, starting with the Garden Tomb and the steps of the Temple of Solomon. I arrived in Jerusalem at about eleven thirty in the morning and walked to the Garden Tomb, which was closed. Its opening time was two o'clock in the afternoon. So, I headed for the steps of the Temple of Solomon. I walked downhill along the right side of the Wailing Wall, but I couldn't see any step. Two young armed guards were standing by. I asked them, 'I am looking for the stairs of the Temple of Solomon. Could you tell me where they are, please?' 'The Temple of Solomon doesn't exist anymore. What remains is just the supporting wall called the Wailing Wall.'

"I insisted. 'A friend of mine told me that he had already visited the stairs of the Temple of Solomon.' 'No. The temple was entirely destroyed. Now there is only the Dome of the Rock there.' The two guards seemed to be irritated by my insistence. I didn't want to bother them anymore, so I gave up. Maybe the Neapolitan engineer gave me wrong information, but he looked very informed.

"While waiting for the opening of the Garden Tomb, I strolled about the area. I crossed the street and bought a ticket to visit the archeological area. I entered there. A few ruins were scattered here and there. Then I arrived at the entrance to a cave. There was also a group of tourists guided by an English-speaking guide at the entrance. A lady from Australia came close to me and asked me to join the group. How strange! Whenever I was in need, someone appeared and helped me. I joined them and listened to the guide. 'We'll cover a distance along a narrow underground tunnel with shallow water, which can sometimes rise up to the height of your trouser pockets.'

"Actually, at the entrance the water was high up to the pelvis. Then, it shallowed. The tunnel was narrow and low. Sometimes we had to bend ourselves forward. If I had suffered from anxiety and claustrophobia as before, I couldn't have walked through the tunnel. I was happy that I could walk underground without fear. The tunnel was long and seemed to be never ending. How many laborers left the marks of their pickaxes on this tunnel! Three thousand years ago they were alive and worked to dig the tunnel. But they disappeared like a dream. Did they vanish into thin air? Were they reborn? Did they go to heaven or to hell? Nobody knows, and maybe we will never have an answer to such questions. Only saints and enlightened ones can know the truth.

"Walking through the tunnel, I compared it to the tunnel of my life. I had spent my life without seeing the light of joy, like a fish swimming in the water of a dark cave. I didn't know that the tunnel was connected to the stairs of the Temple of Solomon, a place where Jesus had been definitely, but, to my surprise, it led me there! How mysterious it was! After about ten minutes, the tunnel ended. We kept walking underground and gathered in a place with several stairs. I sat on one of those steps and listened to the guide. 'According to more than one archeologist, these are the stairs of the Temple of Solomon. As you can see, the stairs are neither too distant from each other nor too close. So at that time, people could go up to the temple easily, and in the meantime, the sacrificial animals could walk up without difficulty.'

"Were these the real stairs of the Temple of Solomon on which Jesus had walked? I can say only one thing: I was attracted to these stairs by a mysterious energy. When I came to Israel, I didn't know about this place, nor had I a map to locate this spot. I arrived there naturally. I think those were the real stairs of the Temple of Solomon.

"Beyond the stairs was an open space with a pool that could be the Pool of Siloam where Jesus performed the miracle of healing a blind man, according to John's Gospel. At the Siloam Pool I left the group. It was almost three-thirty in the afternoon, and I had to hurry to get to Gordon's Calvary in time.

"Passing by the Wailing Wall, I wanted to meditate for a few minutes in front of it. I washed my hands and took a kippah from the provided basket. While I was walking quickly toward the wall, a boy with traditional Jewish garments came to me and asked, 'Would you like tefillin?'

"I looked at him. Maybe he doesn't know that I'm not Jewish, I thought. Instead of speaking, I just nodded at him because I didn't want him to know that I couldn't speak Hebrew. He started to roll the tefillin around my left arm. Thinking he was wrong, I pointed my finger at my right arm. Apparently he already knew that I was a foreigner. So he said in English, 'Which hand do you use for your writing?' 'My right hand,' I answered. 'Therefore it is correct to put the tefillin on the left arm if you are right-handed.'

"The boy noticed my inexperience and called an adult Jew. Now, he'll notice that I'm not Jewish and won't allow me to wear the tefillin, I thought. To my surprise, it didn't happen. He coiled one tefillin around my left arm, my wrist, and my middle finger. He took the other tefillin and rolled it around my head. He set one of the two small leather boxes which contained passages from the Torah on my upper arm and the other on my forehead. After setting the tefillin, he said, 'Repeat after me.' He pronounced some words, and I repeated them. The words I could understand were only Adonis and Elohim. I guessed that they were names of God. Maybe the other words that I repeated after him and I couldn't understand were also names or attributes of God. Then I gave the tefillin back to him.

"When I got to the Garden Tomb, I was surprised at the silence in that place. I turned to the right and headed for the skull-shaped rock. It was a cliff with two big holes and a nose-shaped stone between them. To my eyes, it didn't look like a skull. On the railing was a picture of the cliff. Looking at it, the whole cliff seemed to be skull-shaped.

"I turned left and walked to the tomb. Entering it, I saw three stone beds. One of them was a bit higher than the others. The ceiling of the tomb and the right wall had been plastered. I was alone inside the tomb. Turning my eyes to the wall on the right, I thought I saw Jesus's face slightly imprinted on the wall. It was similar to that on the Shroud of Turin. I didn't see the whole face but only some features like the eyes. At that time I felt that the real Holy Sepulcher was there.

"I got out of the tomb and looked for the winemaking press. I couldn't spot it. So I asked a lady who was sitting on the bench. She got up and pointed out a pool where in the past the grapes were pressed by feet and the juice flowed into a smaller basin. 'Do you want to see the real place where the Lord was crucified?' 'Yes, of course!'

"She led me to a rocky wall on one of the sides of the garden. 'This cement covers the crack in the rock caused by the earthquake that happened when Jesus passed away. Underneath our feet there is no rock but a wooden floor. The rock is hollow. Digging is in progress. Jesus's blood fell from his bleeding body into the Ark of the Covenant. He established a new covenant between God and humans.'

"I was puzzled by her words. How is it possible that the Ark of the Covenant was below the cross when Jesus died? I thought. She noticed my doubtfulness, so she took out a pen and a postcard from her purse and wrote something. Then she gave me the postcard. 'Do your research, and then you'll find out that I am right.'

"Later, I checked her information. Actually an archeologist had been digging under the rock of Gordon's Calvary. The aim was to bring into the light what was once called Zedekiah's Cave, a vast underground quarry which supplied the stone for the Temple of Solomon. Therefore, nothing can be excluded. I still keep the postcard the lady gave me. Besides the name of the archeologist, she wrote, 'Jesus loves you.'

"One of the sites the Neapolitan engineer had advised me to visit was the Tomb of King David. Nearby were the Chapel of the Last Supper, a synagogue, and a minaret. Three religions shared the place. I visited the minaret and the Chapel of the Last Supper, and then I entered the synagogue.

"There were several rows of pews. One side room was a living room with a kitchen. A few boys dressed in traditional Jewish clothes stood inside. They offered me a cup of tea. I told them that I wanted to know something about their religion. Then one of them asked me, 'Why are you interested in Judaism?' 'Because Judaism was Jesus's religion, and I love Jesus very much,' I answered.

"Sitting on a pew, a man with a striped shawl over his head and shoulders was reading a book. The shawl covered part of his grey hair. He had a beard but no curls. His big eyes looked sweet. I approached him trustfully. 'Are you a priest?'

'No, I am not.' 'I'm interested in Judaism. Would you mind giving me an explanation about your practices?'

"He stood up and looked at me in the face. 'Wait a minute. I'll get some sheets of paper and a pencil and then I'll answer all your questions. After I come back, let's go out.' We went out of the synagogue and sat on a bench joined with a table in a wide courtyard. Then I started my interview in a journalistic style. 'What is your priests' habit? How can I recognize them?' 'We have no priests in our synagogues. We call a priest Kohen. Kohens used to conduct their services at the Temple of Solomon, but they haven't had any role since its destruction. From time to time, they come to a synagogue to bless it, but nothing more. When they come, they wear a *tallith*, which is similar to the shawl I am wearing over my head now. They spread their fingers wide and fill the synagogue with blessings.' He drew two hands with widespread fingers and thumbs close to each other on a sheet of paper.

"The word Kohen reminded me of the time when I was a member of the esoteric society. I often heard the noun Kohen in the rituals, but at that time I didn't grasp the meaning. Actually, I didn't care about that word, because it didn't arouse my curiosity at that time.

"The man of the synagogue continued to explain the outline of the Jewish doctrine to me. 'The Kohens are the descendants of Aaron. Do you know who Aaron is?' 'Of course. He was Moses's brother.' 'Nowadays, we have twenty-four thousand Kohens. Their DNA has been analyzed. Surprisingly, they have the same DNA!' said the man."

"Uncle Salvatore, did you trust the Jewish man's words blindly? Or did you check whether his words were true or not?"

"I trusted him. I had no reason to doubt what he said."

"You are too credulous, Uncle Salvatore! It is impossible that twenty-four thousand individuals have the same DNA. How is it possible? Moreover, a DNA test is expensive. Who paid the cost of DNA tests for thousands of people?"

"We don't know the ultimate truth, Benedetto. However, for me it was not important to ask him more questions about the Kohens. So, I switched to other topics. 'I thought the Levites were the priestly order in Israel.' 'It's wrong. The Levites were the helpers in the Temple of Solomon. They were musicians and singers.'

"Then he got up, went into the synagogue, and brought a book with a colored illustration of the Temple of Solomon. 'Can you see the Levites playing the trumpets?' 'Yes, I can.' 'Look at the magnificence of the temple. It was divided into two sections, one for men and the other for women. Nowadays, we have the Kohens, but we don't have our Temple of Solomon!' he said, sighing deeply.

"I asked him, 'What are the main events in your religion?' 'In Judaism, we celebrate *Yom Kippur*. It is a special day that happens in the month we call *Tishrei*, which corresponds to the month of September or October in your calendar. During *Yom Kippur*, food and drink are not permitted for twenty-five hours,' he answered."

"Why for twenty-five hours? A day is twenty-four hours, Uncle Salvatore."

"I don't know. I just heard twenty-five hours. Who knows, maybe I misunderstood his words. Our conversation was in English, and both of us were not native speakers. Therefore, it may be possible that I misunderstood something of his talk. 'Why is *Yom Kippur* so important for the Hebrew people?' I asked the man. '*Yom Kippur* means atonement. On that day, we pray in the synagogue, and then all our sins are forgiven.' 'It's very easy to have all your sins forgiven in your religion!' I exclaimed sarcastically. 'No, it's not easy. Before having your sins forgiven, you must go to those you have offended with your misbehavior and ask them to forgive you. Only after that can you turn to God for forgiveness.'

"His words made me recall my sins. I thought it would have been impossible for me to participate in *Yom Kippur* if I had been Jewish. In fact, I couldn't have at least one of my sins forgiven by the person I had offended. So I asked him, 'You said that one needed to be forgiven by the person one had harmed before invoking God's clemency. Well, if someone caused a girl's suicide, how can he get her forgiveness? She is dead and can't forgive him. Can such a person participate in *Yom Kippur*?'

"The Jewish man got perplexed. 'It's the first time that someone has asked me a question like that. I'm not able to give you an answer. Now I'll ask a rabbi.'

"He went to the other side of the courtyard. Apparently, there were some rooms for people who worked at the synagogue. After a while, he came back with a man with a *tallith* over his head. 'This Italian man wants to know how it is possible for a man who caused the suicide of his girlfriend to participate in *Yom Kippur*. He needs to get the forgiveness of the person against whom he sinned, and in this case he can't be forgiven by his victim.'

"The rabbi answered unfalteringly, 'You aren't responsible. You have no sin to be forgiven. Suicide is an individual action. It is a free choice of the person who commits suicide.' I wanted to interrupt the rabbi and talk with him about the concept of free choice or free will, but I bit my tongue, lest I start a complicated philosophical discussion. Finally he said, 'You don't have to ask anybody for forgiveness.'

"The rabbi smiled at me and crossed the courtyard to go back to his room, but the other man started talking about free will. 'In Judaism, free will is a basic concept. We confront difficult situations which can undermine our willpower, but it is necessary to fight, to struggle with the problems and adversities of life. You need to have problems and trouble to get free will. If everything ran smoothly in our life, we would be like a robot, a machine. But we are men! God gives us good or bad things so that we can achieve free will.'

"Then he wrote the name of Rabbi Akiva on a sheet of paper. He was a poor shepherd and later he became a great sage. After the name of Rabbi Akiva, he wrote *Gam zu l'tova*. 'I don't understand Hebrew. What is the meaning of these words?' 'It means that even this is for good. Accidents also come from God. Everything is in the hands of the Creator. Do you think God, after creating the universe, sleeps? No, it's not like that. God is always present. He looks after all creatures all the time. *Hear, o Israel: Hashem is our God. Hashem, the One, the Only* (Deut. 6:4).' 'What does Hashem mean?' 'Hashem is a name given to God. In our religion, it is a sin to say the four-letter God's name YHWH, also known as the perfect Tetragrammaton. Only the high priest in the Temple of Solomon was entitled to pronounce the Tetragrammaton. The word *Adonai*, which means the Lord, is a substitute of YHWH. When we pray or even when we don't pray, we use the word Hashem as God's name. Do you understand?' 'Yes, I do.'

"His words were clear and easy to understand. His English was good. Then he kept talking about Judaism. 'In our religion, we don't have the Trinity. So the core of our religion is that God is only one and he is almighty and omnipresent. We call the presence of God in our daily life *Shekhinah*. For that, we pray three times a day. This prayer is called *Amidah*. Its meaning is to stand. *Amidah* is a prayer that we should say standing with our body turned to Jerusalem, where once was the Temple of Solomon. Through this prayer, the Jewish devotee is in mystic communion with God and the people of Israel three times a day. The daily prayer consists of eighteen different prayers for peace, for rebuilding the Temple, for healing, for thanksgiving, and so on. We have to pray, moving our body,' he said."

"Uncle Salvatore, what does prayer with a moving body mean? I don't understand. How do Jewish people move their body during prayer?"

"I don't know exactly, Benedetto. I am not Jewish. The man of the synagogue said that prayer was like a dance, like joy. When they pray to God they don't show a sad face, but they express their joy as if they were dancing. For that they move their bodies.

"Then the man resumed the theme of free will and said, 'In our religion, there are two kinds of sins, willful sins and involuntary sins. For example, if a man woos a lady who is already married, it is a willful sin. An involuntary sin can happen if one turns on the light of the living room on Sabbath due to inattention.' 'Do you have to stay in the dark on Sabbath?' 'Not in complete darkness. You can turn on the lights of the bathroom and the kitchen. Sabbath is the seventh day of the week. It is the day of rest for everybody, even for animals. You shouldn't do anything.' 'But you have to eat, so you have to cook,' I said, expressing my wonder. 'No, you can't cook on Sabbath. You must get the food ready the day before, and then you can eat it on Sabbath. In general, there are thirty-nine *Melachos* on Sabbath. *Melacha*, the plural is *Melachos*, means an activity that is forbidden on Sabbath. These activities are cooking, writing, building houses, sowing, reaping, kneading, trapping animals in the forest, hunting, starting a fire, slaughtering, skinning animals, tanning animal hide, and so on.'

"I listened to that man with pleasure, and then he took me to his room in an annex to the synagogue. It was small. I saw nothing else but a simple bed. I guessed that he was the keeper of the synagogue. 'What are all these lines in the air?' 'We use them when we decorate the synagogue for a Jewish feast.'

"He told me the name of the next feast, but I couldn't memorize it. He also gave me a small notebook. On its cover these words were written: *My soul relies on the Lord more than a watchman on the coming of dawn.* (Ps. 130:6)"

"Uncle Salvatore, I can't understand these words. Do you know the meaning?"

"Yes, I know it. As a watchman is certain that dawn will come to relieve him, so my soul relies on the Lord's love. Now is it clear?"

"Yes, it is."

"I said goodbye to the man and left the synagogue. His face and eyes are still vivid in my mind. I can't forget him. I feel like he is beside me, whenever I think of him."

"He impressed you much. Why didn't you ask his name?"

"Benedetto, we were too involved in our talking at that time, and usually I don't ask the names of priests or monks. He dressed like a priest with the *tallith* over his head. But I remember his heart, even though I don't know his name."

"At the hostel in Nazareth I met Anne, a Jewish American lady who had quit her job in America and was studying Hebraic Religion at the University of Jerusalem. We decided to visit the Yad Vashem, the museum of the holocaust, together.

"A few days later, we met at the entrance to the museum. She was very pale. She told me that she had undergone major surgery to remove a malignant tumor from her breast. Apparently, she still had the aftereffects of the surgery. I advised her to breathe deeply and relax. Maybe this advice was a bit effective to her.

"At the entrance to the museum, the origin of Nazism was summarized on a large board. At the beginning, Nazism was illegal, and Hitler was imprisoned. While he was in jail, he wrote the book *Mein Kampf,* which became the ideological basis for the ascent of the Nazism. Maybe the words contained in that book vibrated harmfully, polluted the air, and later they triggered a wave of anti-Semitism, I thought.

"At that moment, I thought of Erez. In my mind I saw him at his kibbutz by the shore of the Sea of Galilee. He cast a stone against the trunk of a tree and said, 'Look at this stone. First it hits the tree, then it bounces and strikes the grass, and finally it lands on the ground. Three effects derive from one action. The same is true of words. Words have vibrations. They trigger a chain reaction when they pass from mouth to mouth or from ear to ear.'

"I went around the museum with Anne, who looked a little bit less pale. 'Do you know that words can give rise to life or death?' I asked. 'Yes, I heard about that in a lecture. It was held in Hebrew, and I couldn't understand everything, for my Hebrew wasn't good, but I caught the gist of the lecture. Yes, words can create or destroy something.' 'Anne, do you think words can cause bad events?' 'Yes, I do. If we speak negative words all the time, it can create bad situations in our life, and vice versa. So, to be happy we need to speak positive words.'

"Anne and I walked around the museum, and then we ended our visit at the bar. We ate ice cream. Then we headed for the tram stop, where we would say goodbye. She remained in Jerusalem, while I went to the bus stop to go back to Nazareth.

"Uncle Salvatore, how was the museum? I think we should write something about it."

"Benedetto, it may sound strange to you, but I can't remember what I saw in the museum. I have a lapse of memory. I didn't write anything about it in my diary. What impressed me was the board at the entrance that described the origin of Nazism.

"Before taking a bus to Nazareth, I went to a bookshop near the bus station to buy Hitler's book, but I couldn't find it. In Nazareth I couldn't buy *Mein Kampf* either. Apparently, in Israel it was not for sale. After coming back to Nazareth, my visit to Israel was coming to an end. The following day I took a taxi to the airport of Tel Aviv. In a few hours my trip to the Israel would be over.

"When I returned to Isola, I went to the biggest bookshop in downtown Isola. I was looking forward to buying *Mein Kampf.* I wanted to read it carefully and then to write an article against Hitler in a local magazine of Isola. I guessed that *Mein Kampf* by Adolf Hitler was the cause of the Second World War as well as of the Shoah. The word Shoah refers to the massacre of only the Jewish people, while the word Holocaust refers to the massacre of all the opponents of the Nazi regime, including the Jehovah's Witnesses, communists, gypsies, and so on. The bookseller, who was a friend of mine, rummaged the bookshelves, and then he found a good edition of *Mein Kampf*. It was the only copy left. I was about to buy the book. But while I was still leafing through the pages, I heard a voice inside me, 'Don't buy it. It is a trap.' 'Why is it a trap?' I asked the voice. I felt like Hitler himself said to me, 'If you write bad things about me, you will contravene the eighth precept Erez gave you. He taught you not to say bad words about anybody. I am dead. If you bad-mouth me, I can't confute your writing or advance my justifications. You will condemn me without giving me the chance to plead my case. Moreover, do you really think I am the only culprit behind the Second World War? Do you believe I am the only one responsible for the Shoah? Do you know the ultimate truth about the tragedy of the Second World War?' At that moment, I thought he might be right. Actually, Erez's eighth precept was quite clear and explicit. It forbade me to speak badly about anybody, whoever he is, whoever he was."

"Uncle Salvatore, we have to keep silent against injustice? Sometimes we have to criticize something immoral, unfair, unjust, or inhuman. You are spoiling your book by writing this idea about Hitler. Uncle Salvatore, how about removing this part from your book? It would be better. I know that you are a man of peace and tolerance, but readers may misunderstand you."

"Benedetto, you misunderstood me, too. I'm not a Hitler supporter. I say again, I'm not a Hitler supporter! I am against Nazism and Hitler. I love the Hebrew people. I just want to abide by the eighth precept Erez gave me: *Don't speak ill of anybody, even the worst criminal."*

"Okay, after this clarification I can understand you. Let's continue with the story now."

"My friend Vincenzo, the bookseller, noticed my hesitation. 'What's happening to you? I've never seen you so pensive before buying a book. You can take it and read it at home. Pay me later. If you don't like it, give me the book back.' 'Sorry, Vincenzo. I'm not interested in *Mein Kampf* anymore. I changed my mind. I won't buy it. Sorry!'

"On the way home, I felt that also Judas had something to say: 'The Christians allege that I was a betrayer, the one who handed over Jesus to the executioners. But it is not true. I was just the one who had the thankless task of negotiating with the Sanhedrin. Furthermore, I couldn't foresee Jesus's crucifixion. I thought he would just be imprisoned. Don't backbite me! Don't backbite anybody, even though he is a monster. You can't know the truth, nor see the core of a human soul. Only God knows the ultimate truth!'

"Finally, Barabbas with his reddish beard appeared in my mind and said: 'Many Christians glare at me. They think I am a bad man. Indeed, I can't be blamed. I'm not accountable for Jesus's death. Pontius Pilate decided that Jesus should die instead of me. What could I do to prevent Jesus's death?'

"Then I imagined that I was inside the circles of Dante's Hell, looking for sinners who were supposed to be there. But to my surprise, I couldn't find any sinners, nor even hell. I couldn't see flames, nor devils with tails, horns, and cloven feet. I just saw a vast, gloomy wasteland without the light of God. It was the hell I saw.

"Since I met Erez, his teaching has been my basic rule of my life. I can't speak ill of others. I've kept Erez's eighth precept in my mind. Ever since the night I spent by the shore of the Sea of Galilee, I've tried to speak positive words. By doing so, I've dropped the quarrels and the lawsuits with my brothers and others. I've purified my soul and I am more serene and peaceful. I smile more than before, and I can open my heart to others. Erez's eighth precept transformed my life."

"Uncle Salvatore, I can see that your trip to Israel transformed your life."

"Yes, you are right!"

"If you make a list of the lessons you learned from the persons you met in Israel, what will you put at the top?"

"Of course, Erez's eighth precept! I can't forget Erez and the night I spent with his family and friends by the shore of the Sea of Galilee."

CHAPTER VIII
THE LABYRINTH

"You have a great spirit, Uncle Salvatore. It is amazing that you recovered your strength after every predicament. Two tragic, fatal accidents made you feel guilty for a long time. In your business you had ups and downs. When the court of law of Isola found you guilty of causing the tailor's death because your truck was not in proper working order and it was even overloaded, you lost your money to compensate for the damage and pay the lawyers. The same thing happened when you lost the case versus your brothers. Because of that, you lost a lot of money and properties. Another time you invested all your money in the Bank of Isola. Then, the bank went bankrupt. That wrong investment made you poor. But you didn't despair, and then you did your best to recover your life. You seem to have nine lives, like a cat!"

"Yes, my past was dramatic. From time to time, a huge landslide of difficulties collapsed on me. I was crushed by the mass of soil and stones that overwhelmed me, but miraculously I survived every time. I got out of the landslide like a little mouse that finds the way out to survive. Then, little by little, I became strong and rich again."

"Uncle Salvatore, in your life success alternated with failure many times. Your memoir is full of arguments and quarrels. You held a grudge against the mayor of Isola. He didn't want to give you the license to build an oil deposit. You sued the municipality of Isola and finally you won the case. One day, you even had a fistfight with the president of the Bank of Isola. You met many girls before marrying Aunt Lucia, but every time you were disappointed by them. Often, anxiety and panic attacks burned your energies and exhausted you. Sometimes, due to your mental confusion, it was difficult for you to distinguish the dream state from wakefulness. How could you endure the death of your young and beloved first wife, who died from leukemia? At that time, you even invited a professor of New York to cure her. But without avail! Nevertheless, all those mishaps couldn't destroy your life, could they?"

My uncle let out a deep sigh, closed and opened his eyes, and said, "In our land of Vittorino, there is an old oak tree. Whenever I pass it, I can't help stopping there. I stand in front of it for a while and admire its magnificence from top to bottom. Sometimes I hug the trunk to get its energy. It hosts a lot of birds. Many cicadas break the silence of the sunny countryside with their continual chirr on the branches of the tree. Sometimes gusts of strong wind challenge its stability, but the oak tree considers them a tickle. What a strong tree it is!

"One day, while I was passing by that tree, I thought, if it didn't receive the rain from the sky, it would wither soon. Without the help of the sky, even though the tree has a robust trunk, boughs, branches, and countless leaves, it couldn't survive. Like that oak tree, I received the rain of love from the heavens whenever I needed it. I think God helped me whenever I was involved in a difficult situation. When my life was wrecked, thanks to God, a helper appeared to me and I survived."

"Your travels helped you a lot, Uncle Salvatore. Traveling around the world, you've learned many things. You've met gurus, masters, and extraordinary persons. From the homeless in Pune you learned something, too. Don't you think so?"

"Yes, I do. My travels broadened the horizon of my mind and spirit. If I had stayed only in Isola, my soul couldn't have grown. Now, I'll tell you a symbol I learned in one of my travels. In Isola I reproduced this symbol. Only you and I know it."

"Only you and I know it? It's a secret! What's it?"

"In a remote corner of our land of Vittorino, I have built a labyrinth. I made it with red bricks on the lawn. The labyrinth is just behind the cave called the Hell Cave. Once, notorious criminals took refuge in that cavern. The place is remote. I made the labyrinth there to be safe from prying eyes. If someone had seen me walking and standing barefoot there, he would have thought I had gone crazy. Do you think my siblings, my wife and children would understand me? Of course not! Looking at me, they would say: 'What happened to you? You've made eleven circuits on the ground, and now you walk there like a madman. You'd better go to a mental hospital!' I am sure about that, because I know them."

"Uncle Salvatore, I can't understand you either! What are you talking about?"

"Listen to me, and then you'll realize the magic power of such a symbol."

"Okay, tell it to me. Suddenly I feel curious."

"One year, while I was traveling across France, I visited the Chartres Cathedral. It's about ninety kilometers from Paris. I entered the church from the royal portal, and I was made curious by a few people that walked around the chairs as if they were looking for something. The next day I went to the cathedral again. This time there were no chairs. About ten visitors were walking on a course of ten circles or so. I took a seat on a pew and waited until their walking was over. Then I approached a lean man who looked like a gentleman. He was old and tall, and he wore silver-framed round glasses. 'Excuse me, sir. I'd like to know why you walk along these drawings on the floor. What is the meaning of these drawings?'

"Hearing me, the man lifted his chin a bit, lowered his eyes and looked down on me. 'I've just walked on the labyrinth.' 'Labyrinth?' 'You don't know what a labyrinth is?' At that moment, I felt like being an uncouth countryman who came to the city for the first time in his life. I opened my arms, lowered my head and admitted my ignorance. 'Sorry, I've never heard about this kind of labyrinth.'

"The man smiled faintly and then held out his hand to me. 'My name is Paul. I'm from London. The bus to Paris leaves in the afternoon. So we have enough time to talk about the labyrinth.' 'My name is Salvatore. I'm from Sicily. Nice to meet you.' I shook hands with him."

"Your story is getting interesting, Uncle Salvatore. At first I couldn't understand you when you talked about the labyrinth, but now I want to know more about this symbol."

"Thank you, Benedetto."

"Paul said, 'I'll tell you what I've done with this old symbol. I've reproduced the labyrinth of this cathedral in the lawn in front of my house. Everyday some passersby walk the labyrinth in front of my house naturally. It attracts visitors as if it were a magnet.' 'What is the meaning of the labyrinth? Why do people walk on it?' I asked. 'The labyrinth is the symbol of the pilgrimage. Walking on it is like pilgrimaging in search of God. Then you get out of the labyrinth with a clear mind. Walking there calms both the body and the mind. You can get rid of mundane worries, and, in the meantime, you feel that you are a true spiritual being. Let's walk this labyrinth together now.'

"We walked the eleven circuits of the labyrinth and arrived at the center, which had the shape of a rose. 'The rose is the symbol of Mary and of love. Let's stand here for a few minutes and meditate on ourselves. Although we can't know the ultimate truth, at least we can purify our mind and body to live a better life. Here, everything disappears, and we can feel the oneness with God, who is love. Now, let's follow the circuits to get out of the labyrinth. We'll go back to the world again with a serener mind than before.'

"After visiting that cathedral, I was impressed by the labyrinth. When I returned to Sicily, I reproduced it on the lawn near the Hell Cave in our land. I walk there whenever I want to. I feel peaceful walking the labyrinth. Can you understand me now, Benedetto?"

"Yes, I can. And I know about another kind of labyrinth. This labyrinth is more well-known than that of Chartres Cathedral."

"Really? You surprise me, Benedetto! Tell me what you know."

"I learned about this labyrinth during a lesson on Greek mythology at school. Our teacher was a young woman with a melodious voice. When she told us the Greek myths, she looked like a nymph or a goddess who descended from Mount Olympus to teach us mortals mythology. One day she drew a labyrinth on the blackboard, similar to a depiction on a Greek vase of the fourth century BC. Then she told us the myth of Theseus, Ariadne, and the Minotaur. Do you know this myth, Uncle Salvatore?"

"Yes, but I can't remember it well now."

"Minos, the king of Crete, appointed the architect Daedalus to build a labyrinth to hold the Minotaur, a creature half man and half bull that fed on human flesh. Daedalus and his son, Icarus, made a structure full of blind alleys, rooms, and narrow streets. The building was so intricate that even Daedalus and his son were trapped there.

"Theseus, the son of King Aegeus, decided to put an end to the sacrifice of young Athenians that were sent to Crete to feed the Minotaur every year. The hero landed in Crete. He was determined to kill the monster. But, how to get out of the labyrinth after killing the Minotaur? Ariadne, the daughter of King Minos, fell in love with Theseus. She handed him a ball of wool. While Theseus was going through the labyrinth holding one end of the thread in his hand, Ariadne stood at the entrance of the labyrinth and reeled the thread off the ball of wool. At last, Theseus killed the Minotaur. By following Ariadne's thread, he found his way back out."

"How fantastic this myth is! Actually, all the Greek myths hide a meaning inside. Somebody calls the Greek myths the psychology of the ancient. Do you know what the myth of Theseus, Ariadne, and the Minotaur symbolizes?"

"Yes, our teacher told us everything about the myth. The labyrinth symbolizes human life on earth. The labyrinth is an open space with no doors or gates. The Minotaur could get out of it and break free, but it didn't because it was prey to instinct and ignorance, which prevented him from following the right way out.

"We humans are not different from the Minotaur. Like it we are dominated by instinct and ignorance. Just as it happened to that monster, we can't get out of the labyrinth of worldly, instinctive life. According to the myth, we can't succeed without Ariadne's thread, which is a symbol. It means that we need a guide capable of setting us free from instinct, ignorance, and error. Thanks to Ariadne's thread, we can get out of the state of animals."

"What's your thread of Ariadne, Benedetto?"

"My Ariadne's thread is love and friendship. Without my friends and my lover, I can't feel like a human. And for you, Uncle Salvatore, what's your thread of Ariadne?"

"My thread of Ariadne is the vibrations of words. Erez taught me how to behave in life. If I don't abide by his eighth precept, I'm not different from the Minotaur. Erez made me understand the vibrations of words. Good words are like Ariadne's thread that guides us out of the labyrinth of instinct. If you backbite somebody, your bad words will come back to you like an echo. They will poison your mind and soul, and then you won't be able to see things as they are. Good words are at the basis of spiritual life."

"Everyone has his own thread of Ariadne. But he has to find his thread inside himself."

"Benedetto, one year ago, when we started writing my memoir, I aimed to hand down a truthful story of my life to my families. So I reported all the details of my life in my memoir. It was my big mistake!"

"Uncle Salvatore, I know your life better than anyone else. Your life has been adventurous, but you had too many lawsuits and arguments, even against your brothers. Your memoir is full of acrimony against many."

"There is a lot of gossip, bad words, and backbiting in my memoir. Don't you think so?"

"Yes, I do. Your memoir is very spiteful when you tell of the lawsuit against your brothers. You lost it, and then you cursed the judge, the lawyers and, above all, your brothers. Your memoir is full of bad words against physicians, politicians, priests, pastors, girls that disappointed you, and even your friends."

"Benedetto, I'm not satisfied with the first draft of my memoir we've just finished writing. We have to change it, rewrite it. I want to eliminate all the bad words and the backbiting. I want to observe Erez's eighth precept. 'Your words,' he said, 'must be creative. Remove backbiting and censure from your mental habit. Drive out speaking ill of others from your life. Words have vibrations that can cause positive or negative effects according to the quality of words.'

"Therefore, be patient, Benedetto! I want you to rewrite my memoir by cutting off all the words and stories such as backbiting, criticism, or censure."

"Are you joking, Uncle Salvatore? It took one year to write your memoir, and now you want to change everything? It was a hard task for me to write and arrange your book. Believe me, we did good work! It's not possible to clean up the manuscript in the way you want now. First of all, if we cut off your quarrels and gossip, the pages of your memoir won't be enough to make a book. Second, it is impossible to make the story smooth. By cutting here and there, we'll hop from one subject to another. It is nonsense to rewrite your memoir. Lastly, you have to write the truth without hiding something. Your shortcomings are also a part of yourself. Backbiting is also a part of this book. I don't want to rewrite it!" I said with an angry face. I was so furious and disappointed that I wanted to stand up and go out. Uncle Salvatore's eyes moistened. He looked discouraged.

"I know it is hard work, but I ask you to do it for me. I want my book to contain positive words. Vibrations generated by written words remain active for a long time. Good words vibrate pleasantly, not only in our heart but also in the air. They are the thread of Ariadne that leads us to a happy life."

I loved Uncle Salvatore very much. I didn't feel like letting him down. "Yes, you're right. Don't worry. I'll try to rewrite the memoir as you want, because I love you. Furthermore, I think you may be right."

Uncle Salvatore's face became bright. Suddenly he stood up from his rocking chair and came to me. He gave me a kiss on my cheek, saying, "Thank you, Benedetto. I'm very happy!"

"My pleasure, Uncle Salvatore! I think first we'd better cut out the part of the memoir relating to the causes of the demerger of the firm Angelo Gagliano & Sons. It has too many resentful words, indeed."

"Yes, cut out that part first, and then my resentful words against my brothers and my friends of the theater group. You have to do the same in regard to my malicious remarks about physicians, lawyers, judges, politicians, and above all, the president of the Bank of Isola that swallowed all my money."

My uncle and I continued our daily meetings to rearrange the book for two months longer. The arguments with his closest friends disappeared in the second version of the book, too. Finally, I cut out his censures against secret societies and exclusive social clubs. Little by little we reduced the memoir by 40 percent. It looked like an olive tree from which pruners had cut off dry and unfruitful branches. It looked very simple and beautiful after trimming. I printed the new version of the memoir and handed it to him. He read and reread it, but he wasn't satisfied with it. Finally, after cutting and rearranging the passages of the manuscript repeatedly, he seemed to be almost satisfied with this present, final version. Looking at his thin lips, I noticed a faint, pleased smile. With all the deletions, his memoir was reduced to almost 50 percent of the original manuscript.

"What a wasted work we did for one year!"

"Sorry, Benedetto. But it wasn't in vain. At last, we did good work!"

"Do you like this final manuscript?"

"Yes, I do. Although it's not perfect, let's try to find a good publishing house for it."

"Perfection doesn't belong to humans, Uncle Salvatore."

"Yes, I know. However, we did our best."

"Now can you go downstairs? There is a room at the end of the first flight of stairs. It is cool and dark, and it maintains the proper temperature for wine. There are many bottles on the floor, but one is on the shelf. Bring that bottle here. I've kept it for a special moment."

I went to the cellar. It was not difficult to spot that solitary bottle. My uncle uncorked it and poured wine into two crystal glasses. Then he smelled its fragrance before tasting it.

"Good wine doesn't keep froth! Look at how limpid it is."

"Yes, Uncle Salvatore. I can't describe the taste of this wine in words."

"Tonight I want to sleep here, in the house where I was born. It had belonged to my father and my grandfather."

"Don't you want me to walk you to your apartment?"

"No. I want to spend the night here."

"Aunt Lucia will be worried if you don't go home. She will be waiting for you."

"Don't worry. I told her that I would stay here tonight."

"Shall I bring you a blanket?"

"Yes, please. Tonight it may be cold."

I went downstairs and took a blanket from the closet. Then I covered his body with it.

"Shall I turn off the light?"

"No. Leave the light on. You know, I don't like darkness."

"Good night, Uncle Salvatore."

"Good night, Benedetto. Have a good dream tonight."

Before leaving, I gave him a kiss on his cheek as usual. I came back home, being worried about him. Although he was in good health, he was ninety-three years old now.

That night, I dreamed of Uncle Salvatore and also of getting out of my body. When I was a child, I dreamed of being out of my body a few times. In a dream I was roaming around the streets of Isola at night. The streetlamps lit up the crossroads. I walked on the streets for some time, and then I hurried to come back home and slip into my body before awakening. I felt that my body would die if I didn't get back into it. After returning into my body, I heaved a sigh of relief.

That night in a dream, I was out of my body again. I walked in the little square that separates my house and the old house where my uncle was sleeping. I saw Uncle Vanni's balcony wide-open, and his room overlooking Via S. Agata lit by a beautiful chandelier. The front door was wide-open, too. I climbed the first flight of stairs and entered Uncle Vanni's rooms. Nobody had stepped in for more than fifty years. I crossed one room first and then stepped into the other room lit by the chandelier where my relatives were celebrating the return of Uncle Vanni from America. The white sheets that covered the furniture had been taken off, the couches had been dusted off, and the mirror of the console looked like new. There was a cheerful party in the room. I saw my grandfather with his thick mustache. He looked happy that his beloved brother had come back to his home on Via S. Agata. I saw Uncle Vanni and Aunt Angelina, who stood beside my grandfather and looked at me delightfully. Then I leaned out of the balcony and saw my father, who wore a white shirt. He entered the house and dialed a telephone number.

"Who are you calling, Dad?"

"I'm calling your brother. He is my son, too."

In the room I saw my family and relatives talking and enjoying themselves. All the irreconcilable conflicts had been settled. The quarrels and lawsuits were over. I saw my cousins, uncles, and aunts toasting the return of Uncle Vanni from Brooklyn. There were no more arguments. The room resounded with the vibrations of their joyful talking. They had many things to tell one another after a long time apart.

I wanted to stay in the room a bit longer and talk with my grandfather. I had never met him, because he died before I was born. I also wanted to talk with Uncle Vanni and ask him something about the life in New York and the monuments of that metropolis. But all of a sudden I heard the balcony panes rattling. I went to the balcony and leaned out. Uncle Salvatore was warming up the engine of his old SPA truck. Thanks to his maintenance, it was still in perfect working order.

I left Uncle Vanni's room and rushed down the stairs to stop Uncle Salvatore from leaving. Oh, my! It was too late! He had already set off for his journey toward new, faraway lands. I ran after his truck as fast as I could, but in vain. I couldn't catch up with Uncle Salvatore.

I followed his truck with my eyes. On the road I spotted several trucks. Uncle Salvatore's truck overtook all of them. He was still the best truck driver in Isola! Suddenly he stopped driving his truck, stuck his head out of the window, and looked at me with his pleased face. Then he waved a farewell, smiling. I also waved to him with tears in my eyes. I kept waving my hand until he disappeared beyond the ridge of Mount Campanito. Then I hastened to get back into my body before the break of day.

CPSIA information can be obtained
at www.ICGtesting.com
Printed in the USA
BVHW071328200519
548789BV00004B/322/P

9 781949 483246